Jim Snyder, a major during the Vietnam War, out-lived his usefulness when America gave up Viet-nam and Southeast Asia to the communists. He was the commander of a search and destroy bat-talion. Unable to find a niche for himself in civilian life, Snyder makes his way back into the military where he is reluctantly accepted. He has one objec-tive, to form a special unit which the country can fall back on when suddenly forced into another war for which it is unprepared. Gradually he gath-ers his old team together.

Then one day Major Jim Snyder and his men roar into the Astrodome to put on a memorable half time entertainment and rip the place off. This is the day about which the book is written. . . .

SEARCH AND DESTROY

ROBIN MOORE

POPHAM PRESS

CHARTER
NEW YORK

A DIVISION OF CHARTER COMMUNICATIONS INC.
A GROSSET & DUNLAP COMPANY

SEARCH AND DESTROY

Copyright © 1978 by Robin More

A Popham Press Book

First Charter Printing December 1980
Published simultaneously in Canada
Manufactured in the United States of America

2 4 6 8 0 9 7 5 3 1

CHAPTER ONE

Colonel Mike Snyder riding through the night in the lead armored personnel carrier brought his brigade, code name Wildfire, to a sudden halt as radios relayed his orders to the rear elements.

"We're at the border now," he said softly to his deputy, Major Jerry Hackett. "Get General Vogel on the side band. This is the last chance to abort this operation."

In the darkness Hackett turned to Major Sorell, the communications officer. "You heard the Colonel, Signals. Point of no abort coming up." Sorell was already calling Division HQ.

In his office Brigadier General Lloyd Vogel had an open line to the Pentagon West, that vast complex of buildings at Ton Son Nhut Airport in Saigon which housed Military Assistance Command Vietnam. And

1

from MACV the supreme commander was in direct touch with the White House in Washington.

The so-called incursion into Cambodia to discover and destroy the headquarters of the North Vietnam Communists had been in the planning stages for several weeks but the delicacy of the operation and the international repercussions that were bound to ensue had given the President and his top security advisors frequent reversals of thinking. First the incursion was on, then it was off, then on again.

Vogel stood transfixed, staring at the battery of radio equipment in the Division commo center. To his right was the channel to Colonel Snyder's search and destroy brigade poised and ready to strike into Cambodia. To his left the communications line to Saigon and ultimately Washington.

"Nothing further from MACV, General," Vogel's Signal Corps officer reported.

"It's a go then. Tell Snyder to take his Wildfire hoods across." And under his breath he added, "If I never see them again it'll be too soon."

Vogel thought of the "neutralization" and "pacification" operations Colonel Snyder's hand-picked brigade of combat-loving officers and men had carried out. It would only require one left-wing bleeding heart liberal reporter to discover how certain areas had been made devoid of the Communists for a major war scandal to break out in the newspapers of the world. And his career, more promising than ever as a result of Snyder's ruthless search and destroy missions, would be blighted. The fewer men alive at the war's end who could personally attest to the means employed to rid Vogel's area of responsibility of the Viet Cong Communist guerrillas and their supporters the better off he

2

was. There was no reason why he shouldn't become Chief of Staff some day.

"Signal Snyder to proceed," Vogel snapped. "Call Air Force liaison and tell them we're operational."

The message was relayed to Mike Snyder by his deputy. "Thanks, Hack. Now all we have to worry about is the enemy. The politics seem to be squared away."

"The politics are never squared away," Hack replied darkly. The column of armored vehicles and truckloads of American infantry penetrated Cambodia territory. Colonel Snyder checked the stars above for direction as they twisted and turned through the abruptly deteriorating roads beyond the border.

"This should be the greatest search and destroy operation Wildfire has pulled off yet!" Mike Snyder chortled.

"We'll kill a lot of gooks, all right," Hack agreed. "The only question is will we get back?"

"I know what you mean. Last thing Vogel said to me was he wanted to get me and all my hoods, as he referred to us, out of his division."

"The hypocritical son-of-a-bitch," Hack growled. "He's gotten himself two citations for the high body count this division has racked up."

"And he knows that we rolled up the score for him," Mike Snyder replied grimly. "I wasn't too keen on what we had to do myself. But we've wiped out the Communist infra-structure in this area. Vogel wasn't worried about the women, children, and civilians of uncertain political leaning that we zapped when he was called down to Saigon for his Distinguished Service Medal."

All that night Wildfire rolled deeper and deeper into

3

Cambodia. By morning they had pushed their way twenty miles inside the border and still had encountered no signs of resistance. There could be no doubt but that the Communist command inside Cambodia was aware of this incursion. Armored personnel carriers and half tracks do not move silently. Also the fighter planes circling above ready to provide cover in case of an attack were also whining out a warning that United States and South Vietnamese forces were crossing the border.

Anxiously looking about the countryside in the glow of first dawn Colonel Snyder scanned the area through his binoculars looking for some sign of their quarry, the Communist North Vietnam high command. "We should be on top of General Giap's headquarters right now according to all intelligence we've received," he snapped. "Get the troops dismounted and starting to fan out. The ground underneath us is riddled with tunnels. We want to get in them and wipe them out!"

"Yes, sir." Hackett turned to his radio operator and the signal to dismount and spread out was relayed back along the column. Colonel Snyder jumped from his APC to the ground and began supervising the preparations for the attack against the underground installations directly under them.

Back at division headquarters General Vogel had been watching the progress of the search and destroy column as the radio position reports came in.

"Send word to Saigon that Snyder's column is directly over General Giap's tunnel complex. They're searching for entrances to the system and will be attacking shortly."

Now, Vogel thought with great satisfaction, they were on the verge of destroying Communist headquar-

4

ters. Perhaps they might even capture General Giap himself. Then if Snyder could get himself killed and his deputy too plus a few of those hood sergeants, the division would have mounted a spectacular operation and nobody would be left to talk about the brigade's recent methods of operation. This was a constantly recurring fantasy in Vogel's mind.

In Saigon the Supreme Commander was also intently watching the progress of Snyder's search and destroy brigade. Other units were poised to go in and relieve Wildfire once they had pinpointed the headquarters of the Communist forces which intelligence reported was planning the final assault against South Vietnam. This Communist attack, if successful, would once and for all join North and South Vietnam into one great Communist country and expel United States influence in Southeast Asia.

Such an invasion had to be blunted, halted before it could get started, or ten years of American blood and treasure spent in Vietnam would all go to naught. But the Supreme Commander of American forces was more than a great soldier. He was a political tactician as well. Nobody in Vietnam understood the political hazards that the President was facing at that moment. He had pledged his Administration to stopping the war in Vietnam, not expanding it. Few people in America were capable of understanding that the only way to stop it, and stop it decisively without the defeat of South Vietnam, was to successfully pull off a wholesale incursion into Cambodia where the Communists were waiting for the right moment to strike.

It was a bold move and almost certainly would be successful providing there was no political interference. Tensely the general watched the progress of Snyder's brigade as it was charted on the map in front of him. But what concerned him far more was the mood in the war room at the White House with which he was in direct communication. By now the President and his Secretary of State would have briefed a select group of senators and congressmen on what was happening. His strategy had been to tell the Republican and Democratic leadership of this first phase of the Cambodian incursion after it was a *fait accompli*.

It would be six o'clock at night in the White House now. The supreme commander could picture the tense scene as the President explained what had occurred in Cambodia that day and what the results were likely to be. The Chairman of the Senate Foreign Relations Committee would be bellowing like a stuck bull, the general thought to himself with a chuckle. No wonder they called him "half-bright". Even the Republican senators would be critical.

The congresmen in this election year would be gravely concerned about the effect on their constituents of the news that an attack was being carried across the border and into Cambodia. All they thought about was being reelected. They had no desire to explain the wisdom, the tactical necessity of the move to their constituents.

As the sweep hand on the huge clock in front of him inexorably moved forward the Supreme Commander of American forces in Vietnam was sweating out two struggles. The one in the White House and the deadly battle inside Cambodia.

At General Vogel's division headquarters the signal officer in charge cried out, "Sir, Snyder has found tunnel entrances and his troops are sweeping in."

Vogel nodded silently.

6

Twenty miles inside Cambodia as the day was already becoming hot Colonel Mike Snyder came to a depressing conclusion. Yes they had found Giap's HQ but the mission had been compromised. Throughout the tunnel system there was indication of recent evacuation. Snyder, following his men down into the intricate tunnel system, saw the unmistakable signs of a hasty dismantling of the headquarters. At one point they even thought they were in the actual underground office of General Giap, the hero of Dien Bien Phu, which had been cleaned out no more than twelve hours before. A hospital ward had obviously been emptied in the past few hours.

After two hours in the tunnel system Snyder went back to the surface to report back to General Vogel. The Communists had known they were coming even before they crossed the border. Snyder personally got on the radio to General Vogel. Someone back there, probably certain dove senators in Washington who opposed the war, had betrayed them. Undoubtedly by now a huge ambush was in the making to hit them on their way back into Vietnam. Their orders had been to stay just long enough to clean out Communist HQ and then run back. The search element of the mission had been a success. As for the destruction, at this point it was a question of who was going to be destroyed. And right now that fate looked as though it were destined to befall Snyder's brigade.

Even as the Supreme Commander was receiving this discouraging information in his headquarters at Ton Son Nhut Air Base, a far more shocking signal was on its way to him from the White House. The political pressure had been so severe on the President, especially from the Chairman of the Senate Foreign Relations

Committee that at this moment, before the press had any inkling of the Cambodian incursion, it was necessary to order the men back.

"What about air cover for the brigade that went in?" the Supreme Commander asked the White House. "We can't leave them out there without air."

A few minutes later the reply came back from Washington. "Use extreme caution insofar as penetration of Cambodian air space is concerned."

"Extreme caution?" the four star general asked himself aloud. "What is that?"

Since the first brigade to cross into Cambodia had not succeeded in its mission to search out and destroy headquarters of the Communist North Vietnamese Army anyway, the White House now wanted to deny that a deliberate incursion of Cambodia had occurred at all. If a United States unit had, during the course of hot pursuit, strayed across the border that was regrettable but understandable. But anything that would appear at this moment to be a deliberate invasion of Cambodia must be avoided.

The Supreme Commander talked urgently over the scrambled communications system to Vogel. "Get the brigade back as quickly and quietly as possible. Use minimum air cover. Keep the planes as close to the border as possible so that we can always say it was pilot error if planes strayed too far into Cambodia."

Vogel's curt orders reached Colonel Snyder as he was rallying his troops, bringing them out of the deserted tunnel system and back together in a defensible withdrawal column. He knew that it wouldn't be long before they could expect an enemy attack in great numbers. The Communists had plenty of time to plan it.

8

"What about air cover?" he asked over the radio to General Vogel.

"Negative," Vogel replied.

"Negative?" Snyder shouted. "What do you mean? We'll never get out of here without air cover."

"Those are orders from Washington, Colonel!" Vogel's voice cracked across the air waves.

"Does Washington know that I'm sitting out here with a thousand men twenty miles inside Cambodia about to walk into a preset ambush no matter how we go back?" Snyder shouted over the radio. "Does Washington know that there's no way it can deny an incursion was made into Cambodia when a thousand American bodies are strewn from here to the border?"

"There'll be air cover at the border, Colonel," Vogel cut in. "Get as close as you can to the border and we'll see what help we can give you."

With a string of angry epithets the first few of which managed to get onto the air before Major Sorell, always the prudent commo officer, turned off the radio, Snyder turned and began shouting orders. Then in his command APC he drove from what had been the front of the column all the way to the back, turning the rear into the vanguard of the march back to the Vietnam border.

CHAPTER TWO

Major Snyder had not exaggerated the danger facing Wildfire. He led his column in an angling course towards the border rather than going back in the most direct route possible. The halftracks and armored personnel carriers churned across the dry rice paddies and the trucks following jolted over the dikes, shaking up and almost throwing out of the truckbeds the troops desperately holding on to whatever handholds they could find.

Reaching a rutted dusty road the column turned onto it, proceeding towards Vietnam more than thirty miles away by the route Snyder had chosen. The communications officer sent position reports back to headquarters every ten minutes along with requests by Snyder for air support.

With a sudden blast of artillery the first ambush was sprung on Wildfire. Grimly Snyder gave the order to continue as fast as the column could move. There was no point in trying to change course and attempt to take a new overland route back to the border. They were obviously under surveillance and there was no way Wildfire could escape the North Vietnamese Communist troops.

The quarry, the prey, had now become the aggressor. Fortunately for Wildfire the artillery rounds were poorly directed and straddled the column, only an occasional mortar round falling closely enough to cause real damage.

Still, the change of course had at least caused Wildfire to avoid the first major ambush which had been set for them along the most direct route back to Vietnam. But it wouldn't take long before heavy Communist troop commitments intercepted Wildfire.

Just as Major Snyder expected, it was only another five miles along the route before small arms fire began crackling at them from both sides of the road. At least this was a hastily set up ambush, Snyder remarked to his deputy, Major Hackett. "A well-planned ambush does not have two elements of the enemy firing at each other from opposite sides of the killing ground."

Wildfire pushed on without stopping to engage the ambushers. But now they began taking casualties. Mortar rounds were fired at them from close range and several trucks were hit, wounding or killing the troops inside. Their comrades hastily evacuated them from burning trucks and piled them into trucks that were still operable. Sixty-millimeter mortar teams fired back at the enemy from close range and all along the column M79 grenade launches were fired, further stilling the hastily formed ambush. The disabled vehicles were pushed off the road and Wildfire continued towards the border.

For a while Mike Snyder thought they had successfully evaded the main enemy force. But then ten miles from the border they were hit in force. The enemy had successfully calculated the route that Wildfire would be following and by now were waiting for them.

Mortar and small arms fire poured into Wildfire. A blocking force ahead forced Snyder to halt his column. Now they would have to fight their way out of the ambush. All along Wildfire's flanks American and South Vietnamese troops were pouring heavy machine gun and rifle fire into the ambush. Mortar teams were feeding their charges into the tubes as fast as they could drop them in.

"Give me that microphone," Snyder shouted to his commo man. As calmly as possible he outlined the situation to General Vogel. "Send air cover. We'll never get out of here without it."

Desperately Colonel Snyder surveyed the sky above him in the direction of the border. Surely General Vogel would not deny them air cover at such a crucial time. Yet no planes came in sight. Repeatedly Snyder made requests for air cover. Meanwhile his casualties were increasing. The enemy had managed to entrench itself solidly while it waited for Wildfire to come into the killing ground.

The fire power directed at them was awesome. Mike Snyder could see his entire brigade being wiped out in this engagement. Back on the radio he repeated his pleas for air cover but was confronted with silence on the other end. Apparently General Vogel was going to let Wildfire perish in this ambush without offering air cover. Mike Snyder shook his head, reached for his

M79 grenade launcher and added his own firepower to that of his men. There was nothing to do but fight it out to the end.

Suddenly the whining roar of the most welcome sound of his life shot through the air above him. A jet fighter was coming in to assist. Mike looked skyward and saw a single jet streaking towards them. Only one fighter? he thought. We could use a squadron but one is better than none at all.

The fighter banked into a snarling dive and laid down a coating of napalm covering the ambushers with a sticky inferno. Snyder grabbed the radio from the communications officer and switched on air to ground frequency. "Try to clear the road ahead of us," he called out to the pilot. "Don't use napalm this time. We've got to go through it ourselves." Obligingly the jet wheeled and made a pass at the armored force ahead which had halted Wildfire. The fire from eight 20mm cannons raked the enemy and in one strafing pass the blocking force was cleared out. Snyder gave the order to move out and a crippled Wildfire limped onwards, the troops climbing into the operational vehicles piling the dead and wounded aboard.

First Sergeant Jimmy Medford, who had fought his first battles in the Korean War, and had served for three years with Mike Snyder during his meteoric rise from major to full colonel, took the opportunity of the brief lull in enemy fire to run forward to Snyder's command vehicle. His eyes followed the arcing path through the air made by the single fighter plane. "I don't know who he is, sir, but if we get out of this alive it's because of him."

"That's right, sergeant. And we've got a long way to go before we reach the border where General Vogel

14

has deigned to give us real air cover." Snyder turned and looked back over the crippled column behind him. Smoking vehicles littered both sides of the road as the operable vehicles proceeded slowly forward.

"Have you any casualty count, sergeant?" Mike asked as though not really wanting to receive an answer.

Sergeant Medford shook his head. "Hard to tell sir. But we're hurting bad. I don't know if we'll get out of another one."

"As long as our angel stays above us we might make it," Snyder replied, raising his eyes as though in supplication.

At division headquarters Vogel was following the fortunes of Wildfire, a grim smile on his face. "I guess we've seen the last of that unit," he remarked to his deputy, Colonel Creech. At that moment the radio liaison with Air Force crackled into life.

"This is blue leader one, blue leader one flying along the Cambodian border. Blue leader one reporting that one jet has broken formation and flown into Cambodia. He's now assisting the column caught in ambush."

A sudden rage gripped General Vogel. He turned to Creech again. "Find out the name of the pilot. I'll have his ass flying Hercules transports the rest of this war."

"Yes, sir. But as long as a fighter plane is already in Cambodia and maybe saving Colonel Snyder, wouldn't it be just as well to leave things as they are?"

"Get that insubordinate airborne bastard out of there. Now! Doesn't he know that we have orders not to violate Cambodian air space?"

"Last night the orders were to give Snyder air cover inside Cambodia, sir," Creech reminded General Vogel.

"Well, things changed back in Washington since then.

15

Get that son-of-a-bitch back here. I could be relieved of my command for getting us into World War III."

"We're about there now, sir," Creech replied. And then he saw the look of rage tinged with fear on General Vogel's face and knew better than to pursue the matter further. "I'll find out who the pilot is and we'll deal with him, sir," Creech hastily agreed.

Mike Snyder also wanted to know the name of the pilot who had saved them from the ambush. "Ask that pilot who he is," Snyder commanded Major Sorrel. "I have a bottle of Johnny Walker black label scotch I've been hording for an event. I want to send it to him."

"I already asked him, sir. It's Captain Robert Murray, Third Tactical Wing. And he's in deep trouble now, sir, for breaking orders and coming to our rescue."

"I'll bet," Snyder snapped out. "Vogel would really like to see the last of us." He turned to Medford. "Right, sergeant? Who else but us knows how many villages we wiped out for Vogel so he could claim there were no Viet Cong left in his area of command."

Medford nodded grimly. "I reckon if the press got hold of what a search and destroy mission like Wildfire really does, and saw some of the results, there'd be a lot of hell to pay with the general's future."

Snyder reached for the radio. "Switch onto the air-to-ground frequency again," he ordered.

"Yes, sir." The communications officer turned a knob and static crackled from the receiver.

"Captain Murray, this is Colonel Snyder. We appreciate what you have done."

"A pleasure, colonel," a cheerful pilot's voice broke through the static. "I'll stay with you. Might as well be

16

hung for a sheep as hung for a goat. There's an ambush forming up ahead of you. Keep going. As long as I have rounds in my machine guns, napalm and bombs, I'll stick with you."

In less than ten minutes a barrage of mortar shells and artillery smashed into Wildfire and once again Colonel Snyder's men were fighting for their lives. Angrily the jet fighter piloted by Captain Murray streaked down at the North Vietnamese and raked them with machine gun fire, dropping napalm, incinerating whole enemy elements. Sergeant Medford was standing with Colonel Snyder, both of them pumping M79 grenades into the ambush areas as the column continued to push ahead.

Each time a blocking force of enemy started to cut them off Captain Murray destroyed it with napalm, bombs, and his deadly machine gun fire. Suddenly, in a blaze of smoke and flame a mortar round landed on the hood of the armored personnel carrier in which Snyder was standing, shouting orders and firing back at the enemy.

Searing pain followed by blackness descended upon him. He lapsed into a state of semi-consciousness. "Medford, Medford. I can't see," Snyder cried.

"This vehicle has had it, sir. Let me help you into another one."

"Something's wrong. I can't see," Snyder repeated weakly.

"Stick with me, sir. Come on. Climb out of here. You can make it, sir."

With Medford's help Snyder managed to climb out of the disabled armored personnel carrier and was aware of being half led, half carried to another vehicle in the rear. The fire fight raged on all about him as

Wildfire continued to fight its way towards the Cambodian border with Vietnam now only five miles away. "Still no air cover?" Snyder's voice quavered.

"No, sir," Medford replied. "Just our man above. Captain Murray. He must be getting low on ammo but he's still giving them hell and we're moving."

Mike Snyder felt himself falling over the brink into the dark abyss of total unconsciousness. He tried to stay with the situation but could not hold on. So this is it, he thought. There is no more. The shattering explosions about him became muffled in his ears and then stilled.

CHAPTER THREE

The tips of Miguelina's delicate long fingers followed the scar from forehead down along his cheek to his chin as Mike slowly came awake. Once again his mind had relived the ambush during the moments of deep sleep, bursting into sudden awareness in the bright morning light. He turned his head slightly and smiled at the exquisite face looking down at him seriously from the tangled raven tresses that curled about her neck and shoulders in delightful disarray. He was in love, really in love. For the first time in his life. Hard to understand. Hard to believe.

"You should have seen it before the plastic surgeon got at me," Mike grinned at her.

"I would have loved you just as much then," she replied solemnly. Mike reached for her, pulled her close to him and they kissed for many moments. Then she laughed softly. "No, my colonel, not again. We have

19

breakfast with my father in an hour, I have to get back to the palace and pretend I was there all night."

Reluctantly but knowing it was necessary Mike released her and watched her push back the covers and slide her beautifully formed body out of bed. He resisted the impulse to reach his hands out and caress her. He sighed as she took the peignoir from the bed and slipped it around her bare shoulders. Then she smiled down at Mike. She threw back the sheet exposing his nude body and the overwhelming evidence that he was ready to make love to her again.

Gently she became serious. "You will not really leave me today, will you, Mike?"

The smile disappeared from his face. "I have no choice, Miguelina."

Briskly she took her hand away from him and turned. "We'll talk about it again at breakfast."

He watched her disappear into the bathroom and then sat up and pulled on his own bathrobe. This would be the last day of this "hardship" tour. Tonight he would return to the United States. And that meant going back to Cookie and her old man. In fact it was undoubtedly old J.J. Cookson who had gotten him transferred out of Costa Vacca and back to Ft. Hood, Texas where he would be near his little wife who hated Costa Vacca and would not join him here.

Costa Vacca was as far from any active US military scene of action to which he could have been posted. General Vogel and the Pentagon high command echelon had wanted to take no chances on Colonel Mike Snyder being available for newspaper interviews should any investigation of the search and destroy missions be mounted. So here he had spent a two-year tour advising the strong man of Costa Vacca, Miguel Alamen, on anti-communist guerrilla bush tactics.

Miguel's daughter, Miguelina, had made the assignment a delight. From the begining Mike and the old man, General Alamen, had gotten along well. But then, as inevitably it must, criticism of the dictator's treatment of dissidents, communist suspects, and prisoners in general caused a furor in the United States. The United States was withdrawing its military support and Mike's assignment was abruptly terminated.

The door to the bathroom opened and Miguelina, fluffing her hair, walked out fresh and shining, her nude body glowing from the shower and toweling.

"Oh my God," Mike mock-groaned. "How can you expect me to just stand here doing nothing?"

"You can have the bathroom now, *mi amore*," she laughed. Then she was serious. She said, "You know you don't have to go back if you don't want to."

"You know I have to, Miguelina. I'm in the United States Army. I have no choice." Unsteadily he walked into the bathroom and closed the door after him.

The old headache was coming upon him. He had never dared tell the army medical examiners about it or the hallucinations he sometimes endured. And there were sudden mad impulses to do something outrageous like assassinating General Vogel or giving out the whole story of his missions in Vietnam, or taking off in a jet plane and crashing it into the Pentagon. Perhaps there was some drug he could take to ease the sudden pains or cleanse his mind of the wild images which possessed it from time to time. But if he confessed the extent of his troubles to military authorities he would undoubtedly be branded as unstable and find himself prematurely retired. And this he did not want. Not yet.

21

With the reduction in force immediately after the shameful abandonment of Vietnam and the American Ambassador's evacuation from the roof of the embassy in Saigon by helicopter, he had been reduced to the rank of lieutenant colonel. He hoped to regain his old rank on a permanent basis before retirement.

Mike swallowed the headache pills, chasing them with a concoction distilled from cocoa leaves, the source of cocaine, and soon felt better. He had provided himself with two years' supply of this Costa Vacca special medication to take home with him. After a shower and shave he felt better, and dressing in his starched suntans he left his quarters for the palace.

Mike picked at his breakfast in desultory fashion as General Alamen concluded his final plea. "You know you don't have to go back, Mike. Stay here. I will make you the general of my army. That wife of yours you don't love, whose family tries to run your life. . . . I make the rules here. You will be issued a divorce and you and Miguelina can be married."

When Mike didn't reply, Alamen continued. "Mike, the seismic information from the exploration barges was put on my desk yesterday. A formation just off our coast looks as though it could be developed into a field with reserves of several billion barrels of oil. And back in the plains behind the coast there are three potential fields. We are going to drill our first wildcat well next month. You should be here for this. I will let you buy or lease a hundred square miles in the oil plains. You will be rich beyond anything you could dream of. You'll make your father-in-law look like a poor man."

Eagerness shone from the dictator's eyes as he importuned the man he hoped would become his son-in-law. "We need you, Mike. The Communists, when they hear about the oil, will be organizing guerrilla forces again to try and take over my government."

Miguel sighed deeply. "Why is it that Americans don't understand that if we fail to take harsh measures in this part of the world we are asking for communist takeover."

He chuckled and grinned cagily. "Once we have the oil there will never be a problem about so-called human rights again as far as America is concerned. You don't see the President of the United States bothering Venezuela or Nigeria, do you? No, of course not. The United States needs the oil."

After a silence Miguel turned to his daughter. "Even you could not persuade him?" he asked, a hopeless tone in his voice.

"Don't you understand me?" Mike finally replied. "I'm an American, an American soldier."

"Yes, a soldier who has been reduced in rank from full colonel to lieutenant colonel," Miguel said acidly.

"Actually I am a major. That's my permanent rank. I was only a colonel while the war was going on. They have what they call a RIF in the United States you know. That means reduction in force. Colonels go back to being lieutenant colonels or majors. Some majors go back to being sergeants. And many men are RIFed out of the army altogether. Until the next war, of course. Then they all came back in at high ranks."

"So when you go back to the United States you may even go down to major. And you could be a general of my army, permanent general," Miguel observed.

Mike looked from Miguel to his daughter Miguelina. She was more beautiful than ever. What a contrast this vibrant, aware, truly worldly young woman was compared to his wife Cookie. But of course when he married Cookie she had been the toast of Texas. Runner-up in the Miss America contest. Her father, one of the richest oil men in Houston. And certainly one of the most powerful politically not only in state but in national politics. Of course that was why Mike had so quickly been given temporary rank of full colonel, he now saw. Cookson's daughter couldn't be married to just some ordinary officer. And that had also been his problem with General Vogel and others. Political influence, the infamous initials PI, on his service record. It meant you were an officer to be reckoned with. It also meant you were an officer who had been promoted over the heads of others not necessarily for outstanding merit. He had hated it.

"I have to go back, Miguel. I think Miguelina understands why I have to go back. Certainly it's not because my wife is waiting for me. There's something about being an American that's hard to explain."

He looked into the eyes of an uncomprehending president. "One of my best friends was offered the job of general in King Hussein's Jordanian army. Fifty thousand dollars a year plus all of his expenses, his private jet and a free trip a year back to the United States to see his old country. He preferred to stay a lieutenant colonel, a permanent lieutenant colonel incidentally, in the U.S. Army. And he was killed in Vietnam just before I left there. That's the way we are. I'm sorry. I'm probably wrong. But I can't help myself."

Impatiently the dictator pushed his chair back, stood up, shaking his head, and brusquely left the dining terrace of the palace overlooking the azure blue waters of the Caribbean Sea.

"My plane leaves in a few hours, Miguelina," Mike said sadly. Then he smiled gently. "I guess we can be grateful that Cookie hated this 'bug-infested jungle' as she called it, where they don't even speak English."

Miguelina looked at him searchingly, silently, for some moments. Then she said, "You'll be back, Mike. You'll be back to stay. I'll be waiting."

"You will come up and visit, won't you? I mean we could meet in Houston or Dallas, someplace like that."

"The way things are going neither I nor any of us will be allowed into the United States. It seems your government is trying to express its disapproval of us here."

"I wish I could make them understand that you don't stop Communists from overrunning your country by inviting them in and treating them as honored visitors. Well, if they give me a job that doesn't require a secret clearance I'll be able to travel to Mexico. We could meet there."

"We'll see, Mike, we'll see," Miguelina replied. Then, with a quick smile she said, "Would you like me to go back to your quarters and help you finish packing?"

"Yes," he replied huskily.

CHAPTER FOUR

Sally Cookson, better known to her friends as Cookie, was at the Houston Airport to meet the Braniff flight bringing her husband home from Latin America. She was standing outside the customs and immigration entrance when Mike Snyder walked through the doors.

"Mike!" she cried shrilly and threw her arms around him. "At last you've come home. And Daddy says they're not going to give you any more nasty assignments to those foreign jungle countries where they don't even speak English and there's nobody you want to see there."

Mike sighed, remembering how just this morning he had described Cookie's attitude to Miguelina. He held Cookie to him for a moment, kissed her and then gently pushed her away and supervised the porter bringing his suitcases out. Customs hadn't asked him about the distilled cocoa leaves.

"Jason will take them," Cookie said gesturing at the tall black chauffeur. "Wait 'til you see Daddy's new Mercedes. He's had it up to a hundred and twenty miles an hour."

This Cookie, this blonde wife of his was something to see. That was undeniable, Mike thought. Everybody at the airport was staring at her wondering who the lucky man with her was. She was braless, the nipples of her breast clearly outlined under the sheer sweater she was wearing. He really couldn't blame himself for the intense affair he'd had with her before he had gone to Vietnam for his first tour of duty. She'd been the most beautiful, the most desirable woman Texas had to offer and everybody had been intensely jealous of him for having captured her total affections. Now, he felt nothing for her except pity and distaste.

They settled into the back seat of the air-conditioned Mercedes and Cookie casually reached over, putting her hand on his crotch. "Sorry, honey," he said. "I— uh—need a little time." Cookie snatched her hand away angrily. "Well! Pardon me!"

She'd made that one trip to Costa Vacca, stayed three days and hating what she considered to be a backwater banana republic, had mercifully left. It was then that the affair with Miguelina had begun in earnest.

Not that he and Miguelina hadn't tasted deeply of each other prior to Cookie's visit when she'd planned to stay with him during the remainder of his tour as a military advisor to a friendly Latin country. All it had taken was that one series of articles that appeared all over American newspapers about the alleged brutality inflicted on political prisoners by the dictator to turn

28

America against Costa Vacca and eventually terminate his assignment.

Cookie darted a mischievous look at Mike. "What are you looking so thoughtful about?" she asked. "I'll bet I know. You're thinking of that black-haired spic girl, that bloody dictator's whore of a daughter."

Instantly Mike's aroused state dissipated into annoyance. "It's not fair for you to talk that way about a charming, intelligent, and very pro-American woman."

"Oh, did Cookie hit an exposed nerve, darling?" she taunted.

"All right, Sally, enough of that."

"Oh, she was married twice before she was eighteen," Cookie blazed. "I always know when you're mad at me, Mike. That's when you call me Sally instead of Cookie."

Mike looked at her coldly.

"You know damn well Miguelina was forced to marry the favorite illegitimate son of the dictator of Costa Vacca when she was sixteen, and she hated him. He used to force her to watch when he had her previous suitors tortured in prison. That was the motivating force that caused General Alamen to overthrow and execute Pruhillo. Young Pruhillo was killed shortly after that, and Miguelina married the man her father picked out for her. A dutiful girl. And he was assassinated by the Pruhilloistas when they tried their abortive return." Mike could feel his anger rising and knowing he would give himself away, he stopped talking and let himself calm down.

Cookie rapidly changed the subject. "Wait 'til you see what I've done to our bungalow. You'll love it, Mike. Daddy was so good to us. They're having a party for us tonight. Just some close friends—oh, and you know who?" Mike shook his head without answering. "Your new commanding general."

"What!" Mike looked at Cookie in shock. "How does your father know who my next commanding general is going to be?"

Cookie smiled wisely. "You know Daddy."

"Even I don't know what my next assignment is going to be," Mike shot back, trying to keep the annoyance from his voice. He thought a moment. "I wondered how come I was going to be stationed so close to Houston."

"Well, just between the two of us—and I'm not supposed to tell you, but you know, Mike, I never can keep anything from you—Daddy and the Governor did have something to do with your new assignment."

Mike groaned to himself. So it was going to start all over again. Couldn't they realize how deeply he resented the political interference in his career? Whoever the commanding general was, Mike would have two strikes against him going in.

As the slick black Mercedes sped from the airport toward River Oaks, Mike reflected on the offer Miguel had made him. If he was going to be plagued by political interference, why not take on the job as general of the army of Costa Vacca?

The patio party at the Cookson compound in the world's most expensive bedroom community, River Oaks just outside of Houston, was underway when they arrived. "We'll go around to the bungalow first and then walk across the lawn," Cookie said.

"Good idea," Mike agreed. "I might as well get unpacked and changed before appearing at this little homecoming your father is so kindly throwing for me." The edge of sarcasm in his voice was unmistakable but once again Cookie wisely chose to ignore it.

As they walked through the front door of their bungalow Mike could not help whistling at the elaborate decorating and renovations that had been made in the house they had spent very little time in together. Shortly after Mike had married Cookie, a move not only encouraged but almost forced by her father who felt that Mike was the sort of material he could mold a successful man from, Mike had left for his second tour of Vietnam. "So this is the bungalow? Some bungalow! Christ, your Dad must have spent a hundred and fifty thousand dollars on this shack."

"I'm glad you like it, Mike. You haven't seen anything yet. Actually, it was over two hundred thousand. Wait until you see the art, some of the sculpture he gave us, and the bathroom."

Mike walked up the thickly-carpeted stairs to the second floor and turned left into the master bedroom. The old sash windows had become lead casement tudor style panes which gave the room a baronial appearance. "Take a look in the bathroom," Cookie suggested.

Mike walked in. The bathroom had been enlarged to include what had been a small guest room. "All the fixtures are gold, 18 carat gold, Mike," Cookie continued enthusiastically. "Too bad we'll have to leave it for an ordinary lieutenant colonel's house on the base," he remarked.

"You're near enough to the base so you can drive out there," Cookie replied. "Daddy fixed it that way."

"I need a drink," Mike said weakly.

"Go down and look at your den. Daddy had the

31

most beautiful bar put in for you. You make us both a drink and then we'll carry it out to Daddy's patio."

"I've been wearing this same suit since I left Costa Vacca. Mind if I change?"

"Of course not. Take a shower and put on something comfortable. What do you want to drink? I'll make it for you."

"I suppose there's a bottle of Johnny Walker black label down there somewhere."

"A case, Mike. Wait till you see the wine cellar. All the wines you like best, all the wines you couldn't get down there in that jungle. Daddy had the wine cellar specially air conditioned to keep all the wine at the right temperature. He and the biggest wine merchants in Houston designed it and stocked it."

"Just give me a double Johnny Walker black and soda. I'll be down in a few minutes."

He carried his overnight case into the ornate bathroom, took out a bottle of coke juice, gulped a long swallow, popped two aspirin, and undressed.

By the time Mike had showered and changed and accepted Cookie's scotch and soda at the bar, he had recovered from the transition from Costa Vacca to Cookson's River Oaks compound.

With Cookie holding his arm he sauntered out of their lavish patio and across the acre of manicured lawns and hedges to the Cookson mansion. About forty people were clustered on the Cookson patio and around the large kidney-shaped swimming pool.

"All my dearest and closest friends," Mike remarked dryly.

"Now be nice, Mike," Cookie whispered.

From across the lawn boomed Cookson's basso voice. "Here they are now, folks! Mike's back from the wars.

32

At last we've got the children with us again. Come on over here, Mike, y'hear. Yep, that's my son-in-law. Already sucking on a drink. Wouldn't even let me make the first one for him."

The big burly form of J.J. Cookson, florid-faced, white hair and ear-to-ear grin shining like a beacon, moved towards them. Reaching Mike he put an arm around his son-in-law in a bear hug and slapped him so genially on the back that Mike almost dropped his drink. "Good to have you back. Great to have you. We missed you. And Cookie, why Cookie hardly lived while you was away. We gonna have us a real time now. Come on and say hello to your old friends."

Mike did recognize most of the people that had been at his and Cookie's wedding, although he hadn't known them then and certainly knew them no better now.

As J.J. Cookson, his daughter and son-in-law walked back to the party in progress, suddenly Mike stopped short. He stared unbelieving at the plump, balding man in the garish Hawaiian sports shirt topping a pair of madras slacks. "Welcome back to CONARC, Mike," the brusque voice of General Lloyd Vogel rasped.

Mike continued to stare in disbelief at the General who smiled wryly back at him.

"I knew you'd be happy to see your old commander from Vietnam," J.J. Cookson boomed. "Lloyd here has been telling me they've got great plans for you, Mike," he went on cheerfully. "We've just been getting to know each other. I thought you'd like it that your wife and family are getting along just great with your new boss."

Mike took a long pull from his drink, switched it to his left hand and walked over to the General. Vogel stretched out his hand and Mike took it for a moment.

He had to struggle not to relive the last moments he could remember of the ambush. Wildfire had taken seventy percent casualties because this political general had not given him air cover when he needed it most. "Good afternoon, General Vogel," Mike said in a subdued tone.

"Glad to have you back in the division, Mike," Vogel said heartily. "I'm really enjoying getting to meet your father-in-law. I hope Mr. Cookson and I will see each other quite a bit."

"Now Lloyd, I told you it's J.J." Cookson corrected the general genially.

"Right, J.J.," Vogel chortled.

Mike was beginning to feel as though the walls of his world were moving slowly, inexorably in on him and would soon crush him, leaving him a different man, all the vitality of the old Mike Snyder squeezed out of him to dry in the hot Texas sun.

"Let me freshen up your drink, son," J.J. continued genially. "Now come on and say hello to all these good folks here who came to welcome you home."

Mike handed his glass to his father-in-law who took it to the bar and instructed the bartender to make his son-in-law a good strong Johnny Walker black and soda.

"I guess you didn't get much of that down there in that banana republic, did you, son?"

"Oh, General Alamen got pretty much what he wanted," Mike murmured, taking the new drink and immediately downing a good portion of it. Then for the next half hour he walked around shaking hands with Cookson's cronies, their wives, and the friends they'd brought with them. Collectively the group was probably worth well over a billion dollars, Mike estimated.

The second scotch became a third and Mike began to adjust to his new life. Actually he was readjusting to an old life he had started that day when Cookson had taken him aside almost five years ago and on this very patio had said to him that now he'd had a pretty good sample of what his daughter had to offer, why not do the right thing and marry her.

Mike wanted nothing more than to have this luscious girl for a wife. He could hardly believe that her father, the big Texas tycoon was actually standing there proposing the very thing Mike hadn't quite believed could happen. Love? He was no theorist about the fine points between infatuation and the deep, abiding kind of love that lasted. He wanted Cookie. She obviously wanted him. And if J.J. Cookson wanted them married, why not indeed? It didn't occur to him that it was "advantageous" or a stepping-stone to a life style most young men would find quite comfortable. Mike's life style was going to be his. His and Cookie's. An army post, simple, adequate—but one that he was responsible for. They would live on his salary, depend on no one else for anything. How wrong he'd been, he thought. . . .

Late in the evening as the last guests were leaving, Betty Lou Cookson finally said to Mike, "Now I know you're tired, Mike. It's been a long trip up here and then this party." She gave her daughter a sweet understanding suggestive smile. "And I know you two can't wait to be alone together away from us. So you go on back to your bungalow and enjoy the rest of the evening."

"That's right, Mike. I guess I wasn't thinking right. Keeping you and Cookie away from each other when you first got back." He smiled lewdly. "Now you two just forget about me and Betty Lou, go back to your bungalow and we'll see you when we see you. You have five days as I understand it before you have to report to Lloyd at Ft. Hood."

Somewhat numbed by the events of the day Mike nodded and taking Cookie by the arm led her across the compound back to their bungalow.

CHAPTER FIVE

Thanks to the cozy relationship between General Vogel and J.J. Cookson, it was a week before Mike Snyder reported to the division headquarters for his new assignment.

Cookie was her old self—fuzzy and contemptuous in her perception of the world outside River Oaks. If it wasn't happening in Houston, it wasn't happening. She babbled on about Mike's assignment to Costa Vacca, his probable relationship with Miguelina and her father, and seemed not to know or care that she no longer was important to her husband. Cookie had always bought what she wanted, and the man didn't live who could resist the combination of her assets. Money, a body that was straight out of any man's fantasies, and the powerful connections of a daddy who chewed up bankers and politicians for breakfast. Cookie wasn't worried about a thing. Maybe Mike didn't seem all that excited about making love to her now. But he was probably just tired or something. She would change all that. And soon.

After a week of Cookie's vacuous chatter Mike was just as bored with her as he'd been before leaving for Vietnam. During his period of recuperation at Ft. Sam Houston Medical Center the indifference had set in again and continued back in River Oaks prior to his assignment to Costa Vacca. He had been bitter but unsurprised at being RIF'd from full colonel to lieutenant colonel, but that was the way the system had to work.

By the time Mike threw a crisp salute to now Major General Vogel, both of them in uniform, he was ready to resume his army career, unconcerned about whether or not he would continue to stay at the bungalow instead of an officer's home on post. It was a two-hour drive from River Oaks to his station and he felt that probably he would have to secure quarters and stay at least half of the week at his new station.

Mike Snyder was still a military man and realized he would have to let bygones be bygones with General Vogel. In the back of his mind he'd never forgive the general for what had happened, but it was best to forget such things now.

After fifteen minutes of amenities, Vogel, the old army politician, expressing his pleasure at becoming friendly with J.J. Cookson and part of Cookson's milieu consisting of the political powers and financial powers of Texas, got down to business.

"As the old joke goes, Mike, I've got news for you. First the good news. At a meeting of the Joint Chiefs recently it was decided that in the immediate trauma following our evacuation from Vietnam the military had made a mistake in almost totally wiping out our counter-insurgency capabilities. The Green Berets have been relegated almost totally to a training force and it was suddenly realized that if we should get into another war, if we were threatened from down south of the border by Communist insurgency, we have no way of coping. Therefore it has been decided to establish, perhaps I should say reestablish, a unit with the capabilities of your old Wildfire group in Vietnam. In other words we must put together the means of transporting a well-trained group of jungle fighters into any country in this hemisphere threatened seriously enough by Communist insurgency that we have to step in rather than let the Russians or Communist Chinese take over."

"It's about time they realized that!" Mike snapped. "How come they've withdrawn their support from Miguel Alamen in Costa Vacca? He has a Communist insurgency problem that is multiplying every day and now, with the discovery of oil in Costa Vacca, it's only going to get worse."

"Your friend General Alamen has adopted tactics not popular in this country," Vogel replied. "Those newspaper stories, those pictures, did incalculable harm to him and his regime."

"How the hell are you going to stop the Communists if you can't aggressively track them down, interrogate them, and with intelligence from interrogations continue wiping them out? That's what we did in Vietnam. Don't you remember, Lloyd?" The general winced at Mike's use of his first name. "How do you think I made your area of responsibility totally free from Communist subversion? We worked with the Koreans and some of the best South Vietnamese units to exterminate the Communists." Snyder laughed mirthlessly. "How the hell many MyLia situations do you think happened in your command? I had to laugh when I was reading about those generals whose careers were terminated as a result of the MyLai massacre. Hell, that was a clambake compared to what we did in your area and you know it."

For an instant a look of terror came across Vogel's face. It was quickly supplanted with a fearful and finally an angry demeanor. "That war, that period is behind us now, Major. Forget it. I don't even want to hear you discuss it with me or any other officer again. It was indeed fortunate that you spent two years in Costa Vacca during the incipient investigations into our search and destroy activities in Vietnam."

"What did you say, General Vogel? What grade did you call me?"

"That's the bad news, I'm afraid, Mike. The good news is that you are going to head up a new Wildfire unit. The bad news is you've been RIFed down to major, your permanent rank."

"Just like that. 'Colonel, you're a major now,'" Snyder exclaimed angrily. "You know, I don't have to stay in the army. You know what I've got waiting for me in Houston. I don't have to take this kind of treatment."

A slow smile came across Vogel's face. Instantly Mike realized he'd trapped himself as the general laconically drawled, "Of course you're free to resign anytime, Major. Nobody can make you stay in the army. But I should point out to you that many officers and non-coms who very much wanted to stay in the army were RIFed out altogether. I might further point out, as you are undoubtedly aware, that your file has PI stamped on it very distinctly. Were it not for certain connections you have, you never would have made it to lieutenant colonel or full colonel. You're lucky to have major as your permanent rank in a peacetime army at age 35. So you have two choices—either accept the RIF and organize a new Wildfire unit or resign. I would advise you to think carefully about your decision."

For a moment Mike thought about being a general in the Costa Vacca army, owning oil property that would have made J.J. Cookson drool if he knew about it, becoming as rich as any Texan that ever bought a big home in River Oaks. But still, he was an American, an officer, albeit drastically reduced in grade. It took only a few seconds for him to control himself and reply to General Vogel. "Sir, I accept the assignment."

"I thought you would, Mike."

"What have I got to work with to start this unit? I lost some of my best officers and men in Vietnam. I'd like to find the remnants of them. Maybe I can find Sergeant Medford. He's the one who saved me in Vietnam. And I'd like to find Major Hackett as well. In fact all the men still alive from that unit would be useful in forming the new Wildfire."

"I'm afraid that Sergeant Medford was RIFed down to corporal and quit. Major Hackett did stay in as a first lieutenant. I don't know where he was assigned. You put together a Table of Organization and reform a company with the capabilities of your Wildfire unit out of men that are still in the army. They will continue to serve in your new unit at the same grade you find them."

"I want Sergeant Jimmy Medford back in and I want him back in as a master sergeant."

"I can't do that for you. We went to a lot of work to cut the military budget. I have no authorization nor

41

would I give authorization to increase a budget we've just cut."

Snyder controlled his temper. What is this shit about there being no room on the roster for one more highly experienced noncom? he asked himself. But he also realized that Vogel would be more than happy to see Snyder out of the army permanently and he couldn't afford to antagonize the general now if he were going to be successful in putting together his old Wildfire unit. It was a great challenge, just the assignment he would have asked for if given the opportunity. The only problem was he had to work under this fat-assed politico general, Vogel.

Mike felt a sense of mission, a sense that had been long gone within him. He would put up with Vogel, kiss the old fart's ass if he had to but if there was anything needed in the United States of America today with the war in Vietnam lost, with the humiliation and degradation of the entire military being exacerbated by the American public, nothing could be more important than to have a Wildfire unit such as he had led successfully into Cambodia, Laos, and even North Vietnam. A unit which had totally, and yes, he had to admit, ruthlessly destroyed the communist infra structure in the areas assigned it. What could be more challenging than implementing such a unit, making it operable and once again, being able to provide a deterrent to Communist overt infiltration of countries like Costa Vacca. General Vogel was giving him the opportunity to institute such a unit and command it. This general didn't understand the essentiality of such an outfit. But Mike Snyder, during his exile period in Costa Vacca during which time he'd visited many countries in Latin America, knew how important it was to have such a brigade, an airborne brigade, at the fingertips of the President if he had to make a fast decision.

Well did Mike Snyder remember May of 1965. He had been on his way to Vietnam then when suddenly orders were switched. He was a captain with the 82nd Airborne at the time and suddenly found himself on a transport plane headed for the Dominican Republic. Disappointed as he'd been at not going to the war in Vietnam, he found that his unit of paratroopers had been the saving force that prevented the Communists from taking over in Dom Rep. It had been his proficiency in Spanish—his father had taken him to Spain when the advertising agency received the Spanish Tourist Board account shortly after World War II— that had won him the assignment.

Mike had begged his family to give him trips to Spanish-speaking countries. He understood the Latin temperament although he neither agreed with nor could condone the Latin outlook on human life and violence. Since to this day the operations of the United States troops in the Dominican Republic were classified top secret need to know, his highly successful activities in exterminating the Communists had never been declassified. This was an assignment for which he would always be grateful. He had been a soldier, he had taken orders, he had done his job, he had killed, he had conducted interrogations and acted on the intelligence received. Only a few people, not including General Vogel, knew the extent of his activities on the missions to the Dominican Republic in 1965.

One of those aware of his successes in the Dominican Republic, his ability as an American to personally interrogate Spanish-speaking prisoners, had been Ambassador Cabot Lodge's personal appointee to CIA operations chief in Vietnam in October of 1965. General Lansdale had personally requested that Captain Michael Snyder join his special unit consisting of such CIA stalwarts as big Hank Miller and Daniel Ellsberg who had later blown all the operations in the sudden burst of liberalism almost eight years later.

So Mike Snyder realized he had too much behind him, too many people he could call upon to help him, to jeopardize the possibility of producing a unit that could save the United States from one more close-to-home communist encroachment.

"J.J. says you want to stay at home and drive out here every morning," General Vogel said after a long pause. "I know it's a two hour drive, Mike, but if that's what you want it's up to you. Incidentally, this entire operation is classified top secret so you will discuss it with nobody."

The admonition was the last thing Mike had to hear. Nobody knew better than he how important it was to preserve the secrecy of such a unit being formed. "You can be sure I will guard the secrecy of the existence of Wildfire II with my life, sir," Mike said, knowing he was being over-dramatic. What worried him was the General's ability to keep the operation secret, particularly when Mike started pressing him for the personnel and equipment he would need.

"Sergeant!" General Vogel bawled out, "Escort Major Snyder to the area designated for Wildfire II."

"Yes, sir!" the sergeant bawled back. He looked at Mike Snyder's silver oak leaves, signifying rank of lieutenant colonel and then questioningly back at General Vogel.

"We're all caught in this new RIF, Sergeant," Vogel explained.

44

"I've got the old gold leaves in my little souvenir chest at home, General," Snyder remarked curtly. "I'll have them on tomorrow."

"Why don't you go by the PX and get a set right now, Major," Vogel replied sharply. He handed Mike a file folder. "Here's the documentation on the RIF. But you'll get up there again soon, Mike. You know how these things are."

Mike did not bother to reply. He turned neatly on his heel and followed the sergeant major out of General Vogel's office.

CHAPTER SIX

Mike Snyder wearing civilian clothes had been driving over two hours on Route 10 when he finally passed the little Texas town of Seguin and knew he was close to his destination outside of San Antonio. He left Randolph Air Base on his right and sure enough there on the outskirts of San Antonio was the strategically located Texaco station. He turned off the highway into the large service station and pulled up to a halt beyond the gas pumps.

Stepping out of his car he walked into the gas station and through the door to the mechanic's stand behind. Four or five apparent locals were lounging around watching one man standing under a car which had been elevated on the hydraulic lift working two wrenches on the underside of the vehicle. A television set in the dark corner of the cluttered greasy service area was blaring forth a late afternoon interview show.

Nobody paid any attention to Mike as he walked in and stood quietly in an out of the way corner of this service area. The body of the man under the car was familiar to him; the wide shoulders, lean whip-like body, and the inordinately big feet. Mike said nothing, not wishing to disturb the mechanic at work.

Two of the locals were watching the television show, the others engaged in conversation with the mechanic who talked to his friends as he did his work on the underside of the automobile six feet above the floor of the garage.

"Whatta you think of that kraut Jew boy getting the peace prize?" chortled one of the observers.

A string of curses emanated from under the car on the hydraulic lift but the work went steadily onward.

Another local took up the cry. "At least the gook cocksucker was honest enough not to take it. He knew them fuckers was going to zap us."

"Fuck those Vietnam War peaceniks!" another member of the group swore. "What the fuck did we give it away for? We could have won anytime they let us. First war in American history we lost. What you think Davey Crockett's thinking about now?"

"He's thinking America ran out of guts, that's what he's thinking," came from underneath the automobile. "What the hell are we talking about that for? It's over. We lost! No, we didn't lose, we walked away from it. Just when we could have won. My unit, if they'd let us go, could have wiped out the enemy and destroyed them right in their own home. But would those political generals, those left wing Communist liberals in the United States let us win the war? Fuck no! So here I am putting in new transmissions." The mechanic ducked his head and came out from underneath the car. "I

48

make more money running this garage than I did in the Army. But I'd still rather be back there. Now let's get off the subject of the war and talk about poontang or something that makes sense today. We fucked ourselves around the world. Let's at least have some fun at home. I'm going to get me all cleaned up and go into town tonight. I told the old lady I had to meet with a big customer of her brother's. It's a good thing both of us chase cunt and give each other excuses for being out."

He turned to one of the locals watching the car. "OK Earl, it's fixed. You ought to get at least another 20,000 miles out of this piece of iron before it collapses. Why the hell don't you get a new car anyway?"

"I get me a new car and either the old lady or my boy will crack it up again," Earl replied. "When I need a nice car I rent one or borrow one. No point buying me a new Chevy for the family to wreck."

"I know what you mean, Earl," exclaimed another member of the club that peopled the garage.

"The whole fuckin' world is going to hell," another loiterer contributed.

"Everytime I go by the Alamo I say to myself I'm sure glad those guys can't see what the country's come to today. Shit! Three tours in the Nam and where are we. Old Jimmy's got the right idea. Let's go into town and find us some tang. Forget all this shit."

The mechanic whose work on the car had been casually observed by the loafers suddenly spotted the newcomer to his garage club. He stared at Mike, incredulity and a tinge of shock in his expression. The words poured out of his throat. "Jesus Christ Almighty. Son-of-a-bitch it's the colonel!"

Mike smiled and walked towards his old first ser-

49

geant, Jimmy Medford. "How you doing, Jimmy? And by the way, it's major now."

"You got caught in the RIF too, did you, sir?"

"You're damn right I did. And I can tell you I had one hell of a time finding you. So you decided not to re-up, huh?"

"They offered me corporal, sir. After all those years of service comes the RIF and I get caught."

"I heard there was a little problem too," Mike smiled.

Jimmy Medford looked sheepishly at his feet. "You know how things happen when you get back from four years of combat and the dick-heads back here don't understand what you were doing."

"Sure, I understand, Jimmy. Any chance of getting you back?"

"Shit, sir, I heard that General Vogel was back at Ft. Hood, the rumor was he was putting together another Wildfire operation under his division. I went up to see him. Asked if he could use me. Let me tell you that general is very touchy about any of us who were back in the Nam serving under him. He covered up about ten MyLia operations and now he's scared shitless."

"I know that, Jimmy. So what happened when you asked to come back?"

"Same thing, sir. They'd take me in as a corporal. Hell, running my brother-in-law's garage here makes me more money."

"What do you feel about coming back in as a buck sergeant?"

"With you as commander, sir?"

"That's right. I can't tell you much about it now but they seem to be getting a little sense in Washington.

They figure they might need a unit like we had before. What about it?"

"Buck Sergeant in the peacetime army?"

"Take my word for it, Jimmy, you won't be sorry." Mike looked around the garage, eyed the idlers and then turned back to Jimmy. "I have a couple of ideas that could be good for you and everybody in the new Wildfire operation. You saved me once, Jimmy. I still don't know how we got out of that ambush."

"If it hadn't been for that pilot, Murray, we never would have made it, sir," Medford replied.

"I guess so. I found him again a few days ago. He's still in the Air Force. Still flying Hercules transports. They really racked his ass when he flew over into Cambodia and gave us that cover. But he'll be part of our plans."

"Sir, I don't know what's on your mind. But whatever it is I'd like to be part of it. Get me those stripes and I'll come back. You've got to have something more than bird turd on your mind."

"That's right, sergeant. Come in as soon as you can. Report to me at Ft. Hood. We'll take it from there."

Jimmy Medford took two steps to the wall, reached for a lever, pulled it and the hydraulic cylinder began to recede into its casing, slowly dropping the car he'd been working on to the floor of the garage.

CHAPTER SEVEN

When Major Mike Snyder reported for duty the next morning he went directly to the office of General Vogel. Snyder did not mince words.

"Sir, I found three of my best men from Wildfire in civilian life. They're all willing to come back. Most of all I need Sergeant Medford. He was offered corporal when he was RIFed."

"Yes, Medford's case was a strange one. At one time he had a warrant giving him permanent rank as master sergeant. The warrant was revoked for misconduct on Medford's part—"

"He was always a precipitous type," Mike cut in. "That's how he pulled off so many successful combat missions. You can't expect a great combat man to be a compliant peacetime soldier, sir."

"What are you trying to do, Snyder? Bring all your old hoods back together again?"

53

"I can't do that, sir. Most of them were killed in that ambush when you left us out to die. If it hadn't been for a certain Air Force pilot, Captain Murray, who disobeyed orders, we all would have died."

"That sort or talk borders on insubordination, Snyder," Vogel growled menacingly. Then he relaxed slightly. "If I didn't know your father-in-law, your wife, and on top of that have respect for your ability in a combat situation, I would have you out of the army right now."

"What are you going to do about Medford?"

"He can come back in as a corporal. That's the best I can do."

"How the hell do you expect me to put together a Wildfire unit that the Chief of Staff will pronounce ready to go anywhere in the world and pull off any mission necessary if you won't let me bring the best men into the unit that I can find?"

"You should understand it, Snyder. Politics. I know my budget, I know my TO, I know what I can do. I'm not sticking my neck out for a bunch of hoods. You might as well know right now it wasn't my idea to get you into my division and let you start up another Wildfire unit. That came from somewhere in Army Intelligence. And don't think I couldn't get you out anytime I want to. In the last month since you've taken up your new assignment there hasn't been two days go by that you have not proved yourself insubordinate in one way or another."

"I may appear to be insubordinate, sir, but I'm also trying to carry out my assignment. I expect that some of the reports of what I did in Wildfire have reached rational eyes in the Pentagon. Eyes belonging to men, generals, maybe even admirals, who know what we are going to be facing again around the world. It takes an officer who has killed a hell of a lot of the best men the enemy could throw at us to organize a search and destroy team. You should know that, General. I went from full bull colonel back to major. You went from brigadier general to two stars, major general. Why? I'll tell you why. Because my Vietnamese officers wired up Communist suspects to field telephones, threw them in a barrel of water, cranked out the electricity and we followed up the information they screamed at us. That's how. How the hell do you think I wiped out the entire Viet Cong Communist cadre in Tay Nhin? Your headquarters, sir. We killed everyone. No suspect was left alive. As a result, no more attacks on hamlets and village chiefs and schools, and the administrators reporting to Saigon. Why? Because my brigade, my intelligence men, my Vietnamese, and I myself, sir, kept up a quiet little counter terror offensive. Would you like to know how many women and children who were taking information to the Communists we killed on your behalf?"

General Vogel slammed his fist on his desk. "That will be enough, Major. That's enough to put you out of the army permanently," he shouted. "I could put you in Leavenworth!"

"You probably could, sir, and you'd be my cellmate. If they put generals and majors together in jail. We were certainly together when we wiped out the communist infra structure in your command."

Slowly reason, perhaps even surrender took the place of General Vogel's fear-inspired ire. He sagged back into his chair behind the desk. For a long time he stared up at Major Snyder standing at casual attention in front of him. Finally, choosing his words carefully, his eyes hard as he met Snyder's implacable gaze, General Vogel said, "I don't know what quirk of fate threw us together again, Major Snyder. I certainly didn't plan it. When the orders came in from Washington and your name was cut to command, under my jurisdiction, a new Wildfire team, I will admit I fought it. I hoped you'd stay down there in Latin America as a military advisor until your retirement. And let's get something else straight between us, Major Snyder. I went to West Point. My stars are permanent." Almost unconsciously his index finger of the right hand outlined the five points of first one of the stars on his shoulder and then the second. "I intend to make two more before I retire. I will not subject myself to another of your hysterical harangues. Probably you should be in the psychiatric ward at Ft. Sam Houston. But you're here. And you know why?"

Mike Snyder nodded, a rueful look coming across his face. "Yes, sir. My father-in-law wanted me near Houston. And for the political influence in my case I am truly regretful. I never went to West Point, sir. But I believe I'm as much a part of the United States Army as you are. Perhaps I look at it differently. I don't ever expect to become a member of the general staff in Washington. All I want to do is a good combat job. Sure I've got PI stamped all over my military records. Ever since I started going out with J.J. Cookson's daughter and he figured I would marry her, he used governors, senators and even a president from Texas to advance my career. I didn't like it, I don't like it. So let's you and I get one thing straight, General. All I'm interested in doing is creating Wildfire II. I need your help to do it. I need you to bend one or two regulations for me."

A cunning look came across Major Snyder's face.

"And I might be able to help you, sir. Who knows what J.J. Cookson could do for you at a time you needed a strong dose of PI as you're going after that third star? At least we're not in competition. We should be working together. Now how about bringing in my old master sergeant, Jimmy Medford? And bringing him in as a buck sergeant and allow me over the next few months to promote him back to master sergeant. And while you're at it I'm not asking for a push back up to lieutenant colonel but my former deputy First Lieutenant Hackett certainly deserves to be a captain."

"Bring in Medford. I'll authorize rank of buck sergeant on the TO for him. But no other promotions, none." General Vogel looked at Mike Snyder, almost a pleading expression in his eyes. "They watch my budget like hawks in Washington, don't you understand, Snyder? I'll have to explain bringing a sergeant back in after he has been RIFed."

"I guess I understand, sir. I understand they give out the distinguished service medal for stringent budget cutting. But you work with me, and I will produce the Wildfire II that you have been ordered to develop. Do we understand each other, sir?"

General Vogel nodded, deflated. Mike Snyder stared down at him and after a few moments of silence he played one last political card. "By the way, sir, the University of Houston is opening its football season against Rice. Just a college game but very interesting. J.J. asked me to extend you an invitation to bring your wife and join him in his skybox at the Astrodome. He puts on a better show than goes on below on the Astroturf. I'm sure you'd enjoy it. Can I tell him you'll join us?"

The atmosphere in General Vogel's office immediately lightened. Vogel smiled, stood up and nodded. "Yes, Snyder, tell J.J. I'd like to join him."

"Good, sir. I'll tell him to expect you. I'll leave the tickets with your orderly tomorrow."

"Thank you, major. And, yes, let's try to work together." The General smiled tightly. "Wildfire II could become an important unit in the Army. We never know when a trained counter insurgency unit will be needed fast."

CHAPTER EIGHT

An elderly, gentle black butler dressed in starched white mess jacket and knife-creased black pants above patent leather shoes carried a silver tray of drinks from the butler's pantry to the lounge of the luxurious skybox perched high above the multitudes in the Astrodome.

"There you go, Lloyd, Lurleen," J.J. Cookson genially greeted General Vogel and his aging Southern belle wife, handing them their drinks from the tray. "Sure good you could come up here for the game."

"Oh, we're thrilled to be here, J.J. I always wondered what the skyboxes at the Astrodome were really like," Lurleen gushed.

"They make it handier to watch the game," J.J. allowed modestly.

The butler continued to make the rounds of Cookson's guests who alternately watched the football game on television or stepped out of the skybox to the seats in the mini-grandstand allotted to each box to see the game in actuality.

"Not much of a game, really. Rice and Houston," J.J. commented. "However, we ought to get some good betting in. What do you think, Henry?" He turned to Henry Hodge, President of Hodge Drilling Bits. "Second down and long. Hundred dollars Rice doesn't make its first down. You're an old Rice man. Whatta ya say?"

A hundred dollar bill appeared in Henry Hodge's hand. "You got it, J.J." J.J. put a hundred dollar bill into his guest's hand and both of them watched the play below intently.

Mike Snyder with his deputy Jerry Hackett standing beside him also peered down at the game below. The blocking and tackling in this hard-fought game between two traditional rivals reflected Mike's mood. "What a fight I had to go through to get Jimmy Medford back in with three stripes," Mike growled inclining his head toward General Vogel. "And three of my best officers from Vietnam he wouldn't let me bring back in at all. Don't they know what they're doing to the Army when they get rid of some of their best combat men in a RIF?"

"Take it easy, Mike," his deputy advised. "Why don't you enjoy the day. This is some sight up here." Hack looked around the brilliant assemblage in Cookson's large skybox. "Christ, you'd think these women were at some ball. There must be a quarter of a million dollars of jewelry in this box alone."

"Yeah, it wasn't until I married Houston that I saw the ladies' approach to football. They hate the game but they wear every sparkler they ever had when they come here. Look at that emerald pendant my mother-in-law is wearing. Or take my wife. Her Daddy gave her that diamond necklace for a wedding present. I used to tell her, hey Cookie I'd say, you don't wear expensive jewelry to a football game. You know what she'd say back to me?" Snyder chuckled mirthlessly. " 'What other reason is there to come to a football game?' she'd ask." Snyder nudged Captain Hackett surreptiously and motioned toward Henry Hodge and his wife.

"Hodge over there, his granddaddy started the Hodge Drilling Bit Company. Henry's daddy took it over and now Henry runs the show. He's as rich as Cookson. Look what his wife's got on. Check those diamond bracelets and look at the pearls. You know old Henry Hodge wouldn't give his old lady cultured pearls. Each one of those is a real pearl brought up by pearl divers in the Arabian Gulf."

Hack laughed in a self-deprecating way. "I guess I don't know my jewelry. I'll just have to double my estimate."

"At least."

"First down!" Henry Hodge cried out jubilantly.

"Two hundred they kick on third down in the next series," Cookson rasped pulling two more bills from his pocket.

"You got it, J.J. I don't know why you want to bet against a winning team."

J.J. walked over to a telephone on a wall hook, picked it up, dialed three numbers and listened. Turning to Henry Hodge and the others in his skybox he said, "I'm gonna get Frank Bogelson, see how much his box wants to bet against our box on the score at the end of the first half." He paused. "Hey Frank, how much your box want to put up that Rice isn't seven points ahead at the end of the half?" J.J. chuckled uproariously at what he heard coming over the phone. "I didn't think you Houston U folks would put up with that. Five grand your box will put up? We'll match you." He listened for a moment. "Of course cash, you old bastard. When the half's over bring your five grand and I'll give you a drink." He listened, laughed again. "Yeah, our five grand will be ready but you won't be taking it away with you." He hung up. "OK, everybody who wants to get in on the bet and double your money, put it up now."

There was a commotion at the open door to the box and Cookson looked over. The Governor of Texas, his wife and two aides walked in and were greeted effusively by J.J., Henry Hodge, and the other guests. The governor allowed as he'd have time for one bourbon and branch and then with Cookson, Hodge and the others wandered back out to look down at the game.

"You just lost you another two hundred! First down again!" Henry Hodge chortled.

Mike Snyder turned his back on the assemblage. "The whole U.S. Army going to hell, we've destroyed millions of our friends in South Vietnam turning them over to the Communists and we're going to do the whole thing all over again," he grumbled to Hack. "And look at everybody here. Even the governor. Do they give a damn? Hell no. All they think of is money, and more money. Someday when we don't have a country their money is not going to do them any good."

"Oh come on, Mike, don't be so serious. At least wait until Monday."

"I don't understand Vogel," Mike went on. His head still ached despite the generous gulp of liquid cocaine

62

he'd swallowed. "For that matter I don't understand the army. Here they are asking me to build up a new Wildfire unit and they're RIFing everyone that I need to make it a success. Looks to me like we've been ambushed again."

"And what are you going to do about it?" Hack asked ruefully, seeming to accept the situation.

Mike shook his head. "I'll work it all out, you wait and see. One way or the other."

"Yeah, yeah, I know you will, Mike." Hack gave his commander a worried look and turned back to the game.

Cookie came up to her husband, slipped on arm around his and said, "What y'all looking so serious about there, Mike? Why don't you have a drink?"

Mike looked at his wife, her blonde coiffed hair, the dress more suitable for a garden party in Monaco than a football game in Houston. "I was just talking to Sally Hodge," Cookie went on. "She and Henry want us to come over tomorrow night. They're having a little party for Billy and Marie Hodge. You know Billy's little boy will be five years old tomorrow. And I'm his godmother. So we've got to go."

"Of course we've got to go," Mike agreed. "You go tell them we'll be there." He watched Cookie laughing and prattling emptyheaded nothings with the Hodges and then he turned to the door, walked out and took a seat. He always had loved football but now he was finding it hard to concentrate on the play below.

As he watched the game he was conscious of the constant betting among the Texans in this box and also that Cookson frequently went to the skybox telephone calling other boxes and making bets. Cookson's voice bellowed out odds he was giving or taking on the bets.

Occasionally he let out a lusty victory yell as his guests won a big bet against a sister box.

At the end of the first half Cookson added up the bets he had outstanding and let the other guests know that they were ahead of all the others. Then, during the hiatus between the halves with the college bands strutting up and down the field below, Cookson sidled over to his dour son-in-law.

"I hear you're having some kind of a dispute with General Vogel, son," he began.

Mike turned to his father-in-law. "I guess that's a fair statement," he replied, adding no further information.

"What's it all about? Something to do with you wanting your friends to get back in the army and Lloyd says he can't do it because of the budget. Now why do you want to get yourself all hot and bothered about a few measly sergeants? In fact, I don't know why you don't get out of the army altogether anyway. If you don't like what's happening, get out. It was fine to wear a uniform and play soldier when there was a war, but boy, the war is over. Men have better things to do with their time than fool around playing war games. You could be doing something important now."

"Like what?"

"Like making your fortune. How long do you think you're going to keep Cookie happy running back and forth to that military base like a Boy Scout. It's time you think about making it big, son. I could make you governor, boy. You could become senator," he paused thoughtfully, "or at least a congressman to start." He looked at Mike from under beetle eyebrows. "I made you a full colonel there for a while. But like I say, the war's over now. It's either business or politics. I think you'd do best in politics. I got several laws I need passed, we all need passed, here in this oil business."

Mike looked at his father-in-law coolly. "Do you remember what Mark Twain said? The only place you find a truly criminal mind is in the Congress of the United States. I'm not a politician, I'm a soldier."

Before Cookson could reply there was another stirring at the door to the box. Cookson turned and greeted the newcomer, a portly man who appeared to be in his late forties. He was wearing a dark suit and a lemon colored vest and flowered patterned tie. His round chubby face fairly crackled with a good humor and his eyes twinkled as he moved towards Cookson.

"Now we gonna get us the real odds," Cookson chortled. For the first time that day Mike Snyder smiled and seemed to enjoy his surroundings. Big John Dykes always had that affect on people and he and Mike had become friends since the first time Houston's vaunted oddsmaker and gambler and Mike had met several years before. John Dykes and J.J. Cookson greeted each other and then John shook hands warmly with Mike. "You enjoying the game, Mike?" John asked.

"They're both playing good football."

"So what are the odds the professional is making?" Cookson asked heartily.

"I'll take Rice and give you six points," John answered.

"Six points!" Cookson complained. "Eight points would be more like it."

"OK J.J., eight points," John agreed. "And furthermore you've had a first half to see them fight it out to a tie. How much you want to put on it?"

"God damn," Cookson grumbled. "You trapped me into a bet. OK, I'll take a thousand on Houston."

"You got it, J.J."

"John, can I get you a drink?" Mike asked.

"You sure can. Bourbon and branch. You gonna have one with me?" John asked, looking at Snyder's empty hands.

"Now that you're here, yes."

John watched Mike walk over to the bar where Cookson's skybox butler was making drinks. "You got you a good son-in-law there, J.J.," Dykes said sincerely.

"Oh yes, Mike's OK. I've just got to get him over this army thing and back into civilian life. No soldier gets to be a hero when there's no war going. He's already done that. Now we've got to get him doing something important."

Mike returned with the drinks and he and John clicked glasses, took long swallows. Then Mike asked, "How's sporting life in Houston?"

"Oh can't complain, can't complain. There's always something to bet on and always plenty of bettors, right, J.J.?" John took another long sip of the drink.

J.J. nodded and watched his vivacious daughter as she made her way around, charming Cookson's guests and pleasing her father greatly. Then J.J. shifted his gaze to Mike. "I've got a bet for you, John. I'll bet all the money that's wagered on the Houston-Dallas pro game on Thanksgiving that the major here won't be able to hold on to Cookie another year unless he gets out of the army and gets down to business."

Big John Dykes whistled. "That's a lot of money, a lot of money you're talking about. More money than is bet on any other sporting event in the U.S. of A.!"

66

CHAPTER NINE

Mike Snyder and his wife, Cookie, sat in their king-size bed in the air conditioned master bedroom of the River Oaks bungalow reading before turning out the lights to go to bed. Impatiently Cookie threw her book onto the floor and turned to her husband. "Why can't you be more friendly to Daddy and the folks he invites to come over?" she suddenly blazed.

"What do you mean? I'm perfectly polite to everybody."

"You seem to be somewhere far away, in your own world. What's the matter with you, Mike?"

"I guess I'm thinking of the job that's been assigned to me," he replied after a moment's thought. "Yes, I guess that's it. I'm supposed to form a whole new unit and Vogel won't give me the people I need."

"So why don't you get out of the army then and do something useful," Cookie challenged. "My father says there are a lot of things you could do. I could help you, Mike," she began. "Why don't you run for

Congress or help Daddy in the oil business or something like that?"

"Yes, I guess I had better do something positive," Mike conceded. Cookie smiled and stretched her lithe body arching her back and reaching out with both arms.

"Don't you like me, honey? We haven't done anything for ages."

Mike turned to his wife, admiring the body that had once so thrilled him before they were married. Those were the days when he thought he was the biggest lover in the country, with the gorgeous Cookie Cookson choosing him as the man she wanted. Cookie was certainly the most photographed and written about society girl in the state. Now at 27 she was still as pretty a woman as Texas or any place else boasted. So why wasn't he aroused? There was nothing wrong with Cookie, it must be him. He reached out for her and she snuggled to him. "Come on, lover, take me. I need it. Yes, that's better, Mike," she sighed.

Hours later when he should have been sound asleep Mike still restlessly tossed in his side of the bed. Finally, he crept out of the bed, found his robe in the darkness and walked out of the bedroom and down to the den on the floor below. He turned on the lights and sat down in the easy chair and started to shuffle through the newspapers which he hadn't read that day. Then suddenly he got to his feet, walked to the desk, looked through the leather bound book of phone numbers and finding the one he wanted lifted the telephone receiver and dialed. The phone answered on the first ring. "John, this is Mike Snyder. No, I'm not putting a bet on anything but I'd like to talk to you. How much money is bet on the Dallas-Houston game?"

CHAPTER TEN

Mike Snyder stood with his deputy, Lieutenant Hackett, and Sergeant Medford watching the men of Wildfire teaching recruits how to repel. The ropes were dropped from a fifty foot platform and the novices hitched their harnesses to the ropes and fell off the platform backward, sliding down, the friction rings controlling the rate of descent.

"Of all the men I had in the Nam who had pledged to make a career of the army I guess there's only about a hundred and fifty left," Snyder mused. "That's not so good."

"And things may be getting worse," Hackett muttered. "Look who's chugging across the field toward us."

Sergeant Medford and Mike turned and spotted General Vogel. "I'll see you later, sir," Medford said and started off in the direction of the unit's headquarters.

When General Vogel reached him Snyder tossed a salute which the general returned. "Just had word from Corps to implement a further RIF, Major," Vogel began abruptly. "Since the officers and men with most time and grade are in your unit I'm afraid we'll have to begin with Wildfire."

"But General," Snyder protested, "we're cut to the bone now. I can't afford to lose any more of my experienced men. It just won't be possible to create another Wildfire unit without them."

"Sorry, Snyder. Orders are orders. I want to go over your TO and see where we can cut."

"There's no place left to cut if you want a unit with the capabilities we're supposed to develop," Snyder snapped angrily.

"Are you saying you can't carry out your assignment, Major?"

"Nobody could without a cadre of experienced, combat-tested men." Snyder controlled his anger. Obviously General Vogel would like to get him out of the division, out of the army for that matter. But already the big plan was shaping up in his mind. He had to remain on the inside to carry it off.

"If you feel your job is too much for you we could begin this new RIF with you." Vogel's steel gray eyes bored into him.

Mike shook his head. "No, I'll carry out the assignment, sir."

"Then let's go back to your HQ and decide where we can cut."

Mike flashed a hopeless look at Hackett and started across the training field with the general.

Big John Dykes looked around Mike's den and bar

in the bungalow with obvious approval. "Yes sir, old J.J. did real well by you, didn't he?"

Mike nodded. "A little George Dickel and branch?"

"That's me," John agreed. "Well Mike, I don't suppose you brought me all the way over to River Oaks just for a drink. Although it's worth the trip to see this compound." John accepted the drink and paced about the den, then out into the living room looking across the casement windows and the lawn to Cookson's home beyond. "All in all I'd say this is a fine place to talk about money. Conducive, you know." He took a sip of the drink. "All right Mike, what's it all about? I must admit I'm curious. You want to know how much money is bet on the Dallas-Houston game?"

"I guess what I was really interested in is how much cash is inside the Astrodome for the betting?"

"Depends a lot upon how Dallas and Houston are doing when that game comes up on Thanksgiving Day this fall. Everybody likes to bet something on anything. But Texans, well, they do it bigger. I'm not a Texan myself but I feel like one. And Dallas-Houston is something every Texan will bet everything on—if the odds are right."

"And you have a lot to do with making them right, don't you?" Mike asked.

"I suppose that I have something to do with making the odds, yes," John replied modestly.

"So if the odds were made right, let's say managed, how much cash figures to be in the Astrodome when Houston hosts Dallas on Thanksgiving?"

John gave Mike a questioning smile. He hadn't become kingpin of the United States oil capitol sporting life through any lack of native shrewdness. But he was puzzled as to what Mike Snyder was getting at.

"It's hard to answer that question, Mike. A lot of the betting is done before the game by telephone. But a lot more takes place in the dome itself. And you know Texans. They like to bet with hard cash. They don't even like checks, no matter how good they might be. You know the old saying, cash and dead men tell no tales. And of course most of the people like me who take bets and lay them off, go to the game ourselves. What are you getting at?"

"Nothing really. I was just wondering. Ever since Cookie's father said he'd bet the same amount of money as was wagered on the Dallas-Houston game that I wouldn't be able to keep her interested another year unless I got out of the army and started wheeling dealing, I've wondered how great his lack of faith in me really is."

It was patently apparent to John that there was much more to Mike's questions than how little his father-in-law thought his chances were of keeping Cookie. A good gambler trusts his instinct, and John's instinct told him that something very big was on Mike's mind.

John took another long pull on his bourbon and water and then, sighing, replied to Mike's question. "I guess I can guaran-damn-tee you that come kickoff on Thanksgiving Day that Astrodome will look like the whole pot of gold at the end of your rainbow." John stared at Mike shrewdly. "I don't know what you have in mind but whatever it is I should know. I might be able to help you."

"Oh, I'll keep you informed. I'm just playing around with some wild ideas."

"Well, don't get too wild without talking to me, son," John cautioned. "I've had a wide range of experi-

ence in many things and you don't do anything without
letting me hear what you're thinking."

"You can count on me, John."

Half an hour later the portly gambler walked out of
the bungalow and onto the street where his car was
parked. As he got in behind the wheel he noticed another car parked behind him at the end of the street.
He did not think anything of it at first but when he
started his car and drove off the other car also started
up. John made a right turn and had gotten only a short
way before he noticed the car turning right and following him. He wondered who was keeping him under surveillance now. He was a little behind on paying off
some of the bets he'd layed off, but that wouldn't be
enough for any of his associates to have him followed.
There was always the matter of his jumping bail in Illinois and Massachusetts but that had been six years
ago. It didn't seem likely that the local authorities
would have caught up with him here. Well, someone
was after him, that was for sure. There wasn't much he
could do except go on about his business and wait until
his surveillance team decided to make itself known to
him.

CHAPTER ELEVEN

It had taken two weeks for Mike Snyder with the help of his father-in-law to set up this golf game. As Mike, General Vogel, J.J., and the Governor stepped up to the first tee to make their opening drives, Mike Snyder felt an exhilarating sense of accomplishment. This would be the day that would decide whether or not his grand scheme could go beyond the dreaming phase. But once an objective has been decided upon, actions and attitudes fall into place. Cookson had been pleasantly surprised himself by Mike's change in outlook and demeanor.

General Vogel as well had come to the conclusion that Major Snyder was fitting into the system and perhaps would become a good peacetime soldier after all. This golf game in itself was a clear indication of Snyder's desire to work in harmony with his commanding general. To be playing golf at the River Oaks

Country Club with J.J. Cookson and the Governor of the State of Texas was a tremendous accomplishment. The corps commander would be pleased, and Vogel's relationship with the governor as well as one of the most important oil men in Texas could not fail to be mentioned in dispatches to Washington.

The Governor allowed as how he played golf to get exercise, eschewing the golf cart offered him. Naturally Cookson and the others followed the Governor's example. All of them were walking the course as they played.

The game proceeded evenly with Mike Snyder perhaps winning the most honors as they holed out on each green. It was a hot Sunday and after the first nine holes they stopped for refreshments at the clubhouse before going out to play the second nine. Cookson made a remark about its being too bad that Mike Snyder stayed in the peacetime army instead of doing something important in the great state of Texas. "I thought he should run for politics," Cookson said to the Governor. "Not your job, of course," he added hastily. "But he's ready to flex his muscles, maybe run for congress."

"Well, J.J.," Mike interjected, "you might not realize it but I'm trying to do a very important job for General Vogel now. We're setting up a special unit. Even though it's peacetime you never know when we're suddenly going to need to show some muscle some place in the world, particularly the way things are going down in South America now."

The Governor looked interested, "What is it you're doing, Mike?"

Mike gave his commander a questioning glance and Vogel nodded assent. "During the war I was a specialist in running search and destroy missions." Mike noticed a slight look of alarm coming across General Vogel's face now. "We had the means to find the enemy fast and destroy them before he could attack our installations." There was a moment's silence, then Mike went on. "I'm trying to use the nucleus of our old search and destroy units to build one stationed here in Texas that could fly anywhere in the world and destroy or badly damage any enemy force the United States deemed a threat to our security."

"You mean for a while we didn't have such a capability?" the Governor asked, surprised.

"Well, Governor, you know what a RIF is. The Army's been suffering a RIF every few months and there are not many units left that are up to their old strength. To answer your question, sir, no. There is no light, fast-moving strike force available at this minute to fly into a country, take for an example Costa Vacca, and destroy a Communist guerrilla army fixing to take over the government."

"How long will it take to build up your unit, Mike?" the Governor asked. He was obviously interested.

"Well sir, despite the RIF that hit us most recently and some of our other problems I'd say we'll be fully combat ready by mid to late November. A little over two months from now."

"I'd like to see one of your exercises," the Governor said. "This certainly is an important capability, particularly to Americans living near the Mexican border. You never know what's going to happen in those Latin countries. And as for the Mexicans," the Governor looked around and lowered his voice conspiratorially. "Tell you the truth, I never trusted those Mexicans. Never have, never will."

"Governor, it would be an honor to have you come over to division headquarters," General Vogel chimed in. "We'll set up an exercise for you."

"It's too bad all the people of America can't see what we're doing," Snyder added. "Maybe it would give them a little more confidence in the army, particularly now in the time of peace if they knew what we could do if we had to."

Vogel nodded. "Yes, that's always our problem. Letting America know that their military is alert and prepared at all times to protect this nation."

This was the conversational moment Mike had hoped he could precipitate. He took the opportunity and ran with it. "When Houston and Dallas play on Thanksgiving Day in the Astrodome there will be 67,-000 people there and of course all of America will be looking at the game on television. Wouldn't that be a hell of a time to show the United States what we can do?"

Mike paused and seeing he had a rapt audience of three he went on. "There it is, the day Americans commemorate the earliest event in the settling of what is now our nation. What a time to show them what their armed services are doing for their security."

"That's quite an idea you just had, Mike," the Governor mused.

"Yes, Mike, a fine thought," Cookson echoed. "Let America see a new unit in action. And it will dramatize what kind of different shows we can put on in the Astrodome."

"The Chief of Staff would really love a chance to show America what his army is doing for it," Vogel contributed.

"That's right, General," Mike added to the momentum. "Let America realize we're still the best in the world if a push comes to a shove."

Playing the last nine holes Cookson, the Governor, and General Vogel frequently referred to the idea they had hatched at the end of the first nine. When the game was over and they went back to the clubhouse to tally up the scores and have a drink, the conversation returned to the possibilities of the big show in the Astrodome.

The political implications were very clear to the Governor. He would make a speech at the end of the demonstration. As Commanding General of the division in which the search and destroy unit Wildfire II had been formed, General Vogel would be introduced by name.

Cookson made a play for Major Mike Snyder also being introduced. He was already planning his son-in-law's political career.

After two drinks and a club sandwich the Governor was called to the telephone but not before all four men at the table had started to plan their own assignments in bringing this halftime show to fruition.

A highly enthusiastic and excited General Vogel finally took leave of Cookson and Snyder to return to his post, promising he would immediately start putting the idea of the halftime demonstration into the army system of channels.

Cookson and Mike Snyder rode the short distance back to the Cookson compound from the River Oaks Country Club in the golf cart which had not been used for the game. For the first time since Mike Snyder had returned from his last assignment, in Costa Vacca, Cookson seemed totally pleased with his son-in-law. "Boy, now you're beginning to think like a Texan. If you didn't talk so much like a damn Yankee I think everybody would think you were one of us."

"Well, maybe when I'm around a while I'll pick up the lingo," Mike replied cheerfully.

Cookson dropped Mike off at the entrance to his bungalow, reminded him they were having cocktails at six at the big house, then drove on.

CHAPTER TWELVE

The River Oaks bungalow provided the scene for Mike Snyder's first Wildfire party. "It isn't often that Cookie and her parents go off and leave me alone," Mike confided to Hack. "And this Friday they picked just the right time to go to see the Governor in Austin for the weekend. I sure wouldn't want to be having this meeting on a military post."

After finishing off the fried chicken the group adjourned to Mike's den for the real purpose of the gathering. The spontaneous camaraderie turned to tense attentativeness as Mike Snyder addressed his men sitting around the room.

"First, it's a go. General Vogel received enthusiastic permission from Washington to stage a military exercise during the halftime of the Dallas-Houston football game on Thanksgiving Day, five weeks from now. The Astrodome management has given the plan its OK and the front office of both teams has agreed to let us stage a six minute simulated combat show. The rest is up to us. You men are the key leaders of this operation. Now is the time to make up your own minds whether you want to go ahead. On Monday, after the weekend, we get started and there's no turning back. So you have tomorrow and Sunday to think it over."

"We're with you, Mike, or we wouldn't be here," Lieutenant Hackett's tone was forceful. Other assenting voices were raised and Mike nodded and smiled.

"I appreciate that, men, I just want you all to realize the jeopardy we are putting ourselves into. And for that matter the hazards we are exposing over 67,000 spectators to. It will be a hairy day for everybody and you must evaluate the risks against the rewards."

"Getting away from the dickheads who run our lives and the country from Washington is a hell of a reward," former Captain Leroy Thompson's bass voice boomed out.

This sentiment was greeted with general agreement. Mike nodded and went on. "All it takes is one man to blow the whole thing and land us all in Leavenworth. Every leader in this room must be absolutely certain of each man in his group. Now let's get our individual assignments straight and code names memorized. From now on when we're referring to Operation Dome you will call me Astro Leader. Captain Hackett, deputy leader, will be known as Two." Mike looked across the den to the tall, thin, sad-looking man quietly sipping a drink.

"Bill Sorell is a genius in signals. He was also, as many of you know, the original Wildfire's expert in expedient devices. He will be in charge of all our communications. He's out of the army now but he will train with us for Operation Dome."

Sorell's lips twinged into a smile. However, he said nothing. "Sorell's code name is Signals. Another touch of bourbon?" Mike asked turning back to Sorell.

"Don't mind if I do, Astro Leader." He stood up and carried his empty glass over to the bar.

Snyder focused the attention of the room on the muscular black man. "You all know Captain Thompson, former Captain Thompson I should say. He was the commander of the Special Forces A-team on the Cambodian Border where we were stationed."

Thompson looked around the room and nodded to the others present. "Thompson has got a very special mission to carry off. It is a crucial one to our operation but it involves only him and his men. When his primary mission has been completed, maybe a week before we implement Operation Dome, he and his group will join us in the repelling section of the operation. The code name for Captain Thompson is Joshua." Thompson smiled inscrutably as the others looked at him.

Snyder pointed to his sergeant. "Jimmy Medford will be in charge of the repelling section. This will be one of the key aspects of our entire exercise. Sergeant Medford's code name is Rope.

"And Lieutenant Anson who, like Medford, is on active duty will head up the skybox team with Two. When we have the scale model of the Astrodome to work with next week, you'll be able to see how intricate this particular crucial phase of the operation is. The skyboxes are loaded with jewelry. Therefore, Anson's code name will be Ice.

"And Captain Murray," he turned to the Air Force

officer who was standing in a corner watching the proceedings. "Murray saved us during that ambush that Vogel would have let us all be killed in when we went in to Cambodia. Murray was flying fighter cover that day. He was the only man, the only pilot who disobeyed orders, came into Cambodia and gave us the cover we needed so we could get out. Now he flies heavy transports. It will be Captain Murray in a Hercules transport who will get us out of this operation and on to our final destination. Naturally Murray's code name is Hercules.

"And former Master Sergeant Williams sitting beside Hercules is our Director of Personnel. Sergeant Williams will be the man who schedules transportation for families, girlfriends, wives of all the members of Wildfire who wish to take such dependents with them. Williams is also working with the men who were partially or wholly crippled in our search and destroy missions back in Vietnam. We are taking those of them who want to come with us to our final destination. Williams' code name is Roster which will undoubtedly become Rooster.

"And finally there's Lieutenant Tichman also active. He will be in charge of the guards outside the Astrodome when our operation starts. Also it will be Tichman who secures the armored cars we're going to need and the tanks. His code name is Steel."

Mike Snyder surveyed his group of leaders. "Any questions?"

"What about the men in Wildfire who will not participate in the operation?" Sergeant Medford asked.

"Good question, Jimmy," Snyder answered. "The answer is we are gonna have two Wildfire teams—one will be the team that actually goes into the Dome and pulls off this caper. The other team will be made up of those who we have not chosen to participate. At the last minute they will find themselves waiting at Fort Hood for transport while we are actually moving into the Dome. That's why I keep bringing up the importance of being absolutely sure that every man picked for this operation is totally trustworthy. Now we have exactly five weeks to practice this exercise until we are making our moves in our sleep. Everyone of you leaders will walk through your moves at least once in the Astrodome itself. This is something I will arrange in conjunction with the exercise we're putting on. Because we have the cooperation of the Astrodome authorities, thanks to my good father-in-law," he chuckled, "and can show every man his precise assignment directly on site, we will successfully stage the most intricate light infantry raid ever conceived."

Hercules raised his hand. "Dome leader, where do I land and take off with the plane?"

"I have been thinking a lot about that," Mike answered. "I believe we have a solution. We'll talk to you about it separately."

"I guess the big question on everybody's mind is the security of our final destination," Hackett observed. The others nodded agreement.

"I'll have a great deal more information on that in a week," Snyder replied. "I'm on my way to Mexico for the weekend. I can only tell you that we will not have to worry about extradition and half the money we take with us will be invested in oil fields which will bring our group collectively a large yearly income over and above what each individual takes as his personal division of the spoils."

"I guess what we all think, what we're all saying, is

that we trust you, Mike," Thompson said. "We all face very heavy time if this doesn't work."

"I'm aware of that, Thompson, and as your leader, the Chief of Planning behind this whole Operation Dome, you can be sure I will get the worst if we fail."

"It's worth a try. What are your choices, anyway?" Sergeant Williams asked the group. "It's life in limbo here. We'll never rest easy. If we answer honestly the question, what did you do in the Vietnam War? we're dead in the job market anyway. What have we got to lose?" Williams looked around the assembled leaders of Operation Dome and shrugged.

The others nodded and walked over to the bar helping themselves to another drink.

"The big question on my mind," said Captain Tichman, "is why Mike Snyder wants to pull this thing off. He's got it made. A rich beautiful wife, a daddy-in-law that will always see that he's well taken care of. This house," Tichman gestured around the bungalow and went back to mixing a drink for himself. "Why, Mike?"

"That's a fair enough question. I think I've answered it to some of you." He looked around the den of the bungalow which had been decorated at such great cost. "None of this belongs to me. I didn't earn it. More than any of you in this room I am not my own man. I'm owned. Lock, stock and barrel. My wife and my daddy-in-law own me. Sure, I could walk out of here, kiss off my wife, her family, stay in the army and help generals like Vogel politicize the military. You know what happens to a soldier that opens his mouth. The more truth he tells the deeper shit he's in. Let some general who really knows what's going on out there, in Korea, in NATO, in South America, just let him speak up and see how fast his ass is retired. If he's lucky. He's more apt to get court martialed. What can you do to stop America from giving itself away? I don't suppose any of you ever read *The Decline and Fall of the Roman Empire*?" He looked around the room.

"The what?" Sergeant Medford asked.

"The strongest nations on earth were never defeated from the outside. They were destroyed by the decay within their own population. The Roman Empire lasted a thousand years before it atrophied away. The American Empire will be lucky if it goes 225 years the way things are now. Maybe, just maybe, Operation Dome will accomplish more than making us all rich, giving us a satisfying life in a country that will appreciate us, and sparing us the frustration of watching the United States destroy itself from within. Maybe our demonstration, if you want to call it that, will start people thinking. Every nation in the world is shaking down the United States. Look what happens in the United Nations when an anti-American resolution is passed. Those apes jump up and down in the aisles screaming, laughing like chimpanzees because they fucked America again. We who give them everything they have, we support the United Nations, the world's most anti-American establishment."

Mike looked around the group, his eyes gleaming, compelling. "We who worry more about the rights of military deserters, rapists, murderers, muggers, dope peddlers and thieves than we do about the rights of law abiding citizens—how much longer can we hope for a stable America? Have you seen the United States stand up to anyone who threatens force or violence against us? Any week our United States government had asked us to, we could have won the war in Vietnam. And with a minimum loss of lives. Ask those guys maimed and crippled at Ft. Sam Houston, at the other veterans' hospitals what they think about the strength of America. Any Communist black country in Africa can get more out of our government than the black citizens inside the United States. Anybody who cocks a fist at the United States, at its President, is immediately bought off.

"What kind of leadership have we had in the United States in the last decade when we have been treating our friends like enemies and our enemies like friends? The only difference is that the enemies do not become friends. They become even more hostile to us the more we do for them. Whereas our friends suffer. My guess is that five years after we pull this caper off we'll be brought back to the United States as heroes. If that time ever comes we'll know the United States has again become a country we'll want to be part of.

"In the meantime, let's face it, the people in America that stand for cowardice and appeasement, the head-in-the-sand ostriches, have won the day in the area of demonstrations. Now maybe we can make a point." Snyder walked over to the bar, poured himself an ounce of his special formula, sipped it and looked around the assembled men who would implement Operation Dome.

"Does that answer your question?" he asked finally.

"Yes, sir," Tichman replied. "I guess we all have our reasons for becoming part of this thing and even if they're not all the same they all add up to the same thing."

"Good. We're together. Now in one hour I drive out to the airport. I'll be back from Mexico City Monday afternoon. I won't see you all again until Tuesday out at Wildfire. We've got the momentum going for us

now. Let's just keep it moving. I've arranged with a local motel to house all our RIF'd and discharged men
so they can train with us." He turned to Sergeant Williams. "Rooster, I've got it set with General Vogel that
nobody, but nobody, messes with our Wildfire training.
You just reintegrate the old guys as they come back
into our Wildfire force. Nobody outside will know the
difference. We've got a hell of a lot to do and not
much time in which to do it. And Thompson, you
and your men have the toughest mission of all to pull
off. I'll work with you on that next week. OK troops,
drink up. Have a good weekend. Every one of you who
reports to Wildfire headquarters Tuesday morning is in.
Nobody quits after that."

"Ain't going to be no quitters coming out of this
room, Mike," Thompson avowed.

"Thanks, Joshua. Everybody let their men know
that once they're in nobody gets out. We may have to
shoot a few men between now and Thanksgiving Day
but there's a great big desert out there in which to lose
the bodies. Understand?"

"Yes, sir!" the men replied vigorously.

CHAPTER THIRTEEN

At midnight Mike Snyder checked into the Reforma Hotel in Mexico City and asked for the suite of Miguelina Alamen. "Si, Senor Snyder," the room clerk said, "Senorita Alamen is waiting for you upstairs. Shall I have a boy take your suitcase to the room reserved for you?"

"Si," Mike agreed, anxious to get up to Migi's room. "Just tell me the number of my room." He pulled a five dollar bill from his pocket in his eagerness, handed it to the bellhop and received the key. He noted his room was a different room from Migi's. Latin discretion, he smiled inwardly. There was no doubt where he would be for the next twenty-four hours. His toilet kit was in his briefcase.

Migi was waiting for him. His heart leapt and the business aspects of their meeting utterly forgotten, he reached out his arms. She pressed her body to his and for some moments they held each other. Finally she pulled away from him. "I told you we would see each other again, *mi amore*," she whispered. "Now I must hear all about your big plan."

"Is tomorrow soon enough?" Mike asked. "I think that tonight we have better things to do than talk business."

"You are right. I have a bottle of cold champagne waiting if you are interested."

Together they walked into the bedroom and Migi playfully pushed Mike onto the bed and then kneeling, pulled his loafers off. Now in his last moment of rationality he questioned his motive for constructing this whole monstrous plot to rob the Astrodome and escape to Costa Vacca with the loot. Was it just for this woman?

Migi sat beside him on the bed and started to pull his jacket off. Bit by bit Migi undressed him, pouring him a glass of champagne which she refilled as his clothes came off until he was naked on the bed beside her. In an instant they were fused, one being, it seemed, instead of two as the champagne glasses rolled on the carpeted floor, spilling their contents.

It was sometime late Saturday afternoon before Migi and Mike finally were able to discuss the other reason, ostensibly the main reason, for their rendezvous in Mexico City. Miguelina Alamen could not go to the United States without causing attention as the daughter of Costa Vacca's strongman recently on the outs with the United States Ambassador to the United Nations because of alleged human rights violations.

Due to the geography of Costa Vacca it had been one of the early Spanish settlements to import slaves from Africa and the black population outnumbered the white about ten to one. The incipient black leadership which had been encouraged to press for a share of power in running the government had been totally subverted by the Communists who had fled Chile when the Communist dictator there, Allende, had been overthrown. When the Communists who had arrived in Costa Vacca tried to assassinate various ministers of the government, Alaman had dealt harshly with them. As a result of public executions and vigorous pursuit of Marxist terrorists the movement had been all but crushed. And it was this that was causing Miguel Alaman and his government to be severely castigated by some American politicians including those close to the White House seeking the black vote in the United States.

It made no difference that the blacks who had been executed or exiled had been attempting to overthrow the government, using Soviet arms and advised by Cuban guerrilla instructors. The situation in Costa Vacca had been reduced simplistically for political reasons to a racial struggle. The whites, mostly of Spanish, German and to some extent English descent, a population which numbered approximately 250,000, were pitted, according to State Department pronouncements, against the blacks whose population ran, as far as could be determined since there was no such thing as a census taker, to more than two million.

"I'm sorry I couldn't come to see you in the United States, Mike," Migi apologized. "But it is impossible, as you know."

"I'm sorry too, my darling. But in only five weeks, if everything works as planned, we will be together in Costa Vacca."

"Will you miss never being able to go back to your own country?" Migi asked searchingly.

"Probably. But I've made my decision. And everybody with me has made theirs. Besides, I have a feeling that in a few years the men in power in my country will realize what we were trying to say and ask us to come back. Just as the demonstrators of the 1960s against the war in Vietnam suddenly became heroes and today wield influence in the academic world, the political arena, and even in business so will we once again be recognized. As a result of the wavering American policy toward stopping encroaching Communism, we have lost most of Asia, we're in danger of losing South Korea, and almost surely we will lose the southern part of Africa. And by the next generation, before the turn of the century just as old Lenin and Stalin planned, the Communist world will dominate the capitalist western society. Maybe sometime before this actually happens people like my men, who made a decisive statement, will be recognized as having caused influential Americans to think about why we did what we did."

"In the meantime, *mi amore*, I will make you happy."

"I know you will, Migi. It seems like a dreadful, desperate act we are embarking on but all of us believe we're doing the right thing. Now, to be practical, I want your father to allow us to buy cheaply the square miles in the plains area where we know the oil lies close to the surface of the earth. This will give us wealth, security from harassment by America, and the hard work in the oil fields, as owners of our own producing wells, that we are all accustomed to. We are closer to the United States than Nigeria and if, as it appears, we can supply more oil more cheaply to America than can Nigeria, we will not only be immune from American harassment but sought out as an alternative to doing business with Nigeria where the president in the last few years has merrily killed off over 150,000 rival tribesmen in his country. Yet our President calls him one of Africa's great statesmen. Some human rights statement! However, when oil is involved that's the way things are."

"Oh, Mike, I can promise you that my father will keep his word and grant you what you ask. His only request is that you give one half of your time to advising and training our army. In fact he hopes you and the others will let our people work the oil fields on your behalf and that you will develop the finest military establishment for us in South America. It's only a matter of time before we are hit again by Communist insurgents."

"With Costa Vacca's oil riches there's no doubt but that we can hold forever against any type of invasion the Latin Communists can mount against us. I will be bringing with me the finest insurgency fighters in the world. All of them will be devoted to strengthening your father's army at the same time they are building fortunes for themselves and their families."

"There is more than enough money to be made for all of us," Migi replied, her eyes shining. "With your help we can bring up the standard of living of our people. Everybody knows that Americans are the best teachers in the world when it comes to helping poor, ignorant people help themselves. We recognize our weakness in this area and we respect you Americans for what you've done. It was very sad when all your young men and women who worked in our country were called back to the United States because of the way my father fought the Communists. But we did what we had to do."

"Don't worry, Migi, we'll start our own peace corps in Costa Vacca. But we'll add a military training program to it which will truly ensure that peace will always reign in your country."

"What do you need from us to help you make a success of your plan?"

"Does your father have enough influence with the Mexican Government so they could delay giving clearance for American fighter planes to overfly Mexican air space?"

"The new president here is very close to my father. He knows that if the Communists succeed in Costa Vacca it will not be long before they come to Mexico."

"When we take off in our plane we're going to need a three-hour headstart. If the Mexican Government can somehow invent delays for that long a period of time before allowing American fighter planes over its territory, we can get away."

"I will personally talk to the President about this. We all try to make our relations with United States look bright. But, we all know inside that there are times it gladdens our heart to frustrate certain American objectives.

"I have another plan, but if it fails we'll need Mexican government help. We must be careful never to communicate by telephone, telex or cable. And of course letters are out. We will just have to arrange to meet here in Mexico City when we must exchange information," Mike said earnestly.

Migi laughed. "Is that so awful?"

Mike grinned too and in moments they were in each other's arms again.

Later Miguelina pleaded, "Major Mike, please. How are we going to work out our plans before you have to leave tomorrow morning if we keep doing this?"

"You're right, Migi," Mike said huskily. "There's a lot of contingencies we have to cover."

It was a reluctant Mike Snyder who kissed Miguelina Alamen goodbye at 11 o'clock on Sunday morning. For thirty-five hours they had not been apart and now they felt is was bearable to part from each other until their next meeting sometime before Operation Dome was activated on Thanksgiving Day. After the last lingering kiss Mike slipped out of Miguelina's suite and visited his own room for the first time since he'd entered the hotel. He checked out and took a cab to the airport. He would be in Houston at least a couple of hours before Cookie and her parents were due back from their weekend in Austin.

As he looked out the window of the airliner whisking him north he tried not to speculate on the enormity of what he was planning to do. He fought the headache and the hard cold lump in his stomach with a long gulp of the cocaine extract Migi had brought him and then ate luncheon. Arriving in Houston he felt far more sanguine about the whole operation. He of all people, Dome Leader, had to be constantly optimistic and confident in what they were doing.

CHAPTER FOURTEEN

Old J.J. Cookson had given his skybox to Mike and Cookie for the night of the University of Houston—Texas A&M football game. He seldom missed a professional game but the college games were non-priority to him. And since Cookie had been a coed at University of Houston, the game was even more interesting to her because so many of her friends would be there. Cookie and Mike had invited fifteen friends to watch the game from the skybox. The game was a festive occasion and they arrived an hour before the kickoff to take maximum advantage of the Astrodome's amenities.

Mike had invited Anson, Hackett, Medford, and Sorell as well as a group of their most trusted men. When Cookie heard about all the men that would be at the game she invited four of her girlfriends to liven up the party. The tall thin mournful-looking Sorell quickly turned all of Cookie's friends off. Signals was totally engrossed in the layout of the Astrodome. Jimmy Medford, "Rope," usually ready with jokes and small talk, was absorbed in studying the ceiling of the Astrodome and other areas from which his men could repell. Lieutenant Anson quickly saw why his code name was Ice. Not only were Cookie and her girlfriends wearing jewelry that was expensive, but the whole semicircle seemed to glitter in the ceiling lights as the women walked out to the corridor to talk to their friends. The ice was obviously everywhere.

Anson's two men, both urban insurgency experts like himself, men who specialized in guerrilla and antiguerrilla fighting in city areas, studied the situation closely.

"Lieutenant Anson, I want you to meet my friend Mary Lou Sisler. She was a cheerleader with me six years ago at the University of Houston." Cookie laughed gaily. "You know, Lieutenant, to this day neither Mary Lou or I really understand football. Maybe you can explain something about the game to her when it starts."

"I'd be glad to, ma'am. You must forgive me if I seem a little preoccupied. I've never been in the Astrodome before. I was thinking I might kind of wander around and see the place."

"Mary Lou has been here for many football games, Lieutenant Anson. Can I call you Ted? Isn't that what Mike said your name was?"

"Ted, ma'am, that's right."

"Well, why doesn't Mary Lou explain this part of the Astrodome to you and then you can explain the game to her," Cookie suggested brightly.

Anson looked at Mary Lou. She was certainly a pretty girl, much in the mold of Cookie. Light blonde hair, big blue eyes, a friendly smile and, he noticed, a well-filled braless sweater. He also noticed the string of pearls she was wearing around her neck. Those would be the real thing, he thought. Also, maybe it wouldn't be a bad idea to have a beautiful, gushing local girl on his arm as he gave the whole area a very tight inspection.

Anson, like many of his buddies, had been married and divorced shortly after returning from Vietnam. It wouldn't be bad to have a nice piece of fluff like this Mary Lou lined up in Houston. "Mary Lou, you show me this skybox scene, OK?"

"Oh sure, Ted, I'd love to."

"Great. Let's start at the entrance. How do you get in here? I mean I came in through that iron gate over there. How many other ways are there to get in and out?"

"Oh, it's hard to get into the skyboxes. Only two gates. Come on, Ted, I'll show you. As a matter of fact, I know the guard who stands outside one of the gates. He used to come down and try and date the cheerleaders after the games." A beaming Cookie Cookson watched Mary Lou go off arm in arm with one of the more attractive of Mike's friends.

Ice, as Ted Anson now thought of himself, and Mary Lou walked to the gate and waited for it to be opened by a uniformed attendant. "That's not the one I know," Mary Lou whispered.

"You got your card, mister?"

Ted nodded. Mike had given them all tickets that morning. "Now you follow me, Ted. I'm gonna show you the Caribbean Room."

"What about it?" Ted asked.

"Wait till you see. It has a beautiful bar and looks

101

down over the Astro turf. It will probably be taken over tonight by President Hawkins of Houston University and his party."

"Well then, will they let us in?"

"You just leave that to me, Ted, I'll sure know somebody there."

This chick can be quite an asset, Ted thought. To their left as they walked down the hallway was a wall pierced with port holes through which they could look down and see the field below. Then they suddenly found themselves in front of an iron gate through which they could see the Caribbean Room decorated in blue with round iron tables and chairs and a sitting room beyond.

"That's President Hawkins' party," Mary Lou said. The gate was not locked and she pushed it open, walking in as though she belonged, followed by Ted Anson whose eyes flicked about this room high above the Astro turf. It had a superb view not only of the field below but of the entire covered stadium. This would certainly be a prime source of money and valuables, he thought. Only the richest and most important people would be invited to this luxurious vantage point.

An officious looking individual in horn-rimmed glasses bristled up to them. Before he could say anything Mary Lou was rattling along. "Hi, I'm Mary Lou Sisler. Class of '71. Remember I was the cheerleader? We're up in Mr. Cookson's box but we wanted to drop by here and say hello to Mr. Hawkins."

"Mr. Hawkins is busy now. As you can see, the President of Texas A&M is with him."

"Oh that's all right," Mary Lou said brightly. "We'll wait for him."

"Do you have a card for the Caribbean Room for

this game?" the somewhat deflated college official asked.

"Oh, I don't have one for this game but I always stop by. Mr. Hawkins knows me. We'll just wait until he's finished and then I'll say hello and leave."

As the self-appointed faculty security officer looked at them uncertainly, Ted Anson memorized the room and its entrances. Mary Lou took his arm and swept him away from their antagonist and pulled him towards the row of chairs arranged in a line facing out over the field. "If you've never been to the Astrodome before you really needed to see this place, Ted. This is where the real VIPs gather."

"Is there another entrance besides the one we came in?"

"Sure, I'll show you." With that she led him past the row of chairs to another door. "This is how most of the people come in. They take the elevator and it stops just outside. Of course you need a key to make the elevator stop at this level."

"Very interesting, Mary Lou. You really know the place."

"It's always a thrill to come to the Astrodome. No city in the country has anything like it. Do you want to meet President Hawkins?"

"Not really, thank you, Mary Lou," Ted replied. "I think I've seen everything I need to see. Why don't we go back to the boxes where we belong?"

"OK, Ted, if that's what you want. But I'll bet we could watch part of the game from the Caribbean suite if we wanted to. And get a drink too," she added.

"Mary Lou, you're something else!" The girl looked pleased as she led Ted back across the front of the

Caribbean Room to the door they had come through. A few minutes later they were back at the skybox.

"Did you see the layout?" Mike asked.

"I sure did, thanks to Mary Lou. Now I'm going to walk around the other way. If Mary Lou will join me, that is," he added.

"Oh sure, Ted. As a matter of fact I've got a lot of friends we can stop and talk to."

"I'd like to see the other entrance to the skybox circle," Ted replied.

"That's where I know the fellow, if he's still there. Anyway we'll go see."

Mike watched them go down the walkway between the skyboxes on one side and the private rows of seats assigned to each box on the field side. He turned to Hackett. "Well, Ice is getting a good tour."

"We're all getting the kind of briefing we need," Hack said. "Rope is staking out the best areas for repelling. Somehow we've got to get Signals and his number two into the scoreboard control room and also into the television center."

"I had that set up already. The Astrodome is sending a PR girl up here to take those of us involved in the communications end of our demonstration to wherever they have to go to prepare for our show."

Twenty minutes before kickoff a brisk, attractive young lady in a business suit arrived at the skybox. "Is Major Snyder here?" she asked. Mike stepped forward. "I'm Caroline Reynolds with the PR Department. You wanted to go to the television control room and the scoreboard control room, correct?"

"Correct." He turned to Signals one and two. "These officers will be in charge of communications for our demonstration. The three of us will follow along with you. And we certainly appreciate your taking this time to show us around."

"We're all looking forward to your demonstration, Major Snyder. We've had everything from rodeos and bullfights to Billy Graham and boxing matches. But we've never had a military combat demonstration. Are you really going to come down from the ceiling on ropes?"

Mike chuckled. "That's our plan. Sergeant Medford will be most appreciative of a tour of the likely spots for repelling."

"Oh, we'll be glad to show him whatever he wants to see," the public relations woman answered.

"Well, they're just going to wander around at the game tonight. But I'm sure when the Astrodome is empty some day they'd appreciate a personal tour from somebody on your staff."

"It will be our pleasure, Major. Now if you're ready we'll get down to the television booth before the game starts. Then we can spend some time watching the way they light up the scoreboard. If you have any special message you want spelled out in lights during your show just let us know and we'll put it up there for you." Mike, Sorell and his assistant followed Miss Reynolds from the skybox area down to the television booths.

By the time Houston had finally beaten Texas A&M, somewhat of an upset, all of Mike's team had been thoroughly introduced to the Astrodome and were mentally planning their operations. Although Ted Anson and Mary Lou had established a convivial relationship, none of the other girls had succeeded in diverting the Wildfire men from their primary mission which was to thoroughly understand the Astrodome. "They seem to like the Dome better than the dames," Cookie stage-whispered to Mike. She laughed a bit raucously. "What's with your friends, Mike?"

"Well, you're used to the place, you've been here a lot. Us peasants who see the Astrodome for the first time can't help but be overwhelmed."

"Well, at least one of your friends, that Ted, seems more interested in a girl than this covered stadium. Do you want to ask everybody back for a drink?"

"I'll ask them." Mike turned to Hack. "You guys want to come back to the house? The girls are all coming."

At first Hackett looked doubtful but Mike whispered to him, "We don't want anyone thinking we're more interested in the Astrodome than we are in dames. Right?"

"Well, if you put it that way. I was getting pretty friendly with the brunette anyway. What the hell, it's Saturday night, let's see where we go from here."

"That's better. Cookie was beginning to wonder. You all know the way. We'll be expecting you."

CHAPTER FIFTEEN

On Sunday, the day after the Houston-Texas A&M game, Mike and Cookie excused themselves from going back to the Astrodome again to see the Houston Oilers play. Mike promised his father-in-law that he'd watch some of the game on television but basically what he needed was a day to assess the observations he and his team had made the night before and analyze his strategy for the coming four weeks. It would culminate in either the disastrous or triumphant ending of his United States Army military career.

It was nice to lie around the Cookson swimming pool when J.J. and his wife were away. And no sooner had they left for the Astrodome and their skybox than Mike, a towel draped around his nude form, ambled out to the pool and lay back in a lounge facing the sun.

After a half hour's contemplation of the cataclysmic events he was planning to inaugurate, Cookie marched

107

out to the pool in the nude, a towel draped around her shoulders concealing none of her attributes and stood over Mike's prone form. He looked up at her wearily.

"What's the matter with you, Mike? I can remember when you couldn't get enough of me. Remember when we used to make love five times a day? I haven't changed. I'm no different. What's the matter with you? And for that matter what's the matter with your friends? Only one of them, that nice Ted Anson, paid any real attention to my friends. Here I bring four beautiful girls to a party you're giving for the men who serve under you, four girls all of them ready to go all the way with whoever gave them the nicest approach and three of them—no, goddamn it, four of us—get no attention at all. At least I'm glad Mary Lou and Ted found a message for each other. And what about my husband who used to be so horny? All he does is have one big bourbon nightcap and fall asleep snoring. What's the matter with us, you and me, Mike? What happened to that big hunk of verile man I married?"

He had no right to test her, he knew, because even if she passed he still would be through with her in another four weeks. But he couldn't help himself. "I have a great idea for us, Cookie. Let's get out of this exotic bird cage and go out to the base and live on my salary as a major. We'll come see your Mummy and Daddy, but how about doing it my way? Let me pay the bills, all the bills, and let me run our lives."

To his relief Cookie let out a derogatory laugh. "What would I do living out there on that god-forsaken army base. You're not going to stay in much longer anyway. You've got to be crazy, Mike, giving up what we've got. I don't understand you sometimes."

"No, Cookie, I guess not. It's my fault for accepting

it in the first place. I guess I'm a little funny. I have this great desire to make it on my own and not be beholden to anyone, especially my father-in-law. Don't you understand? Between you, your father and your mother, you Cooksons own Mike Snyder. Maybe that's why I stay in the army, it's the last little thing I do myself."

He thought a minute and laughed mirthlessly. "No, goddamn it, I'm a liar. I don't even handle my life in the army the way I'd like to. Or at least I didn't until now."

Cookie gave him a sharp look. "What do you mean? You do now but you didn't before?"

"Oh forget it, Cookie. I can't explain."

"I know you pretty good, Mike. There's something real strange going on in your mind. Sometimes you seem to be all friendly and cooperative with Daddy. He thinks you've changed. He thinks you've got it all together now and are going to get out of the army and work with him. Why can't you do that, Mike? Isn't it what life's all about? We'll have us some children, think how happy Daddy will be with grandchildren. I didn't dare have children until you settled down but now, why can't you go to work for Daddy? You could be a big man, Mike. A lot bigger than any of those generals in the army that push you around. What has the army done for you anyway? In Vietnam you were a full colonel. Now what are you? A major."

"It's the system. You expect it, especially when political influence is responsible for getting you that bird on the collar when wartime promotions come fast. No, I can't blame that on the army."

Mike was surprised at himself to hear his defense of the very institution he was about to degrade. The system. Again the doubts assailed him. Why was he leading almost three hundred men into the most drastic action a military officer had ever chosen in peace time?

Now Cookie smiled tantalizingly. "We're all alone out here. Let's make it on that rubber raft right out in the sun, huh, Mike?" Groaning inwardly he stood up, letting the towel fall from his loins and led Cookie to the rubber mattress beside the pool.

"Well, don't do anything you don't want to do, for God's sake." Cookie's voice grated on his nerves.

"Who says I don't want to, Sally?" he replied.

"You never call me Sally," she pouted.

"The first time we ever made it I was calling you Sally," Mike reminded her. "Come on, lie down."

Cookie lay full length on the mattress, the sun beating down on her golden body, her blonde hair shining up at him. Slowly Mike positioned himself on top of her and closing his eyes imagined it was Miguelina below him. As he fantasized he felt himself growing until he was able to give Cookie the hard strength she wanted. Soon she was whimpering ecstatically and crying out in response to his thrusts. His eyes tightly closed, he was seeing Miguelina, trying to convince his mind that the body under his was indeed Miguelina's. When he felt he was about to ejaculate he opened his eyes, saw Cookie's face staring up at him, her mouth open, eyes wide and instantly his passion subsided even as he continued the motions that were bringing such pleasure to her. He continued to look directly at Cookie's blonde hair and familiar, pouty face until with a loud cry and gasp she finally reached a fierce climax, her hands holding his body tightly to her. Then Mike once more closed his eyes and it was Miguelina. In moments he felt himself let go and climax inside her. It was over, all over except for one ironic thought which streaked through his mind.

Little does a wife know for whom her cunt is surrogate.

Mike left Cookie and dived into the swimming pool. He let himself sink to the bottom of the cold water and then when he could hold his breath no longer he rose to the surface and swam two laps of the pool. He pulled himself out of the water and stood up naked in the sun and walked over to his towel.

"Hey," he called to Cookie who was now lying on a lounge chair dozing in the sun. "It's about halftime in the game. Let's go in and see what kind of spectacle they're showing today. Gotta watch the competition, you know."

"You've got to be kidding. You go in if you want to. I'm staying right out here in the sun." She paused and then opened her eyes and smiled up at him. "That wasn't bad, Mike. Why did you wait so long?"

Mike shrugged. He didn't know how to answer her. He padded off the flagstones around the pool and across the grass to the bungalow. The air-conditioned interior made him feel suddenly cold. He pulled on a bathrobe, turned on the television set and sat down in front of it. His timing had been right. The halftime show was about to begin. The two announcers were making conversation as the Oilers and their opponents left the field. One announcer was saying, "Perhaps it's a little early to talk about Dallas-Houston . . ."

"Ray, it's never too early to talk about Dallas-Houston."

"Well, we're four weeks away from the Thanksgiving holocaust in the Astrodome and that game should be a beauty. Houston has one of the best defensive lines in the league but Dallas is still Dallas. The immovable object is up against the irresistible force."

"Well, as long as Houston's great quarterback Johnny Houricane is playing as strong a game as he is today I'd say that Houston's offense is pretty formidable too."

"And Houricane always has his backup Brian Cotter, always a strong backup quarterback, Ray," the other announcer observed. "Brian hasn't been given much of a chance this season. But he's always been there when the Oilers needed him. Don't you agree?"

"Yes, the Oilers will be in fine shape for that big game. I understand it's already sold out."

"The Astrodome management is keeping 15,000 rush seats open for the fans who couldn't get advance tickets. But it'll be a sellout game all right. Oh there they come, the Houston marching band and look at all those Oiler girls about to march on the field! We have a great halftime show here, folks, so don't go away. After this message you'll be back in the Astrodome for the big halftime show."

Mike sat through the commercial, then watched the band and the strutting girls take over the field. After a few minutes he got bored. They call this a great show, he thought. Well, the greatest show in the history of halftime football is going to be put on by Wildfire. In fact, he mused grimly, it'll be such a stupendous show that there won't be a second half.

CHAPTER SIXTEEN

Some of the plushest offices in Houston are in the Galleria Plaza Office Building out near River Oaks. The office of Tom Dunning, Vice President-in-Charge of Sales of Mid-Texas Life was as luxurious as any office in this exclusive building. In Houston Tom Dunning was boss of Mid-Texas. The home office in Dallas seldom interfered with his operations. And for good reason: Tom Dunning produced extraordinary sales. Perhaps Dunning was unorthodox in his method of operating, but as long as the sales were consistently high nobody interfered.

On Monday, the traditional day off for professional football players, Tom Dunning was having a conference with his protégé, the man he was grooming to fill his spot someday. For the time being, however, Brian Cotter, already Assistant Vice President for Sales, was spending most of his time on the Oilers' bench. Brian

Cotter was still a celebrity, known for some of the spectacular saves he'd made of losing football games as the backup Oiler quarterback. He still had a year or two of good football in him but he was counting on the insurance business to be his livelihood after he hung up his helmet.

"Brian, I got the OK from home office to do another series of television commercials with you."

"Me, boss? The number of minutes I've been on the field this year wouldn't add up to one full game. Who even knows if Brian Cotter's still on the Oilers' bench?"

"Brian, I have faith. I also live by hunches. I have a hunch they're going to need you again before the season is over. That's why I want to make these commercials right now."

"It's all right by me, Tom. If you want to waste the company money doing commercials with that great has-been quarterback Brian Cotter, that's fine. This is probably going to be my last season anyway. I'm getting tired sitting on that bench wondering if I'll ever play. I might as well be in the stands having a good shot of bourbon. At least I'd enjoy the game that way."

"I'm a gambler, Brian," Dunning answered. "I play the hunches." His arm swept about the large thickly-carpeted corner office. "That's where all this came from. Following the hunches. Who knows, maybe the Houricane will get sacked once too often, maybe he'll throw his arm out. One man can't run the whole season himself. And the big game, the biggest of all, is coming up on Thanksgiving. I'm betting $125,000 of the company's money—which is what it will cost to make these commercials and run them statewide—that something's going to happen. Something that's going to put you up front."

"Well, I appreciate your faith, Tom. I'd sure love another chance to show what I can do out there before I become a full-time life insurance salesman."

"How's the wife and kid?" Tom asked.

A broad grin came across Brian Cotter's face. Obviously this was the most important element in his life. "Lucy's just great. And Brian, Jr., he's three years old now."

"Three years," Dunning clicked his tongue. "Is that right! And it was only four years ago that I got you together with that wild sixteen-year-old girl."

"I appreciated that, Tom. More than you'll ever know. But I sure wish we could all forget the situation."

"Oh, of course, Brian. I didn't mean to bring it up. It was just that—" he laughed nervously—"time goes by so fast. Funny thing about that little Lana. Now that's she's twenty years old she's become a mature young woman. She calls me every so often. Naturally I wouldn't tell her a thing, Brian, you know that. But sometimes she does ask how the kid is."

Dunning examined his fingernails a moment and then looked up again. "What the hell! You have nothing to worry about, Brian. She never saw your face. Remember? One week we had her in that motel in Scotsboro. The room was always dark. You went in to her every night and got out before morning. She has no idea in the world that she produced a baby for the star quarterback of the Houston Oilers."

"The star quarterback three and a half years ago," Cotter interjected bitterly.

"Anyway, don't worry about it, don't think about it,

Brian. I don't know why I brought it up. It just seems like it was only yesterday she had the baby and we gave her the five grand."

"To my wife the kid is her own. I was afraid myself that she might not adjust to a baby that we'd adopted. Of course she has no idea that I'm the natural father. Anyway, Tom, the less said about that even between the two of us, the better. Do me a favor and don't ever mention it again. OK?"

"Sure. Of course. Nostalgia, you know. And those two martinis at lunch."

"OK, when do you want me to start filming the commercials? I'll have to clear it with the club, but there'll be no problem."

"I want them ready to show before the Dallas-Houston game."

"But that's only three weeks away," the backup Oiler quarterback protested.

"Don't worry, I've already bought the time. The agency says they can have the commercials ready to go on the air in one week."

"Why are you so sure that something's going to happen that will put me back in the game?" Brian asked.

"I told you, kid, I'm a gambler. Not only a gambler but I play the hunches. Sometimes I win, sometimes I lose. When I win, I win big. When I lose—" He shrugged, a less confident look on his face.

"And in your case, win or lose, you are the best honest-to-god football player pitching commercials on local television. None of the rest of those guys can talk straight. Remember the commercial I tried to do with your offensive tackle? Suddenly he became the best known lineman in the country but the poor bastard couldn't talk. He couldn't even read the cue cards."

Dunning and Brian Cotter laughed at the memory. "Actually I should probably tell you to get a job as a television announcer but you'll make more money selling insurance. I can promise you that."

"I know that, Tom, and I sure appreciate all the encouragement, all the strength you've put behind my career in this business. I'll certainly need it when I retire."

"It's all out there waiting for you, kid. Don't worry. Now get the OK from the club and we'll have the crew down on Wednesday to shoot you throwing some passes and working out with the team."

"The Houricane's going to wonder why you didn't use him," Brian laughed.

"The answer is very simple. His agent, his lawyer, his accountant, and of course his wife. They all think he's worth too goddamn money to us. Besides you are on the Mid-Texas team, not Houricane."

Mike Snyder sat in John's apartment across a long desk from the gambler talking to him in between his numerous phone calls all over the country laying off bets that he received on another phone. Between calls Mike and John were talking about the Houston-Dallas game coming up on Thanksgiving Day.

"Tell me, son," John said, putting down the phone, "what is this really all about? You've been asking me about the betting at the football games, how much money gamblers take into the games with them, how we bookies work on the spot so to speak. But that isn't really what you're interested in, is it?"

"I'm interested in how much money is in the Astrodome when a big game's being played," Snyder replied.

"Why? Are you planning to come in and make some

bets? No, you're not. Come on, Mike, my instinct tells me you've got something on your mind that I ought to know about. I'm a gambler, I play the hunches and I've got one helluva hunch right now about something you know and nobody else does. Maybe we can make some money together if you want to let loose."

Mike gave John the gambler a speculative look. "OK. And just because you're a good old boy and I know you won't go to the cops I'm going to tell you something that maybe can do a guy like you some real good."

"I'm listening. Tell me. And what does me good will do you good too."

"OK. On Thanksgiving Day—there's not going to be any final score in that fuckin' game."

"What are you talking about? No final score?"

"Just what I say. You can take any bet you want no matter how big because there's not going to be any losers on Thanksgiving Day. At least not on the football field."

There was a look of alarm on John's face as he stared into Mike Snyder's eyes. He'd known Mike for several years since before he went to South America after the Vietnam stint. There was a strange glint in the major's eyes, John thought. He recognized the look of a compulsive. A compulsive gambler, a compulsive drinker, a compulsive liver of life.

"Keep talking, Mike. What are you going to do during that halftime demonstration of yours? I know something's on your mind."

"I'm going into the Astrodome with over two hundred highly trained men. Men with long combat experience, some going back to the Korean War and one sergeant even going back to World War II. We're going into the Astrodome and we're going to get our manhood back. That's what we're going to do!"

"If I didn't know you better I'd think you'd slipped a cog and maybe you're ready for a nice visit to an army psycho ward," John said. "I want to know what's on your mind."

"Do you want to join us? Go with us?"

"Where?"

"You've got to trust me on that. But it's a place where there's no extradition. A place where we can live good. The women are beautiful, we can make a fortune, and eventually, when things blow over we'll come back to the United States."

"It all sounds good except that last. I still don't know what you have in mind but I'm beginning to suspect. Where you're going that's where you'll be the rest of your life. Anybody who goes with you, likewise."

"What do you want to do, John?"

"I jumped bail in four different cities in the last six years. I defrauded a bank in Tallahassee, Florida. But it was better that than not paying up. At least I'm alive and my knee caps are where they should be. I'm ready for something besides this." He gestured towards the phones, one of which had started ringing but was ignored by the gambler. "Sure, I'm ready to go with you. They're on to me now. Last time I went to see you I was followed. I've been under surveillance ever since. I don't know who's after me but I guess it's only a matter of time before they get me one way or the other. Count me in."

"We're glad to have you with us. I think you can be a big help, John," Mike replied. "We're taking the biggest gamble anyone ever took."

"In gambling, Mike, as in highway robbery, collection is the key."

"Now you're right on. My Wildfire team is going to take over the Astrodome. We'll seal it off. Nobody gets in, nobody gets out. Then we're going to take all the money, all the jewelry, all the valuables that are in the Dome, and take off for a sanctuary I have lined up down in Central America."

John let out a low shrill whistle. "I was wondering what you had up your sleeve. I thought it might be something like that. Well, you can hold up 60,000 people but how do you get the money out of their pockets?"

"That's the logistical problem we're looking on right now. How do we get the money out of their pockets? We know it's there. We don't have a lot of time. My old psychological warrior in Vietnam is working on that right now. Any ideas you have will be gratefully received."

"As a matter of fact I do have an idea, the beginning of an idea. At least it's a point of departure. Something we can develop."

Mike snapped his finger. "Give, John. Now I'm listening."

CHAPTER SEVENTEEN

Two nights later John Dykes with Mike Snyder and his deputy, Hack, left downtown Houston behind them and continued out the highway beyond the airport to the large still-undeveloped fields and prairies. Ahead of them in the darkness they saw the lights which illuminated a large canvas canopy. It looked like a circus tent. John brought his car to a halt and followed a procession of automobiles into the parking lot where they parked the car, locked it and strolled across the scrub bushland towards the tent. First they heard the deep throated throbbing of the diesel generators which provided power for the lights. Then they heard the sound of a church organ and a choir singing.

"A revival meeting! Why the hell are you bringing us here?" Mike asked John.

"After you've been around for an hour you'll see. Follow me." John continued toward the tent and Mike and Hack followed him under the edge of the canopy's open sides. It was a full scale evangelistic type revival meeting with an attendance of well over 1,000 people crowded into the tent or standing just outside peering at the choir. In front of the singers stood a burly white-haired man in a black suit and clerical collar. The choir, joined by the congregation, were singing an old Baptist hymn, "Bringing in the Sheaves."

"Come with the sheaves, bringing in the sheaves, bringing in the sheaves, come to the Lord with the sheaves."

"That's the Reverend Joshua Carey," John exclaimed. "Cash and Carry, they call him. You'll see why. He could be a valuable man to you, Mike, and I have a sneaking hunch he may need to put a lot of distance between himself and the United States pretty damn quick. There must be at least ten indictments against him around the southwest for various forms of extortion. When you watch him in action you'll see what I mean."

The hymn ended and the Reverend Joshua Carey began to preach. The main difference between 'Cash and Carry' and other revival leaders that Mike had observed in action was that true to his sobriquet, 'Cash and Carry' wasted no time in his appeal for funds to finance the Lord's work. The act of giving in itself would cleanse the soul of every human being listening to his voice, he exhorted his audience.

The Lord had sent word to his servant, Joshua Carey, that he must collect $10,000 this week to use as the Lord directed. The Reverend Carey had a gimmick which neither Mike nor Hack had ever seen before. There was a large lighted tote board behind the choir and at the top of the tote board in lights was the goal

$10,000. Underneath it was the figure $5,210. "Now my friends," the Reverend Carey cried out, "as the sisters and brothers of the movement of Jesus Christ pass among you, give all you can for salvation. As they bring your offering to the Lord's work back here it will be rung up in lights on God's tote board. You will watch as we come closer and closer to fulfilling the Lord's requirement of all of us here tonight."

He paused, raising both hands, and looked out benignly at the crowd about the tent.

"And when you see those lights flash out and those lights say ten thousand dollars we will have accomplished God's will tonight." Reverend Carey's voice rose to a thundering crescendo as once again the chorus began singing "Bringing In The Sheaves."

Mike looked at John. "Ten thousand dollars. He's got to be kidding. There couldn't be ten thousand dollars in this whole damn audience. I guess that maybe there's a thousand people at the most around here. You think they're going to give him ten grand before they leave?"

"Son, you just watch. If the State Police don't decide to hit him tonight he'll walk out of here with at least ten thousand. In all my life I've never seen anybody who could control a crowd the way old Cash and Carry does it. It so happens that the Reverend is a gambler. One of my best customers. At least half of what you see him collect tonight will be passed around the country to the top books in Miami, Boston, Cleveland, Chicago and Los Angeles."

"Yes, brothers and sisters," Joshua boomed forth. "Do the Lord's work tonight and I'll take care of it tomorrow."

The Reverend Carey's eyes lifted to the top of the

tent. "And now as we stand here under the Lord's umbrella, let those of you who are suffering physical affliction come forward and pray with me. Come forward for the laying on of the hands. Whatever you shall suffer, the Lord through his son Jesus Christ will take away. Come forward, right up the aisles, ladies and gentlemen, to the front of the tent. Come stand before me and let me bring the Lord's mercy to you."

He looked over his shoulder at the tote board. The ten thousand figure blinked at the top. Below, the actual amount collected—seven thousand one hundred—sparkled out in lights attesting to the fruits brought in by the brothers and sisters.

"My friends, children of God, we are progressing. We need two thousand nine hundred dollars more. Keep giving. Everything you can give will be greatly used by our Lord for his works in this earthly plane we live in. And remember, as ye give so shall ye receive. The more ye give, the more ye put into God's works, the more God's works will be focused on you," he pointed directly at a ten-gallon-hatted farmer and his wife.

"And you," he pointed at a couple who looked like a business executive and his wife. And so Cash and Carry individualized his appeal for funds to carry out the Lord's work.

The chorus once again burst into song, another favorite evangelical hymn as people streamed forward through the audience to receive the Lord's blessing from the hands of the Reverend Carey.

"Now you'll see some of the goddamndest cures you ever saw," John said to Mike and Hack. "I like to get out here, get a feel of how much he's gonna want to bet tomorrow so I can have my layoffs ready to go. I sure think he's going to make his ten thousand dollar quota tonight," John laughed heartily. "Now look— you see that red-headed girl hobbling down on crutches to receive the laying on of hands? I've personally seen her cured ten times."

"You mean this whole thing is a fake? You mean that the Reverend is a charlatan?" Mike asked, a tone of disbelief and shock in his voice. "He really sounds sincere to me."

"And to everybody else," John added. "The people believe in him. A month ago when he was in Dallas he pulled off one of the most convincing healing acts I ever saw. And made himself about twenty grand, most of which he bet with me. You see the Reverend Carey not only convinces the crowds that he is an apostle of God and Jesus Christ but recently he also sold his spiel to courts."

"What happened?" Hack asked.

John sighed. "Well, if you want to hear the whole story I'll be glad to tell you."

"Yeah, of course we do," Mike reinforced Hack's request. "I'm beginning to see why you brought us out here."

"Well, it seems that this Jew, Julius Goldenbaum, got hit by a car crossing the street in Dallas. Naturally by a big Cadillac limousine owned by none other than Ben Gardner, President of Sun City National Bank and an old wildcatter who controls one of the biggest fields out near Lubbock, Texas."

Hack and Mike listened attentively as John went on. "Ben wasn't too worried. He got out of his car, saw Julius lying on the street and told him he was in a hel- luva hurry but he was well insured. Mid-Texas Life and Casualty would take care of everything.

"Julius played it cool, of course. An ambulance came. Julius never moved, he was put on a stretcher and taken to the hospital where they couldn't find anything wrong with him but he claimed he was paralyzed.

"Naturally his son-in-law is a lawyer and brought a multi-million-dollar suit against Ben Gardner, the bank, and the oil company. It seems the bank owned the car. The driver, an old chauffeur that had been taking care of Ben for years, was on the oil company payroll. So Mid-Texas had a real suit on their hands. Well, old Julius was a patient man. Even though the hospital couldn't find anything wrong with him Julius just couldn't walk. He had himself put into a wheelchair and claimed he was totally disabled.

"Anyway, to make a long story short, just about six months ago Julius Goldenbaum won a three million dollar settlement from Mid-Texas Life and Casualty. Everybody knew that Julius was faking his injury and after the award was made the president of Mid-Texas went up to him in the court room and said something like, 'OK Julius, you beat us on this in court but I want to tell you something. We're going to be watching you every minute. If we see you get out of that wheelchair and start walking around we'll have your ass. You'll be sued for fraud and go to jail.

"Julius smiled at the Mid-Texas president and said that he was going to use the money to get himself cured of this dreadful disability he'd suffered if a cure was possible. Naturally the Mid-Texas people followed him every place he went but Julius kept playing it cool.

"Then one night the Reverend Joshua Carey brought his revival and healing mission to Dallas and old Julius has himself wheeled out to the tent. It was just like it is here tonight. Julius was wheeled up to old

Cash and Carry. 'I want to make a commitment to the Lord, I want to commit twenty thousand dollars to the works of God,' Julius squeaked out. And with that he brought out twenty thousand dollars in cash. Naturally about three detectives from the insurance company were there watching. Well, old Cash-and-Carry did himself proud that night. He must have prayed over Julius for a whole hour. His choir sang five hymns. Everybody in the audience—he had at least two or three thousand people in the tent or milling around it that night—prayed, cried and sang. And then the Reverend Joshua Carey placed his hands on Julius' head, ran them all over his whole body, over his knees, over his back, praying, slobbering all over him. And goddamn if Julius didn't stand up and walk right out of that wheelchair screaming, 'A miracle! A miracle! The good Lord has healed me. I can walk again!'

"As Julius walked out of his wheelchair, out through the crowd praising the Lord, every man woman and child in that audience took every penny, everything valuable they had off of their persons and took them up to the Reverend Carey and donated everything to the Lord's works."

"They got away with that?" Mike asked incredulously.

"So far. Mid-Texas Life and Casualty has brought every legal gun to bear they can. But the Lord's work was done and they can't prove otherwise. But as I understand it, they still have a law suit, and have brought criminal charges against both Cash and Carry and Julius. Needless to say Julius has long since disappeared from Texas with all that money and they'd never know where to find him anyway."

"Do you think the Reverend Carey is uncomfortable about this?" Hack asked.

"Well, there's a lot of power arraigned against him. And because of that the State Police and even the local cops in Texas come into his shows a couple of times a month and break them up. Not that they have any legal right to do so, but Cash and Carry is smart enough not to bring any proceedings against the law enforcement officers who knock over his act. But I think I see what you mean."

"I'll see that you meet him tomorrow. He'll be in my office with a list of all the football games he wants to bet on, college and professional, and of course he'll have horses running all over the country."

John looked up at the tote board, the numbers blinking. They now showed that two thousand dollars was left to collect before the Lord would be satisfied that night. "Oh yes, Cash and Carry will make the Lord's quota tonight and then he'll double it or blow it with me tomorrow."

"What is this Lord's work that he does with the money?" Hack asked.

"Fortunately that's a question that doesn't come up very often. By the time he's healed four or five more cripples, or stroke victims, and there's one blind man who gets his sight restored regularly, everybody figures they've bought God's blessing with the money they've given to the good Reverend and all their troubles will come to an end."

"So he's a complete out-and-out extortionist!" Mike exclaimed.

John gave Mike a long questioning look and Mike couldn't help laughing at himself. "OK, you've got me, John. I want to meet the Reverend Carey. Cash and

Carry. That's our motto come Thanksgiving. The fans bring in the cash, we carry it out. Yes, sir. I think we've seen enough. Let's get back to River Oaks. I think we could all use a little bourbon and branch right now."

One of the Reverend Carey's sisters in the movement for Christ came up to them. "Are you moved to contribute to the Lord's work, brothers?" asked the lovely blue-eyed richly endowed young lady.

"Yes, sister, we want to give to the Lord." Mike Snyder pulled a fifty dollar bill from his pocket and handed it to her. "What are you doing after this is over?"

"Oh we'll be praying all night for guidance, sir," the girl replied seriously.

"How 'bout coming over to our house and helping a couple of sinners like us pray?" Hack asked.

"Well, if that is the Lord's wish I'll be glad to help you pray," the beauty replied. "And what are you able to contribute to God's work now?" She turned a brilliant smile directly on Hack. Sheepishly he reached into his pocket and pulled out twenty dollars. "I'm sorry it's not more, sister. But come on back to my place with me when this is over and I'm sure I can find some more."

The girl took Hack's twenty dollars and put it into the bag she was carrying. "You'll find me back with the choir at the end of the revival meeting," she replied. Then turning to the people standing next to John, Mike, and Hack she repeated her plea for funds to assist the Lord's work.

"You got time to come on home with me, get your car and get back out here, Hack," Mike laughed.

"I'm damn tempted to do just that," Hack answered.

"What a gorgeous thing. I could see myself contributing a lot of money to the Reverend Carey's movement through this girl."

John led the way out of the tent and back to his car. "Did you get some nourishment out of that, son?" he asked.

"Praise the Lord," Mike cried. "I see the way."

CHAPTER EIGHTEEN

Major Mike Snyder, wearing his class A uniform and all his ribbons, stood in the control tower of the Air Force base at Fort Hood looking down on the ramp below. Beside him Colonel Jim Cotten of the Air Force was watching the same scene. "I don't know how you did it, Mike. The Air Force is supposed to have all the good press agents."

"We've got the best show. What can the Air Force do inside the Astrodome? Fly a helicopter around?"

"I heard the Navy got real pissed off. They think they should be in the show. And of course the Marines want in on the act. They ought to give you back a silver oak leaf for setting this one up."

"Meantime Wildfire has got to keep training to do its real job which isn't putting on shows to help the recruiting sergeants make their quotas. Let's see how fast my hoods can get into that thing down there." The

131

giant four engine Hercules transport, the largest in regular usage in the U.S. military arsenal was parked on the ramp below. Its huge tailgate had been dropped to make a ramp into the plane. Mike held a walkie-talkie radio in his hand.

"OK," he said to Colonel Cotten. "My men are ready to swarm aboard in an orderly manner when I give them the order." He held a stopwatch in his free hand.

"Anytime you're ready, Mike."

Mike pressed the transmitter button on the radio. "Board the aircraft!" he barked.

Two hundred men of the Wildfire team waiting at the edge of the runway suddenly double-timed toward the aircraft. Ahead of them an armored personnel carrier and the new T-75 light, high-speed tank with 155mm cannon mounted in its turret sped toward the cavernous opening into the Hercules. The tank mounted the ramp and disappeared deep inside the huge craft. Immediately behind it the T-75, a tank virtually classified and only just beginning to be publicized by the army, rumbled up the ramp and followed the armored personnel carrier into the transport. The Wildfire search and destroy team pounded up the airplane's tailgate and disappeared inside. The Hercules started its engines and they were chasing up the ramp as it lifted from the runway and swung up into place. Immediately the Hercules started its take-off.

As Colonel Cotten and Mike watched the Hercules roared down the runway and angled up into the air. As the wheels left the runway Mike snapped the cap on his stopwatch. "That's the best time yet. Four minutes from the boarding orders until the plane was airborne. We've got us a great unit here."

"And thanks for giving us Kevin Murray as pilot."

"Yes, I understand he was involved in operations with you in Vietnam."

"Affirmative. During the Cambodian operations he saved my whole team from being wiped out in an ambush."

"I heard something about that. He disobeyed orders or something. Wasn't that it?"

"If it wasn't for Murray none of us would be here today. Orders or not."

"Captain Murray has adjusted admirably from fighters to transports. He's one of the best pilots we've got. I hope he decides to stay with us and not go into civilian life."

Mike ignored the comment. "Between your air commandoes and Wildfire I think we've got the team I was assigned to whip into shape. We've added an outstanding capability to the military."

"Let's hope you get a chance to prove yourself in action someplace," Colonel Cotten said.

"We can strike and get out of any place in the world. We could take over a capitol city, pull off a coup and put America's manpower anywhere in Africa or Latin America. Our next job is to sell the Chief of Staff on developing three or four more Wildfire teams like this one," Mike declared.

"Too bad you'll never get a chance to show what you can do. In Washington they seem to think it's better to capitulate than fight."

"Well, the main thing is Wildfire is ready." Cotten and Mike Snyder left the Control Tower, walked down the stairs to the ground and watched as the Hercules finished its circle around the air strip and landed once again. Quickly it pulled up close to where they were standing, dropped its ramp and the Wildfire team pounded back down it.

"I'd sure like to see this operation in a combat situation," Colonel Cotten said longingly.

"Maybe you will, Jim. Well, I've got to join my troops and give them a little encouragement." Mike walked away from the Air Force colonel and joined Hack and his platoon leaders who were gathered around the deputy.

"Damn good show, gentlemen," he greeted them. "Company dismissed until 0700 tomorrow morning." The men, moving at double time, left the edge of the airstrip to go back to quarters. Mike and Hack watched them go. Then Hack said, "Kevin Murray said he'd join us for a drink at the club in a half an hour."

"Good. I want to talk to him." By the time Air Force Captain Kevin Murray reached the officer's club Mike and Hack had staked out a small, quiet beachhead at the far end of the bar. Kevin joined them there. Mike ordered him a drink and then complimented him on the exercise he had just completed.

"I wonder if General Vogel knows who's flying Wildfire," Captain Murray mused.

"It doesn't make any difference. Even if he remembers the Cambodia incident and your name, at this point he's eating out of my hand. Our big halftime show at the Astrodome has made him the fair-haired boy of Department of the Army. He's taking all credit for putting the idea together and implementing it. In this peacetime army, something like this can do us a lot of good. Yeah, we don't have to worry about Vogel. He's as happy as a pig in shit right now."

"Can you really make that landing on the highway

outside the Astrodome?" Hack asked. "To me that seems to be the most hairy part of the whole operation."

"Just get your bulldozers out there doing their job and I'll land the plane," Kevin Murray assured them. "Have I ever let you down?"

"Of course not, Kevin," Mike quickly replied. "You never have."

"I'll land the plane all right and I'll take off. The only question I have is, how are we going to get out of US airspace after your caper?"

"That's what I'm working on now, Kevin," Mike said with a grin. "By Thanksgiving Day we'll have the deterrent to pursuit, our trump card ready to play. The only problem is, to get it we're going to have to steal it. I can assure you, Kevin, that if we do not have the deterrent to pursuit operational we'll abort the whole plan."

"All it would take would be one old jet with a sidewinder missile to drop us out of the sky," Captain Murray reminded Mike grimly. He nodded and took another long drink of bourbon and branch water.

CHAPTER NINETEEN

Major Mike Snyder stood in front of the large scale map of southern Texas showing in minute detail the area from the Gulf of Mexico at Brownsville to McAllen, Texas. The total area was about eighty miles in length and twenty miles north and south. Seated in front of him were Captain Thompson and another black officer, Thompson's deputy on the mission they were planning.

"This is the area of interest," Snyder was saying. With a pointer he indicated a section of apparently desolate wasteland between Brownsville and Port Isabelle protruding out into the Gulf. "It all came together at last about two o'clock this morning," Snyder explained. "My old buddy in the tactical nuke division of Ft. Sill Artillery School finally came across. We've been discussing something like this ever since we could see the giveaway of Vietnam coming when we were

137

over there together. As you know, we had tactical nukes in the country ready to use if we got orders from the White House. They never came of course, and the nukes were withdrawn from the Nam shortly before we pulled out altogether. Anyway, my buddy, who shall remain nameless until he joins us on our Hercules down to Costa Vacca, gave me this information.

"Our tactical nukes on the Mexican border are routinely moved from one station to another every week or so. Security on tactical nukes is almost entirely procedural and not physical. In other words, they don't have a company of men armed with artillery and M79 grenade launchers and all that good stuff guarding the nukes. It is the procedure of relocating them, moving them constantly, and the capability of arming them for use that is what has made it so far impossible for an enemy to capture and use one of our tactical nukes. Even with our friends on the inside it's been impossible until now to plan the successful capture of a nuclear device."

Snyder looked down at his watch. "I've got exactly 1700 5 November Central Standard Time. At 0100 7 November the first of three trucks will be leaving the nuclear station here." The pointer tapped the desolate area again. "At 0130 hours a second truck will leave the station and at 0200 hours a third truck will leave the station. One of these trucks will contain a nuclear device, being transferred from the Brownsville station to the McAllen station." The pointer moved west and tapped an area a few miles beyond McAllen.

"Just like three card Monte," Thompson chuckled. "Where's the red queen?"

Mike smiled back and nodded. "But this time we know. The third truck will contain the tactical nuclear warhead we need. It will be your job to acquire this weapon, Idi," he grinned at Thompson as he used his code name. "We've been planning the details of this little heist for a long time. Now that we have the specific information you will activate your team, follow the procedure we've outlined and you will take what we must have. Is that clear?"

"Yes, sir," Captain Thompson boomed back. "My hoods are ready, Mike."

"Go to it!" Mike instructed. "I'll wait right here at our headquarters until you report success."

Thompson and his all-black team with the exception of Signals were at their posts between Brownsville and Port Isabelle by midnight the sixth of November. At 0100 on the 7th of November, right on schedule, they observed the first of the standard army two and a half ton trucks moving out of the small, nondescript tactical nuclear weapons station guarding the southernmost tip of United States territory bordering Mexico.

Thompson relayed this information to his team members via the walkie-talkie he was holding. At exactly 0130 hours a second deuce and a half pulled out of the station heading west towards Brownsville and its eventual destination McAllen. Once again instructions were relayed to the team and then at precisely 0200 hours the third deuce and a half pulled out.

"The hot truck just left," Thompson reported. Through his radio Thompson received reports from his observers. The first truck had, as scheduled, taken the route just along the Mexican border and had passed a desolate little border town Los Indios and was almost to Santa Maria. The second truck had gone into Brownsville and turned north on Route 77 towards

Harlingen, where it would head west toward McAllen. The third truck was scheduled to follow the border route. The observers reported to Thompson, now in his automobile following at a discreet distance behind the hot truck, that it had just passed through Brownsville heading for LaPaloma.

"Tell the blocking force between LaPaloma and Los Indios to get set," Thompson instructed. With that he speeded up and in a few minutes passed the lumbering army deuce and a half. Thompson, his deputy, and two other black team members headed toward the five mile stretch between LaPaloma and Los Indios where they would cut off the hot deuce and a half and take the tactical nuke. They cruised along the twelve miles to LaPaloma, the Rio Grande River just to their left. Passing through the tiny border village they were soon intercepted by the rest of the team and pulled off the road into the desert.

Glancing at his watch Thompson estimated that the hot truck would reach them in twelve minutes.

"Get the radio-jamming equipment ready. Are you on the correct channels?" Thompson called over his radio to Signals, whose equipment-filled station wagon was parked near the intercept site.

"We'll render their channels totally useless for the minute or two it will take you to pull this off," he confirmed. "But don't take any longer than you have to. The longer I have to jam their radio signal the more suspicious the monitors will be. They're going to be suspicious anyway, but once you grab the truck I'll be able to talk to them over their own channel and with the signal operating instructions that Mike's pal got for us I'll make them think there's nothing wrong, at least for an hour or two."

"We'll be seeing the lights in about two minutes," Thompson announced. "Everybody get ready." It was less than the time Thompson had estimated when the lights of the deuce and a half showed up down the road.

"Go!" Thompson ordered. Two unlighted weapons carriers drove out into the deserted highway and parked across it, blocking the oncoming truck. In his instrument-filled station wagon Signals threw the switches blocking the channel the hot truck radio used to communicate with base. Even as he threw the switch, filling the air with static, the truck carrying the nuclear device jammed on its brakes to keep from smashing into the two weapons carriers. The hot truck came to a tire smoking halt just a few feet from the weapons carriers.

Instantly an armed guard jumped out of the front seat of the truck and two more leaped out of the rear. Through a bullhorn Thompson called out in the strange accent he had been cultivating from listening to some of the black delegates from African countries to the United Nations.

"If nobody moves we will not shoot. You are covered from both sides of the road. You're dead if you pull the trigger." Searchlights from both sides of the road suddenly switched on, illuminating the trucks and blinding the guards. "Throw down your weapons or you die!"

The guards, caught in a hopeless situation, did as they were told. The M16 rifles they were carrying clattered to the pavement. Then, through the bullhorn Thompson issued a series of commands in a gutteral, unintelligible language. Instantly his team of blacks dressed in jeans and blue workshirts emerged from the darkness and herded the guards up against the truck. Thompson turned to the man at his side. "OK, get the driver. Pull him out but don't let the two officers riding in the back of the truck with the nuclear device get away. We want them. And for chrissake, Leroy, don't say 'motherfucker.' We're supposed to be a team from Nigeria, Uganda, some goddamn country over there."

"Yes, boss." Leroy, carrying a 9mm model 59 Smith & Wesson rushed into the bright illumination around the truck and jumped into the cab beside the driver who was wisely holding his hands high. In an approximation of African tribal language Leroy yelled at the driver, who although he could not understand the words, knew what was required of him. Hands still held above his head he slid out of the driver's seat and into the searchlights.

Thompson's strangely disguised voice bellowed over the bullhorn. "Nobody is going to be hurt if you do what we say." Two other members of the team, guns drawn, jumped into the back of the deuce and a half, pulling the canvas aside and confronting a major and a captain. A powerful searchlight was turned in their faces. "Just stay where you are," Leroy ordered, using the same gutteral English that Thompson had mouthed over the bullhorn.

The officers were sitting on a bench against the back of the truck's cab. Between Leroy and the officers was the huge metal box containing the nuclear device. Helplessly the officers raised their hands. In his approximation of some African tribal language Leroy shouted commands. Two more blacks jumped into the truck reaching the officers and taking their sidearms. Neither had a rifle.

"You will be good," Leroy ordered menacingly. "We

do not wish to kill you but we will if necessary." Neither officer replied.

Back in his station wagon Signals switched off the jamming mechanism. It had been needed only for the few moments when the driver and guard in the front seat of the truck were first aware of the danger they were in and when they were captured. It had been a vital move. He realized that when Thompson told him later that the driver actually had the radio mike in his hand when he was pulled out of the truck.

Thompson's team moved swiftly and efficiently now. Two of his men slid into the front seat of the cab, started the engine and drove about five hundred yards to a narrow side road which led northeast to the town of San Benito on Route 77.

The nuclear device guards and the driver prudently remained silent. Handcuffs linked their wrists behind their backs, and then their ankles, so that they could move only as an awkward threesome. They were blindfolded and left by the side of the road as the rest of the team climbed into their vehicles and drove toward Los Indios and McAllen. Far out of sight or hearing of their victims, the team turned off the highway onto the road to San Benito and drove for about two miles before coming across the truck they had hijacked. It had been turned around and backed up to a moving van. Already a crane was swinging the tactical nuclear device in its metal case out of the truck and into the van.

The transfer accomplished, the military vehicle was abandoned and the two abducted officers were put into a nondescript car driven by one of Thompson's men. Another armed man sat beside the driver and a third sitting in the back seat guarded the handcuffed officers.

143

"Nobody is going to get hurt if you act right," one of the blacks said. The captured men looked up in surprise. It was the first time the officers had heard their captors speak pure American.

The man in the front seat turned around, facing the officers in the rear. "We're going to take you to a safe house, it'll be comfortable, and you'll stay there for a couple of weeks. All you've got to do is look at television, read magazines, eat, sleep and don't try to get away." He noticed the alarmed expressions on the officers' faces. "Just relax and nothing's gonna happen to you."

The two officers nodded silently. "We're not terrorists or nothing like that," the black in the front seat said soothingly. "If you two gentlemen cooperate with us, don't give us no trouble, and don't try to escape, everything's going to be fine."

"How long is this going to last?" one of the officers finally asked.

"Before the end of the month you'll be back on duty. Now you can make it easy on yourselves or we can keep you chained. All depends upon your attitude."

Thompson and Signals, following the van containing the nuclear device, drove on north. At San Benito they turned onto Route 77, past Corpus Christi up through Victoria and finally crossing Route 90 between Houston and San Antonio. A few miles beyond, the van was driven into a delapidated barn and parked.

Signals opened the rear gate of the van and the crane deposited the long, heavy metal box onto the dirt floor of the abandoned barn. Just at this moment the car transporting the two officers arrived and drove inside.

Thompson, in worn fatigues, jerked open the back seat of the car and roughly ordered the officers to step out. "OK, gentlemen, you're going to be staying here for just over two weeks. Right now, you can either make it easy on yourselves and open that box, or we'll cut it open with a welding torch. If that's what we have to do your stay here will be just a little less comfortable than if you were captured by the aggressors in a Fort Sill War Games, and last a lot longer."

"You're American!" the major exclaimed.

"Correct," Thompson answered.

"We thought you were some kind of an African terrorist," the captain said, obviously relieved.

"Precisely what we want the men we set loose to report back," Thompson replied. "Now are you going to open the box? I know it takes two of you to do it. Each of you has half the combination."

Dumbfounded, the two officers stared at Thompson. He laughed. "We're still part of the same army, gentlemen. For another couple of weeks. My element here has no desire to hurt our country, but we must see the nuke in that box, with or without your help." The black pupils of Thompson's eyes glowed like two port holes into hell as he stared at the captive officers. "Are you going to dial your combination locks so we can take a look?"

The implied threat was unmistakable. "He can open it with the torch anyway," the captain began.

"If we open it are you going to try and make us arm it for you?" the major inquired. "That we'll never do."

"Don't say never, gentlemen," Thompson replied sardonically. "You've probably never been out of the comfortable confines allotted to nuke heads. But if you'd ever been to Vietnam and seen what search and destroy missions could make people do, you wouldn't be so adamant." He grinned at the fear reflected in the faces of the two officers.

"But to allay your fears, no. We won't try to force you to arm that warhead for us. We only want to get a good look at it. We all know it's harmless as long as you don't apply the combinations each of you knows."

"Who the hell are you, anyway?" the major shouted.

"It's unimportant. Now open the box or your next two weeks will be extremely uncomfortable." He glared at the officers. "Now!"

The major and the captain approached the box reluctantly, each going to his own lock. They looked at each other, the major nodded, and both simultaneously manipulated their combination locks. The lid of the box sprang open revealing a long, cigar-shaped missile with four fins and a rounded nose, about five feet long.

Thompson gestured to his crew and the crane hook was lowered and attached to a ring welded to the side of the warhead. Then the device was lifted from its coffin into the air, and with the help of several of Thompson's men set back down on the dirt floor of the barn, standing straight up. Immediately Signals appeared and began photographing the nuke from all sides, placing a yardstick against it.

"Who the hell are you?" the major's hoarse voice stabbed at Sorell. Signals paid no attention.

"I would advise restraint, Major," Thompson warned softly. "We have nothing against you personally. Under other circumstances we might be having a drink together at the officers' club. But at the moment we are operating under extremely critical conditions."

Signals snapped flash pictures for several minutes and then turned to Thompson. "OK, Idi, I got what I want. Keep these officers under guard until D-Day. They must not escape."

Sorell turned to the nuclear officers. "As you have been told, take it easy, don't do anything rash, and nothing will happen to you two or your nuke." With that he turned and walked out of the barn, leaving Thompson's special guard detail to watch over the prisoners and the nuke.

Thompson and Sorell left the barn together.

"By now the fellows we pulled out of that truck are probably telling the Tactical Nuclear Headquarters staff in McAllen that a bunch of Africans grabbed the nuke and are going to use it in some terrorist activity," Signals chuckled. "With any luck they'll figure Idi Amin really came over here and grabbed it to use against enemies."

"Anyway, we've done our job. I'll see you back at wildfire," Thompson replied.

"Check. I'll call in and report your success to Mike."

CHAPTER TWENTY

Every football fan in Houston who couldn't get to Denver for the Houston-Denver football game was watching it eagerly on television. If Houston could win against Denver the game with Dallas would decide which team, the Oilers or the Cowboys, would make it to the playoffs for the Super Bowl. If Houston, going into the game an underdog, could beat Denver, the Dallas game—besides being a traditional grudge fight—would have enormous significance for the entire league.

John Dykes was sitting in Mike Snyder's den watching the game. J.J. Cookson had come over to his son-in-law's bungalow to join them for part of the first half. He had a large group of his friends, business associates and political allies at the big house watching but he dropped by to lay another bet on the game with John.

"I don't think our Oilers can make it," Cookson

said. "What kind of a point spread are you giving on this game, John?" he asked.

"If you want to bet on your Oilers, Mr. Cookson, I'm giving six points."

Cookson snorted. "Is that the best you can do? Denver should beat them by at least a touchdown and point. Give me eight points and you've got a bet."

"Eight points?" John cried, wounded. "You think Denver can beat Houston by a touchdown and field goal? Is that all you think of the Oilers?"

"All right, goddamn it, six points. I'll take it. A thousand dollars on the Oilers. Denver's got to win by a touchdown and the conversion for you to take my money."

"You've got a bet, Mr. Cookson," John answered.

Cookson pulled ten crisp one hundred dollar bills from his pocket and laid them on the table. "I'm a cash man, John."

John pulled a thousand dollars out of his own wallet and put it down beside Cookson's. "You're covered, sir."

"OK. I'm going back to the house but I'll see you after the game and pick up my money." Cookson nodded to his son-in-law and left the bungalow.

John looked after him and grinned. "That's the way they are in Houston. Cash on the line. And that's the way it will be in the Astrodome on Thanksgiving when Houston and Dallas play. Everybody's going to be putting their money down in cash. And you can bet that I'll see there's one load of cash brought into the Dome that day. No bets on credit."

Together John and Mike watched the game. As the second period drew close to the end of the first half, the usually calm and sanguine John suddenly gripped

Mike's knee. Johnny Houricane was dropping back to pass. It was third and long. The score was tied at 7-7. Unaccountably the great Houricane's protection suddenly broke down under a ferocious rush. He tried to scramble away from the 240 lb. monsters closing in on him. And then one hit him low and as Houricane turned to get away another behemoth slammed into him high. The quarterback's body twisted like a pretzel. He fell to the ground, the ball squirting from his arms. Another Denver lineman fell on the ball, recovering it on Houston's forty yard line.

"Oh. Ouch!" the TV announcer cried out. "Let's see that again."

The mauling of Dan Houricane was shown on the screen in slow motion. Then they were looking at the field again. The quarterback was lying immobile as the trainer and doctor rushed in from the sideline. "That hurt him, Chuck," the television analyst said to the announcer. "He's not moving. Houricane is hurt."

"That's a break they felt all over Houston, Lou," the announcer acknowledged. "He's not getting up. That's the second time Houricane has been sacked in this half. Houston's defensive line seems to be giving." There was silence as every television viewer in Houston watched the stretcher come out onto the field and the trainer and doctor gingerly lifted the quarterback onto it.

"We'll get a report on Johnny Houricane's condition as soon as we can," the announcer promised his audience. "Meanwhile the Oilers' backup quarterback Brian Cotter is coming in. Cotter has not played much this season. Everybody will remember what a star he was before Houricane joined the Oilers and took the starting slot away from him. What a bad break for the

151

Oilers! And next week, when they play Dallas, if they don't have Dan Houricane in shape by then there's not much doubt but that Dallas will win that game and go into the playoffs."

In another home in River Oaks, Tom Dunning, Mid-Texas Life and Casualty's vice president-of-sales, was also absorbed in this football game. He had intended going out to Denver to see it but was unable to leave at the last minute. With him were several executives of the company including the advertising manager who had come down from Dallas for special meetings.

"Well, there goes our boy into the game," Dunning said, a note of triumph in his voice. "I told you all I had a hunch when I made those commercials with Brian."

"Yes you did, Tom," the advertising manager admitted. "Now if he plays a good second half against Denver your hunch should pay off. Maybe they'll forgive you up at home office in Dallas now."

The Houston defensive line lived up to its reputation and held Denver outside the thirty yard line until the half was over.

"We just got a report from the Houston trainer," the announcer reported. "Johnny Houricane appears to have a separated shoulder and was badly bruised in that play where he was sacked for the second time this half. Brian Cotter will be playing the last half of this game. And if Houricane's injuries are as serious as they seem to be he may be out for the rest of the season. So it's all up to Brian Cotter now."

Tom Dunning got to his feet. He paced the room excitedly. "It's up to Brian to save the season. I told you I had a hunch. Always play the hunches. I've got a good mind to call the old man up in Dallas and ask him what he thinks of my commercial now," Dunning said.

"Why don't you wait and see how Brian does in the second half before you do that, Tom," the advertising manager said. "Don't overplay your hand yet."

"Yeah, you're right. We'll wait until the end of the game."

As the second half started, Denver kicking off to Houston, John sat tensely forward in his chair staring at the television set. "If Cotter blows this game away it's going to be impossible to make any kind of odds that will get them betting next week."

"You mean if Cotter doesn't show up good there'll be a lot less cash in the Astrodome?" Mike asked.

"You can bet your sweet bippy on that," John muttered.

The phone rang and John listened a moment making a notation in his pad. Then he hung up, sat down and began figuring on a pocket calculator.

"My assistant returning my call. He gave me Brian Cotter's date of birth."

"I heard you ask for it. What's that got to do with the game except that Cotter's a little older than Houricane?"

"I'm trying to figure his bio-rhythm coordinates," John replied. He punched a few more buttons on the calculator and then looked up, a smile on his face. "Couldn't be better. He's just coming into the cycle where intellectually, emotionally and physically all of his curves come together. That means Brian Cotter is functioning better today and for the next week than he has in the last two months."

"Do you believe that stuff?" Mike asked.

"When you're a gambler you try to work every edge you can. And bio-rhythm cycles, if you can figure them

153

out, give a very accurate index as to how an individual will perform. As a matter of fact I'm gonna call your father-in-law and see if he wants to put down another grand or two on Denver, giving me six points to hedge his bet."

Mike Snyder chuckled. "You don't have to do that. I can see him coming across the lawn now. One thing about J.J. He hates to lose a bet. He'll turn on anyone he thinks is a loser. And that goes for the Oilers."

J.J. Cookson burst through the front door, strode into the den and confronted John. "Tell you what I'm going to do with you, John. I'm gonna take three thousand on Denver and give you six points!"

John struggled against the laughter he could hardly control. Cookson, his voice rising, insisted, "You're supposed to be a professional, John. You gonna take my bet?"

John pulled his wallet from his inside jacket pocket, extracted three thousand dollars from it in hundred dollar bills and placed them beside his other bet. "I've got you covered, Mr. Cookson." Cookson pulled three thousand dollars from his pocket, slapped it on the table and without another word turned and walked out of the bungalow.

"He's one tough betting man," John said with a slow smile.

"You have that much faith in your bio-rhythm cycles?" Mike asked.

"Well, I couldn't very well have said no." He turned to the set. "Come on, Brian," the gambler urged, do it like you did three years ago before Houricane joined the Oilers."

Tom Dunning and his group of insurance executives were totally absorbed in the game as Brian Cotter moved the Oilers from their own 30 across the 50 in three plays, then steadily on down the field toward Denver's goal line. Bullet after bullet shot from his arm into the hands of his recievers. It seemed as though he couldn't miss. He mixed up the offensive drive with great skill. Straight bread-and-butter running plays across tackle around the end, a draw play and then another sharp pass.

Five minutes after the kickoff Houston scored against Denver, giving them a seven point lead. The Houston line held Denver to two series of plays after the kickoff and forced Denver to punt. Brian Cotter was in the game again. And once again the Denver defense couldn't stop him. When they expected a pass he ran the ball. He fooled the Denver line on every draw play. At first and ten on the Denver 45 he threw a long pass connecting with his wide receiver and Houston had the ball on Denver's ten yard line.

Tom Dunning's ruddy complexion was florid with excitement. He pounded the table and shouted at Brian Cotter as though his protegé could hear him through the TV set all the way to Denver. "What did I tell you! What did I tell you! I knew it!" Dunning exulted. "Did I know what I was doing when I made those commercials or didn't I?"

"You knew, Tom. Goddamn if I know how you get away with some of these crazy things you do. But they win for the company," the advertising manager conceded.

Houston scored again in what looked like an easy toss of the ball from Brian Cotter to his halfback who crossed the line with no Denver player touching him. The conversion was made and now Denver was two touchdowns behind.

In the fourth quarter Houston had to fight with every thing it had to preserve its lead. Finally Denver scored and was only a touchdown behind. Field goals would not help Denver now. They had to make another touchdown to win. But once Brian Cotter got his hands on the ball again he maneuvered his team down the field handily. He could do nothing wrong. Within easy field goal range Cotter elected to go for the touchdown instead. Peppering his receivers with short, sharp passes he moved the team down to the Denver eight and scored again. The Houston fans in the Denver stadium were going wild. It was the old Brian Cotter again. When the game ended with Houston the winner by two touchdowns, Brian Cotter was the hero of Houston.

"We'll double the frequency of those commercials, right?" Tom Dunning challenged his ad manager.

"Right, Tom. I'll have the agency do it first thing Monday morning."

J.J. Cookson stalked into the bungalow when the game was over and picked up his thousand dollar winnings on the Houston Oilers bet, leaving three thousand dollars which he lost when he changed over to bet on Denver after the first half. J.J. Cookson had never been a good loser.

"Hey J.J., you should be happy your team won. What's a lousy two thousand dollars to you when your team wins?" his son-in-law taunted. "And who are you betting on in the Houston-Dallas game?" Mike went on.

J.J. brightened a bit. "I'm betting on the Oilers. They're my boys. I knew Brian Cotter could do it but I didn't think he'd do it that big."

156

CHAPTER TWENTY-ONE

Monday afternoon John Dykes was working four telephones for all they were worth. Although a great many Houston fans felt that Brian Cotter had been a flash in the pan in Denver and would go down destroyed by Dallas, the interest in the game had indeed burgeoned.

Handling bets on football and the horses, laying them off when necessary, John never lost an opportunity to tell a customer to show up at the Astrodome on Thursday and bring money. He would be there in his usual box taking all bets and giving odds that nobody could refuse.

"I don't care what happened to Houricane. I'm giving odds. Right now Dallas by only six." He winked at Mike Snyder who had taken the day off from training in order to conduct a meeting between the leaders of his Wildfire team and the management of the Houston Astrodome.

"Yep, I'm going to get all that nice Houston money out and into the Astrodome." Into John's office walked a younger man whose hard, uncompromising countenance made him look older than he was. John looked up from the two telephones he was simultaneously working. "Hello, Larry. What's on your mind today?"

Larry's gaze took in Mike Snyder and he remained silent. "It's all right, Larry. You can talk in front of Mike. We're into something together. What do you want?"

"It's that Tom Dunning," Larry replied.

"What about Dunning?"

"Well, you know he's pretty deep into us as it is and he wants to get down twenty-five grand on the Oilers-Cowboy game."

"Who does he like?"

"Houston, naturally."

John nodded, pulled a desk drawer open, took a pad out and examined it for some moments. "Fifty grand he owes us. What are the chances of collecting?"

"I don't know." Larry shook his head. "Every time I go over and try to see him his secretaries won't let me into his office. I haven't even been able to get him on the telephone. Someone else always answers and says he's out."

A slow smile came over John's face. "Larry, you've laid off a lot of your bets with me. Now because you can't collect from Tom Dunning I'm having problems with my people. But I think I have an idea how we're going to get all our money back from Dunning. You know who works for him, don't you?"

"I don't know who works for him," Larry replied. "What's that got to do with it?"

"It happens that Brian Cotter is going into Mid-Texas Casualty and Life when he retires from football. He'll be working directly for Dunning. Haven't you seen the commercials they've been doing with him on television?"

Larry thought about this a few moments and then nodded. "I think I see what you're getting at, John."

"Dunning can get his hands on all the cash he needs. He has no trouble let's say "borrowing" it from the company without even telling them he's making a personal loan. All he has to do is go to the bank and draw it out. You make it crystal clear to him that we expect to get paid. And we expect to get paid fast. Tell him we'll give him until the day after the Houston-Dallas game to pay off. And you can also tell him that if he wants to make a bet on that game he can bring the cash into the Astrodome. Because unless you see the cash there's going to be no bet. And the day after Thanksgiving, on Friday, we are going to proceed vigorously to collect everything he owes us. You got it?"

"Yeah, John. I see what you mean. But if he gets Dunning to do what he wants him to do, we'll lose the bet."

"I'll take on all the money he wants to bet. Just make sure he arrives with the cash. Understood?"

"I got you, I'll go after him right now."

"And don't be making phone calls. Just walk into his office. No more nice guy stuff. Understand?" Larry nodded, and walked out of the office.

John looked at Mike. "Well I guess that's about another 50-75 thousand dollars cash that will be in the Astrodome on Thursday. I'm gonna make the odds so

159

good, the point spread so enticing, that there won't be a man in Houston that doesn't want to take my action. And I'll tell them to have it all in the Astrodome."

Mike Snyder grinned broadly. "You're a genius, John. How much do you think your people will have on them?"

"My guess is that there'll be a half a million dollars there," John replied. "Just people coming to bet with me."

"This ought to be the biggest heist ever pulled," Mike gloated.

"Certainly the biggest ever attempted," John cautioned him.

"We'll pull it off. It's not going to be easy but we'll pull it off. You wait and see."

"I hope so. Now on another matter, I had a nice talk with the Reverend Carey. Cash and Carry, just as I suspected, is in for some big trouble. There are indictments against him in four or five states and here in Texas they're looking to get something on him. He's getting ready to get out of the God business and I think I've convinced him to go with us."

Tom Dunning stood behind his desk looking down at the schedule for the commercials featuring Brian Cotter that would be run heavily throughout Texas during the coming week. Again he glanced with satisfaction at the handwritten note from the Chairman of the Board of Mid-Texas in Dallas congratulating him on anticipating Brian Cotter's unexpected moment of fame and capitalizing on it. His secretary, a concerned look on her face, opened the door and walked into his office. "Mr. Dunning, there's a man out there who merely identifies himself as Larry and says he wants to see you."

"Miss Pointer, you tell him that I'm—" he stopped in mid-sentence as Larry pushed the door open and walked in. "You can tell him yourself, Tom." There was a menacing look on Larry's face.

Miss Pointer stood in the middle of the office hesitantly until Tom Dunning dismissed her. Then he turned to Larry. "I don't appreciate your walking into my office like this, Larry—" Dunning tried to sound severe.

"Well, Tom, we don't appreciate waiting for our money any longer. What about it?"

"I told you I'd pay you when I could. I've just had a little luck. I should be able to pay off in a couple of weeks."

"You'll pay off Friday, the day after the Houston-Dallas game. And if you don't, the least that's going to happen is that Mid-Texas Life Insurance Company and the citizens that read the newspapers will know that Mid-Texas has a compulsive gambler—I think they call them degenerate gamblers now—as a vice president. Like I said, Tom, that's the least that's going to happen to you."

Dunning's face turned ashen. "Look, I've lost a lot of money. I've always paid. Now you can't do this to me."

"Then pay, Tom. What do you think they'd say at your home office in Dallas if they knew how much you bet with us?"

"My God, Larry, I've got a son at Princeton. Just be a little patient. I'll pay you."

"Patient? We've been patient for three months. I have a hunch, Tom, that you can win big at the Dallas-Houston game. You know what the odds are on the game? You know what big John Dykes is giving? He's betting Dallas and seven points. All that means is that your boy Brian Cotter has got to make sure that Dallas wins the game by more than 7 points. That shouldn't be hard for him."

"Dallas and seven points," Dunning repeated. "Well, that's sure an inviting bet for anyone, Dallas or Houston. He'll have more action than he can take care of. In fact I might put something down with him myself."

"You'll put 50,000 dollars cash in a briefcase and bring it to the Astrodome," Larry growled out the threat. "I'll sit with you at the game. Now your friend Cotter is a hot quarterback all of a sudden. The Houston money's going to be so heavy betting on the Oilers and getting one touchdown, John will be laying off all over the country. All you have to do is make sure that Houston loses by one touchdown. You bet your fifty grand on Dallas giving 7 points, we take Houston and Houston loses by a touchdown and a field goal or two touchdowns you win fifty grand and that makes you even with us. Of course if you want to bet more than fifty grand we'll lay it off for you somewhere. Maybe you'd like to come out ahead. But it's cash, Tom. Do you understand?"

Tom stared at Larry unbelievingly. "Are you suggesting that I try to influence Brian Cotter not only to lose but lose by more than 7 points?"

"You're a very smart man, Tom," Larry said approvingly. "That's exactly what I'm saying. Just bring the money in cash. Now, if I were you I wouldn't waste any time getting over and having a nice talk with your boy Brian Cotter. And Tom, remember, whatever you do, we get paid Friday. If we don't, you'll not only be out of a job at Mid-Texas but your health won't permit you to work for a year. You know what I mean?"

Tom Dunning did not dignify the threat with a reaction. "I heard what you said. Now get out of my office. You'll get your money on Friday one way or the other."

"Good, that's all we want, Tom. You know where my seats at the Astrodome are. I'll be looking for you at the game. And I'll take all the action you want, in cash." He leveled a hard glare at the insurance executive and then left the office.

Tom Dunning sagged into the chair behind his desk, a hopeless look in his eyes.

Back in the windowless caged section of the Wildfire supply room Mike Snyder and his signal and expedient devices expert, Sorell, along with Captain Thompson and Mike's deputy Hackett admired the mock-up of the tactical nuclear warhead Sorell and his men had constructed.

"Christ, it looks like the real thing, Signal," Mike exclaimed.

Sorell nodded, pleased. "When I was instructing at Ft. Sill Artillery School I made several of these mock-ups. We used them for instruction." Thompson, whose group had acquired the real tactical nuke, patted the spurious device several times. "Yep, you could sure fool me with this one." Hackett also admired Sorell's work.

"Well, I'd say we are now ready to put on the halftime show that will be remembered as long as football is played." Mike turned to the model of the Astrodome and pointed to the west gate opening which they would enter and double-time out onto the Astro turf. "This is our key entrance and egress," he began. "If we let anything interfere with using this gate we've had it."

"Signals, have you got your team completely familiar with the scoreboard electronics?"

"I think so, sir. They've been very cooperative out at the Astrodome. Sometimes I wonder why they haven't caught on to what we're really planning."

"The answer is," Mike replied, "that it's inconceivable to any normal civilian that we would even contemplate such a thing as taking off the Astrodome. The nuclear boys think only *they* think the unthinkable. Add Wildfire to the list of those who would perpetrate the unimaginable." Snyder walked over to the mock-up of the tactical nuke and ran his hand up and down the side of it.

CHAPTER TWENTY-TWO

In the middle of the afternoon on Monday, with the big Dallas-Houston game coming up four days later on Thanksgiving, Tom Dunning drove up in front of the neat little split-level ranch house and parked in front of the door. He stepped out of the car, walked across the manicured lawn and around to the back where he knew at just this time on his day off Brian Cotter would be playing with his small son.

Little Brian was there, sitting in a sandbox beside a seesaw and a swing. There was a bench against the fence separating Brian Cotter's backyard from his neighbor's equally modest plot of ground. Brian Cotter and his wife were frugal, conservative people. Most of the married members of the football team had much more elaborate homes but Brian was already saving for his son's education and for the life he and Lucy looked forward to living together.

Tom watched the child throwing small shovelfuls of sand out of the sandbox onto the grass. Then he heard the back door of the house open and looked up. Brian Cotter walked out and smiled, seeing his boss seemingly engrossed in the activities of his little son.

"Hello, Tom. This is a nice surprise. Can I get you a drink?"

"No, but thanks, Brian. I can't stay long. I just had something I needed to talk to you about."

"I hope those commercials are doing you some good," Brian Cotter said. "Boy, we sure had no idea what was going to happen when you took the big chance on me two weeks ago."

"Play the hunches, that's what I say. Listen to that little inner voice talking to you. And do what it tells you. Somehow I just knew that a Brian Cotter commercial would make it again."

"I hope they appreciate you up there in Dallas, Tom," Brian replied.

"I guess they do." Dunning looked squarely at Brian Cotter, the smile fading from his face. He put one foot on the bench and leaned on his knee facing the Oilers' quarterback. "I've got problems, Brian. Big problems."

"Anything I can help you with?" Brian asked innocently.

"You and only you can help me." The seriousness in the vice president's tone of voice and expression suddenly worried Brian. Almost reluctantly he asked, "OK Tom, what is it? If I can help, I will."

"Brian, I'm going to level with you. You know I'm a gambler. I bet pretty heavy sometimes. It seems like my hunches are a lot sounder on business gambling than they are when I bet the local bookies. I'm in deep trouble."

"You got in over your head with the books?" Brian asked.

"That's right. I can't win for losing. Right now I'm into this syndicate I bet with for over fifty thousand dollars. They carried me for a while but now I've got to pay up. If I don't," he shrugged hopelessly, "well, as they put it, the least that will happen to me is that I'll lose my position at Mid-Texas."

"That's impossible, Tom. The business you bring in? They don't have one man in the entire organization that does half the business you do."

"Maybe so. But if they knew up in Dallas that I was a compulsive gambler, if they knew how much I owed the Houston bookmakers, they'd have to let me go. I'd do the same thing if I was the head of the company and one of my men, no matter how good, was a gambler. It's too dangerous. The next thing a man like that does, he embezzles from the company he works for. And he loses and he continues to embezzle. But I've got a plan, Brian. I can get out of it. I can pay off, and believe me I'll never gamble with the bookmakers again." The words were tumbling out of Tom Dunning's mouth.

"I swear to you, Brian if I can get out of this, if I can pay these guys off, get them off my back, and the company doesn't find out what I've been doing, I'll never ever gamble again. But I need your help to get out of this jam. You're the only person in this world that can help me."

Brian Cotter stared incredulously at his boss. It was obvious that he knew what was going to be asked of him and yet didn't want to believe that such a request would ever be made, particularly by the man in whose hands his future had rested for several years. Although

Brian had been an All-American quarterback he'd also graduated magna cum laude from the University of Texas and had planned to go directly into a business career. However, the money, yes and the excitement, had tempted him to go into a few seasons of professional football before settling down to his business career. And right from the first year he'd been starting quarterback for the Houston Oilers, Mid-Texas Casualty and Life had adopted him as their sportsman, spokesman, and symbol.

"They won't stop with just hounding me out of my job," Dunning pursued. "If I don't pay up they'll beat me into such a condition I won't be able to work anywhere for a year." He looked over at Brian's little boy. "I've got a son at Princeton, you know. God knows what will happen to him at this time in his education—if I'm finished." He stared desperately at Brian Cotter. "You've got to help me, Brian."

Brian's eyes narrowed as he fixed his business mentor with a glacial gaze. "I think I know what's on your mind, Tom."

"It would be easy for you, Brian. Just a couple of interceptions at the right moment. It happens all the time, in every game."

Brian Cotter visibly recoiled, a grimace twisting his lips now that the proposition had suddenly been thrown out in the open.

"I wouldn't ask you this, Brian, if I wasn't desperate," Dunning pleaded. "Literally, my life, my future, my son's future depends upon my paying off the books this week. They've given me until Friday. You've got to help me, you've got to do it for me, Brian."

Brian Cotter closed his eyes a moment and turned away from the man who until this moment he had con-

sidered his best friend and the author of his future security. Tom Dunning reached out his hands and, taking
the quarterback by the shoulders, turned him around.
"You've got to do it, Brian. It means nothing to you.
Nobody will ever know."

Brian Cotter shook his head again.

"Ask me anything, Tom. Anything but that. I can't
throw a game. It's not in me. You've been good to me.
Yes, I had planned my whole future around Mid-Texas
and working for you. But not that. I can't do it."

Tom Dunning sagged slightly and then the desper-
ation of his situation seized him, forced him into the
course of action he knew he would probably have to
pursue. "Brian, four years I've been grooming you to
become the vice president in charge of the Houston office of Mid-Texas. I'll be retiring in just a few years. It
will all be yours. I'm giving it to you. For four years
your happiness, your welfare, has been my chief
concern. Remember? You came to me when Lucy so
desperately wanted a child and couldn't have one? I
took you to the best doctor in Houston. Remember?"

Brian nodded miserably. "Yes, I remember," he
murmured.

"Remember when you and Lucy wanted to adopt a
baby? Remember you couldn't find an adoption agency
with a white baby to give up to an athlete? Remember
the girl I found? Blonde? Blue eyed? Anglo-Saxon to
the core? Remember how I arranged it? She met you in
a hotel room every night for a week? She never saw
your face because the lights were never turned on? For
five thousand dollars she agreed to have the kid for the
man she never really saw? Remember, Brian? I was the
buffer. She never knew who you were."

Tom Dunning took two steps towards the child in

the sandbox and patted his head and then stepped away from him again.

"Remember, Lana was under age, Brian. Now, she's twenty. She still doesn't know who you are or where her kid is." A sad yet crafty expression came across the insurance executive's face. "I'm feeling pretty bad these days, the girl wants her child now. She's married, a very sensible kid. And she's pressuring me to find out where her kid is so she can get the child back. But don't worry, Brian. I haven't cracked. All she knows is that she had a baby boy. She doesn't even know if the baby is in Houston. But she wants to take legal action to get her child back. There are precedents, you know, for returning children to their natural mother in cases like this. Oh she's threatened legal action against me if I don't tell her where the child is. I just say I don't know, I don't know anything about it. But of course, I do know. But like I say, Brian, I'm not talking. Now don't you think that's worth something?"

If he had not been so desperate, so consumed with what had become a frantic need to extricate himself from his situation with Larry and his bosses, Tom Dunning would have been stricken at the look of anguish and shock that came across Brian Cotter's face. As it was he merely chalked up a victory. "We're not gonna put Lucy through losing the child, are we, Brian? You never told her the child was yours, of course. That would have hurt her too much, wouldn't it? Knowing you went to another woman to bear you the child the two of you adopted. How does a woman feel, do you think, in a case like that? Is she happy that the child is at least yours even if it's not hers? Or does she feel betrayed, cheated that you're the natural father but she is not the blood mother?"

The barrage was brutal, as vicious as any punishment Brian Cotter had ever taken playing football. Those linemen, rushing in to sack him, those behemoths—if their IQ's were five points lower they'd be geraniums—they'd never inflicted such punishment upon him. Tom Dunning stopped talking. He'd sacked the quarterback all right. Cotter was silent for almost a full minute as Tom Dunning stood waiting for an answer. Finally it came.

"What do I have to do?" his voice was hollow, defeated.

"Dallas has got to win by more than seven points. You know what it will mean, Brian," Dunning went on eagerly. "I'll be clean with those sharks. And you know what I'm going to do, Brian? I'm gonna go to that game with a hundred and fifty thousand dollars in cash. I'm gonna bet it with those bastards. That means when the game's over, when you've done what you have to do, I walk out clean and I've got a hundred thousand dollars. You know what else it means? It means fifty thousand to you and fifty thousand to me."

"If you've got a hundred and fifty thousand dollars, Tom, why don't you pay them off and be done with it? Why do this to me?"

"I don't have a hundred and fifty thousand dollars. I'm broke. But I can get a hundred and fifty thousand dollars of company funds in cash and hold it long enough to take into the game. I need the cash in order to put down the bet."

"That's embezzlement!" Cotter cried out. His little son suddenly looked up from the sandbox at the wounded exclamation from his father's mouth.

"That's how desperate I am."

Brian Cotter realized that no matter what happened

after this game there was no way he would ever go back to work for Mid-Texas. "All right, Tom." He looked at his young son. "You've got me. Just two things I want to tell you. First, I'll throw it away in the second half. And second, you'll do me a big favor after I've saved your ass by never letting me see you again. I'll find a job somewhere after this season. Because I'll be through when I do what you're making me do. But I'm not working for you or Mid-Texas Casualty. In fact, I'm not working in Texas. I'll find a job in some other part of the country. But don't you ever let me see you again."

"If that's the way you want it, Brian, so be it."

"That's the way I want it. And don't you ever forget it."

"I'm sorry it had to be this way," Dunning recited to the ground at his feet. "Just don't change your mind in the second half. Because if I'm destroyed, you go with me."

"Get out! Get out of here before I do something I'll regret the rest of my life. Get out quick!"

The insurance executive turned and strode as quickly as he could without actually running from Brian Cotter's backyard, around the corner of the house and out to his car. He jerked open the door on the passenger side, slid across, started the engine and jack-rabbitted down the street without even bothering to close the door. It slammed shut itself. Now Tom Dunning knew what the phrase "murder in the eye" really meant. But he was saved. Not only saved but ahead of the game. Never, never again would he gamble. Never again would he make a bet with a bookie, he swore to himself. Now he had to plan how he would get the hundred and fifty thousand in cash out of company funds on Wednesday and return it to the bank Friday without company auditors discovering the transaction. But the hardest part was over. This would be mechanics. Mechanics he could handle.

CHAPTER TWENTY-THREE

As Brian Cotter was making the agonizing decision to insure a Dallas victory on Thanksgiving Day, two dozen television sets at Foley's suburban Department Store, all turned to the same channel, were blurting out a sportscaster's analysis of the coming game on Thanksgiving between the Houston Oilers and the Dallas Cowboys. All of the other departments of the store were temporarily deserted as rabid Houston fans soaked up every word of the sportscast.

"And it is my opinion after watching Brian Cotter's amazing victory over Denver on Sunday—was it just yesterday?—that Houston will beat Dallas by one touchdown on Thanksgiving Day." The department store fans applauded and cheered. Scenes from the previous day's football game were shown again. An army of football fans, mostly youngsters and elderly men who did not have to be at work that day, were staring at the game report coming over the television screens. When the show was over chimes sounded throughout the store and an announcement came over the public address system.

"All customers of the self-serve suburban store are reminded that the lucky winner of two tickets to the Thanksgiving Day Oiler-Cowboy game will be named every hour beginning at 2:00 p.m. Your check-out stub is your entry form. The computer will select winners from check-out numbers recorded every hour."

A teen-age boy checked the clock at the end of the store and noticing it was now ten minutes of two, hurried to the hardware department to buy the five yards of plastic tablecloth material his mother had sent him for. He duly paid for his purchase at the check-out counter and then waited until two o'clock for the big announcement. At one minute after two the announcement came over the public address system.

The number was read several times as the youngster, dropping his package in excitement, realized that he held the lucky check-out slip. With a scream of joy he ran back to the clerk who had checked him out and was directed to the check-cashing booth at the back of the store. He galloped excitedly down the aisle to the booth, and presented his check-out slip. The store manager beamed. "What's your name, young man?"

"Billy Weaver," the excited youth replied. Over the public address system came the announcement. "The first set of two tickets has been won by Billy Weaver of 7 Sycamore Terrace. There will be another pair of tickets given out at three o'clock and every hour thereafter."

176

With the two tickets in an envelope firmly clutched in his left hand, Billy Weaver went out to retrieve the roll of oilcloth he had dropped at that ecstatic moment when he heard his number called.

Billy Weaver ran home as fast as his short legs could move. Bursting into the front door, he rushed to the kitchen, dropping the package on the floor, and brandished the two tickets he had won. His mother looked at them skeptically as Billy burbled with enthusiasm that he would take his father to the football game.

"But the game is on Thanksgiving, Billy," his mother reminded him. "Grandmother and Grandfather are coming. We're having a big family dinner. Why don't you give the tickets to somebody whose family are not celebrating Thanksgiving together?"

Billy Weaver was crushed. "But Mom, it's going to be the biggest football game of the year. The whole United States is going to be watching it on television. You mean Dad and I *can't go?*"

Billy's mother saw the disappointment on the boy's face. He had been so excited and now he was clearly crushed. The mother took the tickets and looked at them again. "Well, the game starts at 12 noon. It should be over by three. Maybe we could make it a late Thanksgiving this year. We could have dinner at four, I expect. I know your father would never get over it that his son brought him two tickets to the Oilers and Cowboys big game and you couldn't go. I don't believe I could face telling him."

"I can take Dad then, Mom?"

"You'll have to ask him when he comes home from work. Not that there's much doubt what he'll want to do. But I suppose we could plan dinner later under the circumstances."

"Gee thanks, Mom. It's only thirty minutes from here to the Dome."

"Yes—but think of. the traffic. All those thousands of cars. Anyway, we'll see what your father says."

CHAPTER TWENTY-FOUR

Major Mike Snyder stood across the large mahogany desk from Lieutenant General Vogel. The general was in an uncharacteristically good mood as Mike reported to him. "Sir, Wildfire is ready to put on a spectacular show Thursday. In many ways it should simulate the real thing. The sort of action that you told me Wildfire must be ready to execute if the government of the United States needs the services we can perform. You, as commanding general here and under whose authority we have created this unit, will have cause to be proud of us." Mike was purposely pompous, knowing Vogel would not sense the irony.

"The President of the United States will be watching," Vogel replied, awed at his own statement.

"Well, when the President of the United States sees what we and units like ours can do he will know he doesn't have to take any insults from any foreign leader.

179

Basically our exercise will show how a precision military team, Wildfire in this case, could actually take over any objective assigned it whether that objective be a football stadium like the Astrodome with a capacity crowd, or any city or any presidential palace we might be ordered to seize. An old friend of mine whom you may have heard of, Colonel Mike Hoare in South Africa, said he and his group of Wild Geese—that's what he calls his mercenaries—could take over any country in Africa. Our unit could take over any capitol city in the world if sufficiently expanded from the hard core we have now produced here at Ft. Hood."

"Outstanding, Major Snyder. Outstanding," the General declared, thinking of the reaction in Washington to a unit under his command putting on such a sensational show on television. "I have the entire army recruitment division on the alert to use your halftime show in its drive to expand our all-volunteer peacetime army." The wry look on the general's face eloquently bespoke his opinion of a peacetime army with no draft to force the cream of America's youth into the midst of the United States Army. It was no secret the caliber of soldiers the peacetime army was now getting. It was a constant struggle to keep a fifty percent ratio between black and white troops. And the way things were going it looked as though within two years the army could become ninety percent black since the main appeal of military life seemed to be to the disadvantaged.

"We're handling this just the way we would an actual operation, sir," Mike Snyder went on. "I have established a sanitary cordon around the company and nobody goes in or out. All telephones are cut off. There'll be absolutely no communication between the men going on this exercise on Thanksgiving Day and the outside world. We are putting on an exercise in top secret security at the same time as we're carrying out this exercise."

"Excellent, Major Snyder. However, I expect you will be in communication with me at all times right up until the demonstration begins inside the Astrodome."

"Of course, sir. But I will be the only member of the Wildfire team who will leave the isolation area at any given time. I will call you or come to your office personally every six hours from now until we leave for the Astrodome."

"Supposing I need to reach you when you're inside the sanitary cordon?"

"It shouldn't be necessary, sir. As you'll recall from our actual combat operations in Vietnam and of course the Swift Strike war games at Ft. Bragg in the sixties, there was never any communication with men in isolation."

"Yes, of course, Major. You're really making a serious operation out of this, aren't you?"

"You told me, sir, that the Chief of Staff himself had asked you to implement and develop a unit that could carry out the type of operations that the United States Army Special Forces were trained for in the sixties. Do you remember our operation in the Dominican Republic? As I recall it, you were a colonel in 18th Corps under General Westmoreland at that time. Nobody knew we were coming until we had virtually taken over the Dominican Republic."

"That's right, I remember. That was a fine show, fine show." Vogel smiled at the memory. "President Johnson personally came and congratulated us on how efficiently we carried out his executive order."

"If the President needs an action like that again,

we're ready and we'll prove it on Thursday. Just leave it to me, sir."

General Vogel nodded in satisfaction. "I guess I misjudged you, Snyder. I felt you were a restless type. But your father-in-law and I are friends. And we both have remarked upon how well you have finally adjusted to the changing situation in the United States."

"It was difficult at first, sir, as you must realize. The reduction in force, the reduction in facilities offered men who had sustained both physical and psychological damage in the Vietnam War. And perhaps you'll recall how many of my men were killed on that last incursion into Cambodia which was aborted. But not before we were twenty miles inside enemy territory. It was hard for me to adjust to the fact that you had to refuse us air cover."

"Snyder," the general's voice suddenly became sharp, defensive. "I thought by now you realized what happened in the White House that day."

"Oh, of course I do, General. I just brought up the fact that it was difficult at first for me to reconcile myself to the loss of all those fine men." Snyder realized he had to go carefully at this point. His voice, his whole demeanor became more placating. "I know how hard it was for you to be right there in the middle and give the orders which would have doomed my brigade had it not been for one pilot who helped us anyway. Now, of course I realize what a dreadful decision you had to make."

General Vogel nodded, a self-pitying look coming to his face. "Yes, Snyder, I'm glad now you can understand the terrible strain I was operating under."

"Well, sir, it's a new army, a new era, a new outlook and new challenges to be faced. We must look to the future. And while we don't forget lessons learned in the past, we don't brood over the political practicalities that caused us to surrender in the Vietnam War."

"Right you are, Major Snyder. And just between the two of us, despite your father-in-law's desire for you to go into civilian life I hope that you'll stick with the army. I feel certain that in another three or four years you will advance to the rank of lieutenant colonel. And some day become a full colonel again."

Snyder looked across the desk at the rotund, complacent two-star general and decided he'd better leave Vogel's office fast. He threw a snappy salute, all but clicked his heels and said, "I'll be in communication with you regularly, sir." With that he turned smartly and strode out.

The Wildfire company area was surrounded by concertina barbed wire with military policemen stationed around the perimeter. There was one entrance only into the company area guarded by both military police and two of Major Snyder's most trusted Wildfire officers. Even though Major Snyder was well known both by his own men and the military police, he was required to bring his special pass with his photograph out of his wallet and present it to the guards. They examined the pass and then fed it into the slot of an electronic scanner which guarded against counterfeit passes. The card was returned to him and he was allowed to go through.

Mike Snyder went directly to his office, passing Sergeant Medford who was standing guard in front of it. In his office Mike Snyder changed from the Class A uniform he'd worn during his interview with General Vogel. A few moments later he walked by Medford again. Now he was wearing a black beret and camouflage fatigues complete with webbing on which hung his sidearm, canteen, first aid kit, and two hand grenades attached to the harness. "Are the men ready?" he asked Sergeant Medford.

"Everybody's drawn up in ranks on the company parade ground, sir," Medford reported.

"Any problem keeping them in isolation?"

"Not so far, sir. Of course most of us know what we're going to do. The guys that still think this is just an exercise have been a little restless about not even being able to make a phone call."

"Well, we'll straighten everybody out right now, Sergeant." Major Snyder, followed by Sergeant Medford, strode briskly out of headquarters down the company street to the Wildfire team, now stabilized at two hundred men, drawn up in ranks waiting to be addressed by their commander. It was 5:30 in the fall evening and the parade ground was illuminated by high intensity lights.

"Attention!" Sergeant Medford shouted.

The ranks came to rigid attention as Major Snyder walked up three steps to the platform which the men were facing.

"At ease, men," Snyder called out affably. "Now I want you to listen to me carefully. No American Army commander has ever given his men a talk like the one you're about to hear. Nothing any of you do the rest of your lives will be as crucial as the decision you're all going to have to make tonight, right now."

Snyder paused for a full thirty seconds to let the import of his statement take effect. He searched the faces of his men. He estimated that as many as sixty of the two hundred were not aware of the true culmination of

the Wildfire plan. Moreover he felt it was necessary for
every member of the Wildfire team to once again reaf-
firm their resolve to go through with the mission, as
hazardous a one as any of them had ever participated
in, before the actual operation commenced three days
hence. The eyes of every man on the parade ground
were fixed on their commander. Their attention was total.

"Gentlemen. First, I'm not going to give you any
bullshit. You know something's up—something big—in
fact the biggest irreversible transformation of your
lifestyle you'll ever know. Now I'm going to tell you
what that something is. But first I want to tell you what
it means to each and every one of you. For openers,
$50,000 cash per man!"

A sudden rustling and shifting took place among the
ranks, a few whispers, and then Snyder went on, silenc-
ing them.

"But you're going to give up something that may be
pretty important to you for that money and for other
benefits which I'll soon tell you about. What you're
giving up is the right, for a while at least, to live in or
even visit the United States of America."

Again Snyder paused for effect, his eyes gleaming
out at his assembled troops. "Anybody who feels like
going for a walk right now is free to do so. Let me explain again that we are all on ice here. In isolation that
is. There is a barracks reserved for the men if there are
any who do not want to proceed with this exercise.
However, you will remain in the barracks under guard
until twenty hundred hours of Thanksgiving Day before
you will be released to go beyond the sterile cordon
around our isolation area." Again Snyder paused,

185

staring out at the men. There were no takers of the invitation to walk.

"Good. If at any time any man wants to leave the Wildfire team he need merely report to Captain Hackett who is standing just below me on the ground facing you. Hack will show you to the barracks where you'll stay for the next three days. The barracks are well equipped with K-rations and beer. Nobody will be hungry or thirsty. What I'm telling you is top secret at this point, gentlemen. We can take no chances that any portion of what I have to say will go beyond our isolation area until after twenty hundred hours on Thanksgiving, Thursday, three days from now. Gentlemen, we're marching toward an objective which I promise you will make military history. It will also make the biggest impact on the American public of anything the United States Army has ever done in peacetime."

Snyder allowed a smile to cross his lips and dropped his shoulders slightly in a more relaxed pose. "Now I'm not going to give you that horseshit about duty, lay down your life for it, love the flag and honor your country. Every man here is a combat veteran of Vietnam. You've heard all that rot before and what did it get you ever but shot in the ass, kicked in the ass, and screwed in the end with no honor, no thanks and certainly no love. Every man here knows what it was like to come back from a war we lost. A war the so-called intelligensia of America hated and blamed us personally for being part of.

Snyder smiled bleakly as the troops nodded and mumbled agreement. "The years and the grind in the mud and the blood—the blood particularly. Remember it?" Again a chorus of agreement. "Goddamn it, men, a draft dodger gets more respect than you do. What about the country you got your asses shot off for. What has the country done for you lately beyond insulting you because you did your duty as ordered. Now everyone of you men who goes along on this operation, everyone of you is going to be doing something for yourself personally. Every man of you out there in front of me has seen his buddies die. More than that, every man has seen buddies go into hospitals, veterans hospitals. And there they still are the forgotten men of this generation, the men that didn't run off to Canada or Sweden or some other place, and desert. The men who were maimed for life, physically and mentally. Well, this unit, Wildfire, is going to do something about it. And in a military and orderly way we are staging our own demonstration. A demonstration which will never be forgotten by America. Sure, the creeps and cowards, the hippies, the deserters—they all staged their riots, the ones that were lucky enough to get into college and avoid going to Vietnam had their say on the campuses. And where are they now? They've got the jobs, they got the education. But what did we get? And what did we get when the war was over? If we stayed in the army most of us were RIF'd. If we went into civilian life and admitted we had done our duty as soldiers we were spat upon. Well, when we go into the Astrodome on Thanksgiving Day we are going to give ourselves everything we've got coming."

A youthful trooper whose row of ribbons belied his inexperienced appearance raised a hand.

"Yes, son, what's on your mind? Speak up," Snyder called out.

The young trooper, flabbergasted, stammered, "You mean—*You mean we are going to hold up the Astrodome?*"

Snyder who had taken a cigar out of the breast pocket of his fatigues and jammed it between his teeth, lit it and then replied calmly. "That's right son, we're going to rip off the Astrodome."

The trooper, trying to understand, pursued his question. "Sir? I mean . . ."

Snyder cut in suddenly. "I mean receipts, gate concessions and the money in the audience. Everything that goes into the Astrodome for that game comes out with us. We have determined that there will be as much as twenty million dollars bet during the first half of the game." Snyder took a long drag on his cigar and then looked out firmly at his men. "We're going to take the take. Altogether we estimate there'll be as much as thirty-five million dollars in cash and valuables inside the Astrodome during the Houston-Dallas game."

The men stirred uneasily, looking at each other, exchanging whispers. The men who had known about the final result of the Astrodome exercise trying to quiet the others down. Snyder allowed the excitement to ripple through his men for a few moments and then once again suddenly cut into their conversations.

"You all feel bad about pointing a weapon at a fellow American, I suppose. Real bad?" He looked down challengingly from the platform and then his voice became accusing. "What do you think he's been pointing at you, you the Vietnam veteran? Five years after we retreated in disgrace from the roof of the American embassy in Saigon, five years after the war—and you still can't get all the benefits every other foreign war has entitled its veterans to get. And you know why? Because you're losers. But it was the country, not us, who was the loser."

Snyder's anger added a sharp edge to his voice as he

went on. "But it was our country, the U.S. of A., that sent you over there to Vietnam, it was this country that got you in a fight and then tied your hands behind your back while the enemy, who's suddenly trying to become our friend now, knocked us off with every weapon he had while we were not even allowed to use our best stuff. And now it's this country that's calling you losers, you who did the fighting.

Snyder shrugged and finally a smile came over his face. "Well, such are the hazards of being a professional soldier. What I'm offering you is a sort of fighting man's compensation. It's clean, it's neat, nobody has to get hurt who doesn't want to, there are no forms to fill out or taxes to pay."

Snyder paused looking around at the men many of whom were gaping at him in disbelief. "Where we're going there's no extradition. Only money, security, and fabulous females. Some day even it's possible America will realize what they drove us to and apologize and ask us to come back. Pure reason doesn't seem to add up to much in the United States anymore. Well, we're not terrorists, we're not holding up America to ransom. We're just men who have to make a statement."

Snyder turned from his men and gestured to two sergeants standing behind the platform. They handed up a large board on which was pinned a huge graphic design of the Astrodome. It was placed on the platform behind Snyder as he turned back to the Wildfire team. "So what we're going to do is a little bit more than put on that halftime show. We're putting on a real military operation, the kind you've all been in. Inside the Astrodome on Thanksgiving Day," Snyder tapped the board with his fist, "there'll be sixty-five thousand people carrying an average of $200 each to bet on the game." Snyder turned from the Astrodome graphic to the men listening intently to his every word.

"And I've got two hundred of the best bill collectors America ever trained to go in and collect. And believe me we are going to collect. Now I'm going to explain in detail just how we're going to do it. Your leaders, from corporals and sergeants on up to the officers, have known the true objective of this exercise for the last five or six weeks. Your job is to follow their orders instantly, without hesitation, and happily.

"Now I'm going to run through the entire operation from the moment we walk out of this isolation area on Thursday morning at 0600 until the time we board the Hercules aircraft which will fly us away from the Astrodome and down to our destination, the Republic of Costa Vacca.

"At the end of this briefing any man who feels he does not want to go with us for whatever reason is free to go to the separation barracks where he will be held until after this operation has been executed and the rest of us are all safely on the way to Costa Vacca."

For the next two hours Mike Snyder went over every element of the operation.

While the operation had been rehearsed at some length by the section leaders this was the first full scale explanation of the entire operation giving every individual knowledge of the overall plan.

Mike Snyder finally finished his presentation and looked out fiercely at the men under the lights. He repeated his invitation to walk out on the operation if anyone so desired.

"What about my old lady?" someone shouted.

"Any dependents any man here wants to bring with

him will be flown to Costa Vacca after we arrive. We have a coordinator for dependents who is standing in front of me now and who will make arrangements for transportation. I want to add now that besides the $50,000 cash you'll receive we are, as a group, being given a substantial interest in the Costa Vacca oil industry which is just getting started. We will be on salary to the Costa Vacca army and we will also draw income from our interest in the oil wells. This interest should amount to as much as $50,000 a year per man once the oil industry gets underway. We estimate that Costa Vacca can become the world's number one supplier of oil to the United States. It's in this hemisphere, just a few days away from New Orleans by tanker, as opposed to more than two weeks from the Persian Gulf or the week or ten days the tankers take to get across the ocean from Nigeria, after they've waited a month to load up. Gentlemen, we'll all have a stake in the oil wealth of the Republic of Costa Vacca."

Now a more somber expression came across Mike Snyder's face. "We want to distinguish ourselves from the hippie demonstrators of the 1960s who were nothing more or less than outright terrorists. They threw razor-blade studded potatoes at police and innocent bystanders, they perpetrated violence and frequently death. Yet what happened a few years later? Their leaders are writing books and are respected members of the community, far more respected than we who followed orders and went out and fought for our country in Vietnam.

"That's the way the pendulum swings. But it will swing again back toward us, and that swing will come sooner as a result of our Thanksgiving Day statement.

191

We want to avoid violence if possible but if we are challenged, if it is necessary, we will use all the force at our command to bring off this operation successfully.

"However, I can assure you we will not be attacked by United States Government military force. America is accustomed to being bluffed out. One day it's by some two-bit African dictator who's just killed one hundred and fifty thousand of his own people because they belong to a rival tribe, but whose country happens to have the oil we need. The next day we see our President bow to political terrorism exerted against him by one of his own political appointees—accepting insults, promoting policy that is not in the best interests of this country rather than offend his cabinet member and an Ambassador who threatens him with the loss of all the black votes in the United States if he does not go along with him on all his desires. And by the same token you may be certain that the President, who will be watching our performance on Thursday, will once again accede to force rather than challenge it."

Once again Snyder studied his listeners and felt instinctively they were all with him, in agreement with his philosophy. "Captain Thompson and his element managed to acquire a tactical nuclear warhead recently. The loss of this tactical nuclear warhead has not been announced by the government, probably because of a fear that panic would seize the country if it were known that a potential terrorist group had a nuclear weapon in its possession. Yes, we have this device at our disposal. But we're not using the real thing, even though we could. I don't believe any of us would want to chance its actually detonating. Rather, we have constructed an exact copy of the device, a harmless mockup which we will bring into the Astrodome with

192

us and place in the middle of the Astrodome on the fifty yard line.

"I will have the remote detonating mechanism with me at all times. And it is the real one, but with no device to detonate. This mechanism will be recognized when the television cameras pick it up. Our whole plan is based on the success of this arrogant bluff. If our bluff is called, if America's high command, watching us on television makes a decision to challenge us, our mission will fail and we'll either be dead or in prison for a long time."

Mike stared out at his men. "Make no mistake. If the President decides to call our bluff and attack us full strength either outside the Astrodome or more likely after we've taken off in Hercules, we're dead!"

Major Snyder let this last remark sink in for several moments. Then he went on again, his voice ringing out in the night air deep inside the isolation area. "But we've got something going for us, gentlemen. The United States hasn't called anyone's bluff since President Kennedy forced the Russians to pull their missiles out of Cuba back in 1962. It just doesn't seem to be within the capability of American leadership to call a hand that might be better than what they've got.

"Our leaders are so worried about what the world's going to think, what the third world's going to think for that matter, even what the Communists are going to think, that this country of ours is always tied up in knots of indecision. Considering the stakes we're playing for, considering what we have to gain, considering what we are going to tell the world, I tell you the risk is worth it. America doesn't call a firm bluff.

"Take a look at our former Secretary of State Henry Kissinger, for instance. Gives you some idea of the

American giveaway mentality when he accepted the Nobel peace prize for abandoning Southeast Asia to the Communists. At least the communist gook over there, Le Duc Tho, was not the kind of hypocrite our fearless and wise Secretary of State turned out to be. Le Duc Tho refused to accept that prize. He knew he was going to kill off a million or so of our standard allies.

"And what have we got now? For the last few years every decision has been to give away America to terrorists within and without. Not only give away America but give away our friends. Look at the President's boy in the United Nations."

Snyder looked over at Captain Thompson, his black leader, who had done such an outstanding job in capturing the nuke. "No offense intended, Captain Thompson," Snyder chuckled. The rest of the men laughed with him, easing the tension that had gripped the assembled troops.

Thompson laughed louder than the others. "The man doesn't speak for me, Major. And he don't speak for any brunette I'd ever let serve under me."

"Right on there, Thompson," Snyder called out. "When our leaders finish giving away our friends like Rhodesia and South Africa to the Communists, to say nothing of our friends in South America, there isn't going to be a friend in the world left to the good old U.S. of A. So relax. This isn't the kind of leadership that's going to call our bluff or even worry much about what happens to us. The U.S. of A. sure isn't going to follow us to Costa Vacca with the 82nd Airborne to get us out. Those guys would join us and stay down there if they were sent! So I say our chances are good. But until we land in our Hercules transport plane down there where our friends are waiting for us, we're in jeopardy. Deep shit, that is. So I'm giving you all one last chance. Any man that doesn't want to go on this operation can quit now. Now's the time to walk if anyone has a mind. After this little talk, after I step down from here, there's no turning back. I'm going to stand up here for ten minutes. That's long enough for every man to make up his mind. But when I step down every man still standing on the parade ground is in. And there's no getting out!"

"Hey, we don't need no ten minutes, Major. We're with you!" someone yelled from the group.

A loud chorus of assent followed.

"All right men, I'll tell you what we're going to do," Snyder replied. "Every man who knows he's in, walk off the parade ground, go in and have a drink, eat, and see the movie we've got for tonight. Anybody who wants to stand out here and think it over for ten minutes stay right where they are. There's certainly going to be nothing held against a man who wants to think over whether or not he wants to risk his life, or take a chance on a good long stretch in Leavenworth."

As Snyder looked out over the parade ground his men began to leave the formation in high spirits, laughing, slapping each other on the back and talking about the delights of Costa Vacca. As Snyder had anticipated, perhaps twenty men, most of them the youngest in the group, remained in place on the parade ground. Snyder stood patiently on the platform looking down at them. His hands behind his back, a thoughtful expression on his face. "There's nothing more to say, nothing I can tell you you don't know. You men just take your time, ten minutes that is, and if there's even the slightest doubt in your minds, don't come.

"Sergeant Williams, old Rooster as we call him, is standing right below me. If you have any questions about your dependents, wives, the girl you want to marry, talk to him. As I said, financial arrangements have been made so that you can send money back to the States or take with you to Costa Vacca any dependents that want to come. We'll arrange all transportation and expenses from down there. That's all I've got to say, men. The decision is yours now."

Major Snyder stood motionless for about five minutes, then glanced at his watch. "Four minutes to go," he called out. Five men from the group who had been whispering among themselves turned and walked from the parade ground to the barrack Snyder had indicated as temporary detention quarters for defectors. The remaining fifteen men stood fast for another two minutes. Then three others, troubled looks on their faces, walked to the detention barrack.

Snyder consulted his watch. "The rest of you are with the operation, I take it?"

"Yes, sir!" The reply was a lusty chorus.

Snyder nodded in satisfaction. "Good! You men have thought it over, weighed the risks and the benefits and are with us. Go in and join the others." Sure of themselves and their decision now, the men doubletimed to the mess hall to throw their lot firmly in with their comrades.

Snyder stepped down from the platform and walked around to Sergeant Williams and his deputy. "OK, we have one more matter to take care of. Let's go."

196

CHAPTER TWENTY-FIVE

On Tuesday morning Major Snyder and "Rooster" Williams left at six in the morning to make the drive to San Antonio and the Brooks Medical Center at Ft. Sam Houston. They visited the by now familiar ward which still held some of the survivors of the Wildfire ambush in Cambodia. They then had a meeting with the administrator of the veterans medical center and drove back to Ft. Hood.

"You've talked to all the men who are outpatients, as well as those still in the wards?" Snyder asked.

"Right, sir. The biggest question is Lieutenant Edwards."

"He's with his mother and father now?"

"Affirmative sir. His wife left him. His mother and father don't really know what to do with him. They can't turn him out. He needs a lot of help but there just isn't enough psychiatric care available for men like him, veterans of the Vietnam War."

"He never could adjust to what we had to do on

those search and destroy missions. Edwards just wasn't the killer type. And then the ambush. I guess that's when he really snapped."

"That's right, sir. After you were hit, it looked like half your head was blown off you were bleeding so much, I really thought you were gone, Edwards came up, figured you were dead and we had to knock him out with a gun butt to keep him from leading a one man banzai charge into the middle of the ambush. I guess he screams a lot at night still and he just can't do much."

"Anyway, Rooster, he is coming to the game. Right?"

"That's right, sir. We got him a hotel reservation and I haven't told him what we're going to do, of course, but he knows something's up and today his mother said he's already been better."

"As long as all Wildfire Vietnam casualties are taken care of we've done our duty."

"It's all set, sir. You talked to the guys at Ft. Sam yourself. Special pass to come up to the game. Every one of them knows they're not going back to the ward again. You heard them say they'd rather go with us wherever we're headed than stay in the hospital where they're going nuts anyway."

"OK, Rooster. I feel we've done it all now. It's up to us on Thursday to bring this operation off."

That evening Mike Snyder and his section leaders went through a complete drill of what every individual member of the Wildfire team would be doing during the halftime show. It was a three hour exercise and after it was over and Hack and Mike Snyder went to Mike's quarters within the sanitary cordon and had a drink together. As they pulled at their drinks, Hack shook his head. "You know, Mike, it comes in waves.

First I think it's all a game and then, after our skull session tonight, I realized we're really going to do it. My God! we're gonna pull off the biggest heist in history. It really is all going to happen, isn't it, Mike?"

"Yes, it's gonna happen. We're gonna do it. At least we're going to give it hell."

"All this planning, all the rehearsals, all the logistics we've worked out. It's just got to go down," Hack mused aloud.

"All our work and planning this past two months sure beat hell out of grousing about our frustrations, and worrying about what's wrong with America and the world."

"Is that what it was to you, Mike? A diversion? Something to get your mind off what's eating at you?"

"It sure served that purpose, Hack. Didn't it for you? Didn't it for everybody in our operation?"

"Yeah, I guess it did. But come this time Thursday we might all be dead; going down in a flaming Hercules transport plane."

"Might indeed, Hack. Yep, might indeed." Mike re-lit his dead cigar, puffed on it a few moments and then downed the drink. He stood up and patted Hack on the shoulder. "Now I've got to take me a little trip back to River Oaks. I guess Cookie deserves a goodbye even though she doesn't know it's goodbye."

"That girl, that Migi you talk about, she sure must be something to take you away from everything you could have if you wanted it," Hack remarked.

"Migi is an ancillary benefit, Hack. You don't think I'd expose over two hundred of the best men I've ever known to death or at best long prison terms just because I got me a beautiful woman down in Latin America, do you? Hell no, it's much more than that.

199

Sure, it's going to be beautiful with Miguelina. Just as beautiful as it's gonna be for you and everybody else when we get there. Damn near half the guys are bringing their wives or leaving their wives and bringing their girl friends. The others will find more than they could hope for down there in Costa Vacca. And the girls treat you nice down there. None of this woman's lib shit. A man is king and the women wouldn't have it any other way. But more than that, and this is what I've been trying to get across to you, Hack, you above all who are closest to me and have had the most to do with planning this operation. When we get organized, Costa Vacca is going to have the most powerful military force south of the border. Good men, top soldiers, will be coming from all over the world to join us. We'll be the richest, the best military unit in the world. And we can help change things just by being there.

"Mike, you'll either go down in history as a great world statesman, or the biggest fanatic since John Brown at Harpers Ferry!"

Mike stood up, puffing on his cigar. He patted his deputy on the shoulder, then gave him a hug. "You've got me made, kid. That's about the size of it. See you tomorrow. D-Day minus one."

Hack grinned crookedly at his commander. "D-Day huh? Dome day. Maybe Doomsday. Anyway you've got the best, the most highly motivated bunch of men behind you any commander ever had."

"See you tomorrow, Hack." Mike left the quarters, turned out into the company street, walked to the entrance of the isolated area, presented his pass to the guards who knew him so well. They went through the routine of putting it through the scanner, handing it back to him and saluting.

CHAPTER TWENTY-SIX

It was midnight when Mike finally reached the bungalow at River Oaks. Cookie was up waiting for him. "Mike!" she cried as he came in the door. "I've been waiting for you all evening. Where have you been?"

"There was a helluva lot of last minute details to take care of. This thing on Thursday is going to be one of the most talked about military operations in history."

"Oh come on, Mike, don't take it all so seriously. What are you going to do? Walk in at halftime, run around, shinny up or down a rope? You know as well as I do nobody's going to be watching anyway. Hell, what they're going to be doing is changing the odds and betting the second half. You know that as well as I do."

"Yep, I guess you're right, Cookie. And you know who'll be leading the betting."

"Oh yes," Cookie laughed. "My Daddy. You know he's told everybody that's coming to his box to bring ten thousand dollars with them so that we can out-bet all the other skyboxes on the circle."

"That's your Daddy all right," Mike agreed.

"He's counting on your getting out of the army after your fun and games on Thursday. He's already figuring on getting you into the oil business. You know, Mike, my Daddy's been very pleased at how big an interest you've been taking in his business. He really loves it when you ask him those questions, make notes on what he tells you, and then ask him more questions. He thinks you may be one of the smartest Yankees ever to come into this business since George Bush came down from Connecticut and made a fortune here. For a while there I thought maybe you and I weren't going to make it."

"But now that I'm interested in oil you've changed your mind, yes, Cookie?"

"Well, you got to do something with your life. You're sure never gonna get anywhere in the army. My Daddy got you up to full colonel once and look what happened."

"Yeah, even all that oil power couldn't stop them from RIFing me back to major."

"Well, you'll show them, Mike. A few years and you'll be making more money than the Joint Chiefs of Staff make altogether."

"Yep, you may be right. Do you think your Daddy could buy me the Presidency of the United States?"

Cookie's eyes shown with delight. "Now that's the way I like to hear you talk, Mike. That's the kind of man I thought I'd married. Yeah, I had my doubts for a while but—" she stopped a moment and then went on. "Why not? Old Joe Kennedy bought it for his boy Jack. You just play golf every weekend at River Oaks Country Club and stick with my Daddy. We got more money in Houston than Kennedy had in Boston. You goddamn well know that my Daddy and his friends can buy the White House anytime they got the guy to put in it. And, Mike, you and I are just the people! We sure are, just the people."

Inwardly Mike chuckled to himself. If Rockefeller couldn't buy the White House with all his money and almost sixteen years as Governor of New York behind him, not even Houston could buy it today. Maybe back in the fifties and early sixties . . . but America had changed too much since then.

Mike went over to the fancy bar provided by J.J. Cookson and mixed himself a strong scotch and soda. He took a long swallow of it. He'd have to remember to make sure that Costa Vacca imported enough Johnny Walker to keep his men happy.

"How long are you gonna stay in the army after Thursday?" Cookie asked.

"You know something, baby? By Thursday night I won't even be in the United States Army anymore! What do you think of that?"

Cookie gasped and then let out a shriek of joy. "You mean it, Mike. Honestly?"

"Cookie," Mike said seriously, "I never said a more truthful thing in my entire life. You want to make some money off your old man. You bet him ten grand that his son-in-law, Major Mike Snyder, will be out of the United States Army by nine o'clock Friday morning. You think he'll take that bet?"

Reassured, Cookie let out another squeal of joy. "You bet your sweet ass he'll take it. If you're telling

203

me the truth, Mike, let's bet him more than ten grand. It'll be one bet he'll love losing."

"He'll lose all right. I doubt if he'll love it. Just make sure he bets cash with you. And you got to put up your cash beside it."

"You know what, Mike, I got me thirty thousand dollars cash in my private account. The one you can't touch."

"I can't touch any of your money, Cookie. So what are you saying?"

"What I'm saying is, Mike, I'm going to get all that money out of the bank and take it with me to the Astrodome. And I'm gonna make Daddy put up cash." She gave him a sidewise look. "You wouldn't want to see me lose our money to my Daddy, would you?"

"It's not our money, it's yours. But no, I wouldn't want to see you lose your money to your Daddy. As a matter of fact, I've got eight thousand dollars saved up in my own account. I'll write you a check tonight for it. You get it out and add that to the bet. OK?"

"Oh Mike, I love you," she cried. And throwing her arms around him she nestled in his lap, kissing him. After a few moments he shifted her aside and reached for his drink which he finished quickly. "Mind if I get up and fix me another?"

"Of course not, Mike. I'm so happy. And no matter what you say, Daddy won't mind losing that bet! We'll put it into an investment in oil to celebrate your getting into business with Daddy."

Mike laughed crazily. "It will sure go into oil, I can promise you that."

He slugged himself with one more highball, then wearily followed Cookie up the stairs to the ankle-high carpeting on the bedroom floor and into the kingsized four poster bed. He went quickly to sleep, leaving Cookie gazing at him in perplexed annoyance.

The next morning he awoke first, showered, shaved and put on his Class A uniform with all ribbons, then gently roused the slumbering Cookie. "I got to leave you now. I'll write a check out for everything I've got in the bank. You cash it and make that bet with your Dad."

"Oh I sure will, Mike," Cookie promised.

"You and your Dad are going to be real happy together from now on," Mike remarked.

"I'm so happy, Mike," Cookie gushed. "We'll take him, yeah we'll take him off for forty thousand dollars tomorrow. Will I see you during that halftime show?" she asked.

"You won't miss me, I'll be right out there in the middle of the field. Waving right up at your skybox. I got to go now, Cookie. Take it easy, be happy. I'll be."

"Don't you want me to fix you some breakfast?"

"I got what I needed. I'll eat out at the post. Goodbye, Cookie."

Sally Cookson looked up at her husband, perturbed at the tone of voice. "That sounded so final, Mike."

"See you at the big game." With that he walked out of the bedroom leaving a faintly troubled Cookie behind him.

CHAPTER TWENTY-SEVEN

By Wednesday afternoon the word was out among the sporting folks of Houston and Dallas that big John Dykes had revised his point spread on the Dallas-Houston game. He was giving sixteen points, two touchdowns and at least a field goal on Dallas to beat Houston. Money was coming in from all over the country but Big John announced he would be in his box on the sixth level an hour before the game and he wanted all bets placed in cash. As he said over one of his four telephones to a Houston stalwart, "Sure I'll take your action, all of it, but I want it in cash. I don't want to have to win this bet twice."

"What do you mean, John?" the voice came over the phone. "Win it twice?"

"You know what I mean. Once when I win and a second time when I collect."

Dykes had a similar conversation with Tom Dunning

who at first was horrified. He could guarantee Cotter would let himself be intercepted for two touchdowns but no more. But that was good enough for John Dykes. He'd take his chances on Dallas making an extra field goal.

"I know I'm into you guys for fifty grand, John," Dunning pleaded on the phone. "But I want to put one hundred and fifty thousand on Dallas. And I'm only giving 13 points. Can you lay it off for me, John?"

"Well look, pardner, you just show up at the game with all the cash you want to bet in a satchel, you hear now?" John boomed back on the telephone. "Your record on paying off isn't so good. You come with cash and I'll get your action taken care of."

"But you'll take that action when I'm giving only 13 points, if I bring the money in, won't you?" Dunning asked anxiously.

"You know the old saying, Tom. Money talks, bullshit walks. Whatever cash you bring in—I don't care if it's a half a million dollars—I'll take all your action at that spread. Just bring it up to my box and we'll have us a drink together. Of course I expect you to pay me the fifty you owe me off the top before I take your action, you know that."

"Sure, I understand, John. I'll be up there with everything I can lay my hands on."

"Well pardner, if I know the size of your bank account or at least your company's bank account, you won't have any trouble bringing up as much as you want to bet."

The Houston fans are going crazy trying to get bets down on credit with Big John Dykes but he firmly refused anything but cash brought to him either at the Astrodome or delivered to his office before the game.

Ordinarily, John knew, if there was going to be a cash on the barrelhead bet, the bettors would have preferred to bring it to his office than to the game itself. However, with the point spread he'd made so suspiciously enticing, and the fact that it was beginning to get around that Big John had a past that was rapidly catching up with him, the Houston bettors all preferred to arrive at his box rather than take a chance on leaving it with him and never seeing him again.

As John Dykes mused about opening a casino in Costa Vacca, a concession which Mike Snyder had already obtained from Miguel Alamen, the dictator, he continued to exhort his customers to bring their money with them to the Astrodome and get paid off there. His only problem now was to be able to show the cash to match what was being brought into him. Never before in his career had he ever bet on a sure thing. But here was a clear-cut case where he could not under any circumstances lose. With no second half being played, the worst that would happen would be that somehow Mike Snyder's caper would fail and that all bets would be off. Obviously there'd be no second half to the game no matter what happened with the operation.

To make the situation even better for Mike Snyder's operation, the point spread that John Dykes had given was forcing the other bookies to meet his offer. Some of the bookies were giving only a six or seven point spread and taking the bets on credit, but the greedy big action types in Houston were convinced that it was worth bringing their cash to the Astrodome and getting the extra point protection that "mad John Dykes," offered.

All Wednesday afternoon and Wednesday night, John Dykes was collecting cash. Many of his former associates were willing to lend him cash to cover the bets and he had in his floating account about three hundred thousand dollars. He would be walking into the Astrodome with over half a million of his own money to cover all bets. And his money, the money he brought in, would be inviolate, Mike Snyder had promised him. And then, as he had been expecting for so long, the red phone rang. This was the special line to his attorney in Chicago.

"Hey Earl, what the fuck are you doing to yourself?" the voice rasped over the phone. "You've just made yourself famous around the country giving that sixteen point spread on the Dallas-Houston game. The word's out that Big John Dykes, or should I call you madman Dykes, in Houston is none other than Earl Catona, late of Chicago, Detroit, and Boston. I've kept the Feds away from you for three years now. But they have already been over to see me asking what happened to my old client Earl Catona. You'd better have a lot of money because I'll be fighting three indictments on top of your bail-hopping and even I don't think I can beat this rap."

"How much time have I got?" John asked.

"Well you've got three states filing extradition warrants against you today. By tomorrow, Friday at the latest, you'll have Massachusetts, Michigan and Illinois marshals down there, each one wanting to bring you back to their fair state. If I were you I wouldn't be hanging around your office too long. With the juice you've got, you could probably get the governor to resist one extradition. But three, that's too much. No governor can get away with that."

"I figured they were getting close to me. I've noticed

that I've been followed off and on for the last few months."

"I don't know why they didn't get you sooner. You can't expect to hide behind that Texas accent forever."

"OK, thanks for the call. I'll bust out of the office, walk away from it right now."

"That's the best thing you can do," the lawyer agreed. "Whatever state they extradite you to first I'll get to work there for you."

"I don't think that will be necessary, thank you. How much do I owe you for this call? I'll put a money order in the mail to you today."

"I won't even ask you where you're blowing off to but you'd better be hard to find, real hard to find. Telephone me as soon as you settle down somewhere and I'll see what I can do for you. By the way, this call's on the house. You've paid me enough the past five years. I might take some of that fourteen point action, though," the lawyer chuckled.

"The only way you can do that is to come to the Astrodome and lay it out in cash. And buddy, don't do that."

"So long, Earl. Good luck. Call me when you need me." John heard his Chicago lawyer hang up. He dropped the red receiver into its cradle and stood up. He picked up the large attaché case which was always next to him and walked out of his luxurious apartment for the last time. He took the elevator down to the basement and instead of walking into the garage where his car was parked, he followed the plan he had two months ago evolved. Dykes walked out through the trash disposal room onto the platform where the garbage trucks came to take the refuse away. At the end of the platform were steps going down to the alley behind the apartment building. He walked down the alley to the corner, turned left, walked a block to the cab stand, grabbed a cab and asked to be taken to the Holiday Inn at the Astrodome. Twenty minutes later he was checking in under another assumed name. Up in his room he opened the large attaché case and once again counted the money inside it.

In neat piles of hundred dollar and thousand dollar bills he counted out his bankroll. Four hundred and ninety thousand dollars. He figured thcrc would be seven hundred and fifty to eight hundred thousand dollars minimum of bets being placed with him in the hour before the game began. Now he could only hope that none of the states would be able to have him arrested pending receipt in Austin of the extradition warrants being filed. John had enough strength with the Harris County District Attorney's office, to say nothing to the Houston police, to fend off any arrests that might be contemplated inside the Astrodome itself. Now he was praying for the total success of Mike Snyder's operation. If the Wildfire team succeeded he would go with them and be safe. If somehow the operation was thwarted or aborted—the latter seemed impossible, Mike Snyder was too serious—old Earl Cantona's ass wouldn't see the outside of jail for many a year. He was in the same boat as Snyder and the Wildfire team. Win big or lose big. There was no middle ground.

CHAPTER TWENTY-EIGHT

Billy Weaver and his Dad left at eleven o'clock on Thanksgiving morning to go the big game. They drew a diagram of the Astrodome and showed Mary Weaver exactly where their seats were located so that she could perhaps catch a glimpse of them when the television sets swung around over the audience. Billy and his father were both mightily excited about seeing the game and Billy's mother said that when she saw the game was over on television she would put the turkey back in the oven so that it would be hot for their late afternoon Thanksgiving Day feast.

"We'd better get going, Dad, or we'll never find a parking place," Billy said anxiously.

"There's a parking place for every seat in the Astrodome, Billy," his father assured him. Then to his wife Bill Weaver said, "Some smart son I've got, getting his old man a ticket to the game. Except for the rush seats it's been sold out all season. I sure wouldn't be waiting in line for one of those 15,000 seats. I understand they've been lined up since last night."

"At twelve dollars a seat you can be certain I wouldn't let you be waiting," Mary Weaver replied, laughing.

"I'd sure love to get some money down on Houston. What with the bookies giving fourteen points it's a steal."

"Now don't you talk about gambling, Bill. We do all right but we don't have any margin for anything like that and you know it."

"Well, I've got fifty bucks. If I can find somebody who will take Dallas and give me fourteen points, I'll bring back another fifty."

Mrs. Weaver sighed. "Nothing I can do about that, I guess. Once a year I suppose you've got to have your fling. Now be sure to come right home from the game. Everybody will be starved."

"We'll come home, mother, I promise," Billy vowed.

"And don't eat any of that junk at the Astrodome either. You eat all that cheap popcorn and candy and you won't have any appetite for a good wholesome Thanksgiving dinner."

"I promise, Mom." With that Billy Weaver was already on his way out the front door, his father following.

In the parking lot outside the Astrodome already fifty percent full, the football fans were eating and drinking beside their cars, talking with friends and making bets. And always the betting. When Bill Weaver and his son Billy finally found a parking space in between the picnicking Dallas enthusiasts, Bill was tempted to be drawn into a conversation on the game and the point spread between Dallas and Houston.

While it had become common knowledge that at least one major bookmaker in Houston was giving fourteen points to the Houston fans, most of the private betting was on a more conservative basis. Those betting on Dallas, mindful of the superb half that Brian Cotter had quarterbacked the previous week were only giving six and seven points. But betting fever was in the air. Bill Weaver resolved that when they were seated somebody near him would undoubtedly be ripe for a bet and he'd get his fifty dollars down on Houston somehow.

They walked over to the portal nearest their seats, displayed their tickets and walked in. It was a beautiful clear fall day, not too cold, but then it didn't really matter since the temperature was always the same inside the Astrodome, an even 71 degrees. And of course it never rained in the covered, illuminated stadium.

One hour before game time John Dykes, his heavy attaché case now representing his total worldly goods, walked from the Holiday Inn across the huge parking area and entered the Astrodome, showing his season box ticket to the guard who touched his cap in recognition of this well known frequenter of the sporting events at the Dome.

Inside the stadium John took the elevator up to the sixth level where his box was located just below the ring of the skyboxes. Although the skyboxes start at $80,000 a season and go up from there, it was not the price that deterred Big John Dykes from taking one for the season. Only ticket holders were allowed into the ring on the seventh level and many of the most important bettors John traded action with did not have skyboxes. Therefore he had to be accessible to every-body. It was no problem for a skybox guest or owner to come down one level and place a bet with John Dykes. And anyone in the stadium could get to him if he needed to place big action.

Ordinarily John Dykes was not a nervous person. No matter what the size of the total action he was backing, it never perturbed him. But now, he couldn't help looking around furtively. Would they try to pick him up today? he asked himself. In a way it was fool-ish to expose himself this way. It didn't really make any difference whether he stood here or not.

The big bettors would be coming in with the money to bet with him and if he wasn't there they certainly weren't going to leave and miss the football game. But it was a point of pride with him to be in the middle of the action. A compulsion, an irresistible need to be part of the scene, to actually count money and take bets forced him to stand tall in his box and go through the motions of servicing his customers. They were all going to be taken off anyway, but he felt honor bound to at least give them the excitement of his hoary spiel, his jokes, his observations all made in the Texas accent he had cultivated and loved.

For a kid brought up on Chicago's north side he talked Texan better than the Texans themselves. And he hadn't been in his familiar stand for more than five minutes before his first bettor showed up.

"Hello there, Abel," John greeted his first customer. "Come for some of that fourteen point money, did you? Well, son, I can't blame you. I guess I went a little mad, they're calling me "mad John" nowadays, I hear, but I just wanted to see all that good Houston money turn out."

216

"You got mine, John, I'll take five grand of your action—you're giving fourteen points and taking Dallas. Right? OK, five big ones on Houston." Abel reached into his inside jacket pocket and pulled out a wallet and peeled off three one thousand dollar bills and twenty hundred dollar bills. There's my money, mind if I have a look at yours?"

"Sure thing, Abel. This is the day for cash." John pulled five one thousand dollar notes out of his own inside wallet and handed them to Abel. "I'll even let you hold the stakes, how 'bout that. As long as you sit right here with me, of course," John added with a chortle.

"Oh, I'll be right here, John. I won't walk off with your money until that final gun goes off." He had hardly finished dealing with his first customer than others began coming up to him. In one hour he had put out three hundred thousand dollars with big bettors. And now, as the really magnum force gamblers began drifting to him he realized he might run out of matching funds. Not that it really mattered. Each time a gambler came up and showed him that he actually had ten grand in his pocket—some of them going as high as twenty and twenty-five thousand dollars, everybody wanted a piece of big John Dyke's sucker point spread—he began to write out markers. It was unheard of for John Dykes to fail to pay off a bet within five hours of the win.

By kickoff time John had put out his entire half million dollars plus markers for another six hundred thousand. Each marker had been given to a gambler who showed John the color of his money before John handed out the marker. From the skybox level above, big gamblers were coming down to bet with him. The

217

reason for this was obvious to anyone who was privileged to be watching the game from the skybox ring.

J.J. Cookson set the pace for the spirited wagering among the super-rich skybox owners and their guests. He walked along the ring to a neighboring double box which he knew would be full of Dallas fans. "I understand you're giving twelve points on Dallas," he began. "Of course I can go down to John Dykes and get fourteen, but I'll just take your twelve. Can you handle ten grand?"

The bluff, hearty Dallas banker visiting Houston and sharing the box with his local counterpart laughed derisively. "Now J.J., you know as well as I do that there ain't no one in his right mind giving twelve points and that's a fact. I'll give you six points. I saw Cotter play Denver last week."

"Six points!" Cookson's wounded bellow resounded half way around the ring. "Dallas looks like it's going to the Superbowl. And you only give me six points against our poor little old Oilers here?" he shook a sheath of one thousand dollar bills suggestively. "At least make it seven points. Seven and you've got my ten grand here. What'ya say?"

With a great show of reluctance the banker took ten thousand dollars from his own pocket and put it on the able. "OK, J.J., you're covered. I got Dallas and you've got Houston not to lose by more than seven points."

"I'll be around for my money and a drink after the game," Cookson promised.

The mark John was especially interested in finally sauntered over to his box and clutching his black attaché case, waited for John to finish taking a heavy wager. Then it was his turn.

"I have a hundred and fifty big ones in here, John." Dunning's bravado convinced the gambler that the money was in the case. "Remember, you said I could bet on Dallas and give you twelve points? You'll take that action?" he asked anxiously.

"That's what I'm here for, pardner," John agreed. "Let's see your money." Dunning nodded and sat down in the seat beside John. The insurance executive flicked the combination wheels with his thumb and then snapped the case open. John looked in it. "Do you want to count the money, John?" Dunning asked.

"Might as well. Nothing else to do." Of course it made no difference whether Dunning had a hundred and fifty thousand or even seventy-five thousand. Whatever was there would all go with Wildfire anyway. Nevertheless John counted the money. Exactly a hundred and fifty thousand dollars was in the attaché case.

"All right, I'll take your hundred thousand dollars. You got Dallas and giving me twelve points. I'll also take the fifty thousand you owe me."

"Help yourself."

"Thank you, I will," John replied. He counted fifty thousand dollars out and transferred it to his own attaché case.

"You might as well watch the game here in my box, Tom," John invited. "I don't guess either of us wants to be too far from the other until the game's over."

"You got a point there. I go along with that." Tom Dunning settled back in his chair waiting for the game to begin.

CHAPTER TWENTY-NINE

Just before kickoff, with every seat in the Astrodome taken, the announcer's voice boomed over the public address system, welcoming the crowd to the Dallas-Houston "war for the state." A nervous box office manager, Marty Stang, watched the last of the rush seat crowd file in. Marty tried to derive comfort from the two state policemen who were positioned near the box office watching the fans file past them. The security manager walked up to him. "What's the matter, Marty? You look worried," Tom Shepherd asked.

"Well, Mr. Shepherd, we sold 15,000 rush seats at $12.00 a copy. That's a lot of cash to have around."

"Relax, Marty. In what is it, fifteen years? Whatever, the Astrodome has never lost a penny to thieves. It isn't going to happen now. What's the matter with you anyway, Marty? You're as nervous as a cat in a room full of rocking chairs."

"I don't know, Mr. Shepherd, sometimes I just get nervous. Call it a feeling in the bones. Some people can tell when the weather's going to change by the way their bones feel. I just have this bad feeling about to-day."

"How often do you get these feelings, Marty?" the security manager asked jokingly.

"Not very often, Tom, but when I do something always happens. Like when I was box office manager at the Palace Theatre and we had that robbery. I felt it then. And then there was the time in Detroit when we were hit. I don't know what it is but I felt the same way that morning that I do now."

"Well, Marty, maybe you're just psychic. Only here at the Astrodome, nobody can rob this stadium."

"How come the armored car is late?" Marty asked plaintively. He looked at his wristwatch. "It's never been late before."

"Look, Marty, do yourself a favor and stop worrying, will you? The armored car will be here. Wells Fargo to the rescue. Then you can enjoy the game."

Had Tom Shepherd been able to see the Wells Fargo truck he would have been as nervous and worried as Marty Stang. On a deserted Houston back street the driver of the Wells Fargo armored car turned a corner and found himself staring directly into the muzzle of a 155mm cannon mounted in the turret of a light tank. Even as the Wells Fargo driver and the guard beside him were attempting to assess the situation, another armored vehicle heavier than the money car had pulled up directly behind it. Helplessly the Wells Fargo guard looked about the empty street. It was Thanksgiving, everybody was either at home or the football game. Not even the police seemed to be interested in downtown Houston back streets today.

Through the amplifier mounted in the front of the armored car the Wells Fargo driver shouted out, "You guys have got to be kidding. What is this?"

The tank commander, Lieutenant Tichman, shouted back over his bullhorn, "We're not kidding. One shell and there's no Wells Fargo truck left. Get out of there, with your hands up!"

"We haven't any money in the truck," the driver called back.

"Then why don't you get out and save yourself a lot of trouble?" the tank driver called back.

Inside the armored car the driver looked at the guard beside him. "You know something, he's got an idea there. What the hell, let's get out," he muttered. "This is the first time a tank held up an armored car with no money in it." The driver swung the door of the armored car open and stepped out, raising his hands. The guard emerged from the other side of the armored car. They walked up to the tank. Now Lieutenant Tichman opened the hatch and stuck his head out. "Did you ever see the inside of a real armored car?" he asked pleasantly.

The two Wells Fargo men looked at each other in amazement and then back at the tank driver.

"What are you, nuts?" the driver asked.

"No, not at all. We know just what we're doing. Come on in and look around." The invitation was made more compelling by two men in army fatigues who had jumped out of the armored personnel carrier and were pointing rifles at the Wells Fargo men.

"Well, if you put it that way I guess we'll get our first look at the inside of a tank," the armored car driver replied reasonably. "And by the same token, be my guest, look around the inside of my tank. I hope you won't take your disappointment out on us."

"Oh we're not disappointed, everything's going just as we planned it." The two Wells Fargo drivers climbed up the treads of the tank and into the hatch. Before descending into the tank itself they looked back at their armored car and were surprised to see the men who had leveled weapons at them close the door of the truck without even going inside. As they watched, the two gunmen returned to the armored personnel carrier, backed it up and drove away.

"Come on inside and look around," Tichman ordered. "We're going to take you for a little ride in our vehicle."

"What's this all about now, buddy?" the Wells Fargo guard asked.

"You'll see in a couple of hours. But nothing's going to happen that will hurt you fellows and, as you can see, we certainly are not planning to rob Wells Fargo."

"This is the goddamndest thing that ever happened to me," sputtered the Wells Fargo guard.

"I shouldn't be surprised," the tank man agreed. "Just stay down below here and keep quiet. There's no reason we'd want to hurt you unless you do something silly like opening your mouth at the wrong time or trying to get out of this tank before we let you out. Understand?"

The two Wells Fargo men nodded. The tank officer started the diesel engine and the tank began to roll backwards away from the armored car. It wasn't until the tank had clanked for three blocks that a state police car finally pulled up in front of it and waved the tank down. The tank commander poked his head up through the hatch.

"What in the hell are you doing here in Houston with that machine?" one of the state cops called out.

"Haven't you heard? We're putting on a demonstration at the Astrodome," Tichman replied. "We're heading out there now."

"Oh yeah," the state cop replied. "We heard something about that. Aren't you a little separated from the rest of your people?"

"We brought this vehicle from another post to join up with the others," the sergeant replied coolly.

"Do you know the way to the Astrodome?" the state trooper asked.

"We'll find it, officer. Thank you very much."

The state trooper got back into his car and drove away as the tank continued to clank along towards the Astrodome.

Inside the Astrodome the Houston Oilers and the Dallas Cowboys had gone through their line-up for the television cameras and the kickoff was only moments away. Then over the public address system the Astrodome's announcer called out, "Ladies and gentlemen, will you all please rise for our national anthem." All sixty-seven thousand spectators who were not already on their feet stood up and the notes of the *Star Spangled Banner* echoed throughout the cavernous dome as the words were simultaneously spelled out on the huge scoreboard.

"Oh say can you see . . ."

Mike Snyder watched the football fans standing and singing their national anthem over the portable television set on the seat beside him in the armored personnel carrier. Drawn up beside him were a number of other vehicles from jeeps to armored personnel carriers and even a light tank of the type he had used in Vietnam.

The Wildfire team had established this rally point exactly twenty-five minutes from the Astrodome and when the second quarter began they would start off for the Dome, arriving at the west gate, they calculated, about eight to ten minutes before the first half was over. Once again Major Snyder went over the operation in his mind. Seventy-five of his men were already in the Astrodome with their repelling ropes and their field-stripped weapons which were concealed in their backpacks. Signals and his team were already in their places in the television booth and Astrodome scoreboard control room.

The Astrodome management had been most cooperative, Mike thought. This would be his finest hour, the climax, the high point of his entire life no matter how old he lived to be. And, for that matter, he might not live to see the sunrise tomorrow. Well, the planning, the rehearsals, the entire deception, had all been perfectly executed. Now all that was left to do was pull it off.

As the last strains of the national anthem wafted cacophonously throughout the stands of the Astrodome, the gamblers were getting down more bets throughout the various levels of the stadium. There were many accommodating bookmakers in the stands that day and to them their customers flocked. But the biggest betting was in the skybox circle. Besides all the individual bets being made, the owners and guests in the boxes were collecting pools and entire boxes were betting with each other on the outcome of the game.

J.J. Cookson was in his element. Splashing hundred dollar and thousand dollar bills as he roamed around the skybox circle, finally returning to his own luxurious double box, Cookson was indeed keeping the action lively. He had already wagered fifty thousand dollars on the game when he returned to his own skybox and started gulping down a bourbon and water handed to him by the skybox butler.

His daughter sidled up to him. "You get you a lot of money on Houston?" she asked.

"Enough. I still want to go down to Big John Dykes and get a little of his fourteen point action."

"Well, I'm looking forward to the halftime when Mike comes in and puts on his show," Cookie said. "You know, this is Mike's last day in the army, he told me so himself."

Cookson looked at his daughter unbelievingly. "No, that couldn't be. Hell, Lloyd Vogel would have said something to me."

"Maybe Lloyd Vogel doesn't know," Cookie responded.

Cookson left his daughter for a moment and walked to the other side of the skybox where General Vogel was standing, a drink in his hand, talking to a group of Texans surrounding him who were interested in the halftime proceedings.

"Hey Lloyd," Cookson boomed, "you hear anything about Mike Snyder getting out of the army like tomorrow?"

"No, I sure haven't, J.J.," General Vogel looked in surprise at his host. "I would know if he was getting out. The papers would have to go across my desk.

Even if he resigned his commission today it would take some time to process him out. No, J.J., no reason why Mike would want to be getting out anyway. After this halftime show he's going to be one famous major. He might even get back up to lieutenant colonel again. Sorry to disappoint you, J.J. I know you want him back on civvie street but his heart's in the army."

Cookson nodded and walked back to his daughter. "Sorry to disappoint you, darling, but Mike will not be out of the army tomorrow or next week or I don't know when."

Down on the Astro turf Houston had just won the toss and elected to receive. Dallas was lining up in kickoff formation as the Houston team arrayed itself to receive. The skyboxes emptied as the pre-game revelers took their seats in the mini-grandstand in front of each box on the astroturf side of the walkway. There was an air of tension and excitement throughout the huge arena as Dallas waited for the umpire's signal that the game had started. Then the kicker ran toward the ball, kicked it high and deep where it was caught on the ten yard line by the Oilers' halfback and the game was on. The Houston fans roared approval as their runner made it up to the 32 yard line before being slammed down by the Dallas defense. The quarterback Brian Cotter ran onto the field and called his first play. He handed off to his halfback who charged off tackle for a two yard gain.

Although Dallas was expecting the second down pass, Brian Cotter successfully hit his wide end for a first down. The Houston stands went wild. Two first downs later, the bettors were convinced that Cotter would be as good this week as he had been against Denver and pressed their bets wherever they could.

John Dykes, surrounded by those with whom he was betting, cut the point spread from fourteen to twelve on any future bets. But this did not discourage his customers from coming up to him and having used all their cash importuned him to take bets on credit. Knowing what he did, it made no difference, so John, having personally accounted for over two million dollars being brought into the Astrodome, took bets on markers. As the first quarter progressed it was obvious that Brian Cotter was in top form, as good as he'd ever been in his football career. Up in J.J. Cookson's booth the word was that Cotter is as good as Johnny Houricane.

Tom Dunning wished he could get more money bet on Dallas now. With Cotter looking so good he was one of the many bettors asking John to take their action with markers. What a chance to make a killing, he thought. He was the only person in the whole Astrodome who knew that Brian Cotter was going to be intercepted three times in the second half. Leaving his attaché case full of money with John Dykes for safekeeping, Dunning left the sixth level and walked up to the seventh level Astro box ring. He had a ticket to one of the Astro boxes and the guard at the entrance to the ring allowed him to pass.

Dunning stopped by J.J. Cookson's box and walked down the steps to where Cookson was sitting in the front row of the seats allotted to him. Cookson looked up at Dunning and grinned. "Looks like your boy is doing pretty good out there today, Tom," Cookson remarked. "You sure made a helluva deal when you got him for those commercials. After today, when he beats Dallas, he'll be the hottest quarterback in the game."

"Well, I'll tell you, J.J., you may be right. I sure got

a lot of money bet on Houston. Now I think I might put a little safety money on Dallas." Just as he said the word Dallas, a roar permeated the Astrodome. Cotter had connected with his wide end again and now Houston was knocking on Dallas' goal line.

Cookson looked away from the game and back at Dunning. "Did I hear you say you wanted to bet on Dallas?"

"That's right, J.J."

"How much do you want to bet and how many points are you giving?"

"I'll take Dallas and spot you seven points," Dunning announced.

"How much do you want to put down?"

"How much do you want to take, J.J.?"

"Cash?"

"I got all my cash bet with mad John. Will you take my marker, J.J.? I guess you know I'm good for it."

J.J. Cookson laughed. "You know all the cash I brought in here you've got most of it bet too. Sure we'll take each other's marker. Ten grand?"

"Want to make it twenty, J.J.?" Dunning answered, a challenge in his voice.

"You got it, Tom. Twenty grand. I'm betting Houston, you're betting Dallas and giving me seven points. Correct?"

"Correct J.J.," Dunning replied cheerfully. "See you after the game." With that Tom Dunning continued to walk around the skybox ring.

With half the first quarter gone and Houston ahead seven to nothing Tom Dunning walked out the opposite entrance to the ring that he'd come in. He had given out and was holding a hundred thousand dollars in markers. He could have had two hundred or even half a million if he'd wanted. This was a sure thing. But then he knew there was no such thing as a sure thing. Supposing Brian Cotter at the last minute decided to defy him. Supposing Cotter didn't throw the ball away in the second half. Well, Dunning was through in that case, dead through. He'd be out of Mid-Texas Life—no job. But Cotter would pay too. He would pay with the custody of his son.

CHAPTER THIRTY

"All right men, this is it!" the terse command from Major Snyder went out over the Wildfire command channel and was picked up by every member of the team. In a tank moving towards the Astrodome from Houston the order sparked apprehension in the hearts of the two Wells Fargo men.

"What does that mean?" one of them asked.

"It means that in about five minutes we let you out of the tank," Tichman replied cheerfully.

"And then what? . . ."

"Don't ask questions," the lieutenant interrupted sharply. "Everything's gone real good for you people so far. Let's keep it that way."

The Wildfire section leaders inside the Astrodome also heard the command through the ear plugs they were wearing attached to tiny radio receivers. Via hand signals they alerted their men that everything was proceeding according to schedule.

At the Wildfire mechanized rally point the engines of APCs, jeeps, half-tracks and a tank began to rev up. The column, led by Major Snyder proceeded towards the Astrodome twenty minutes away. Major Snyder sitting in the command seat of his APC waved to the state police escort which had been assigned to the Wildfire halftime operation. A state police car and two motorcycles preceded them to their rendezvous with a new life, or death.

Probably the only person in the entire Astrodome who was not interested in the game was Marty Stang. Nervously he hovered about the box office looking for the grossly tardy Wells Fargo truck. Even the state police officers who had been so reassuring had been unable to resist the temptation to edge their way far enough into one of the portals to see the game being played out below.

The rush seat receipts were still in Marty's office and he was worried. He picked up the phone in the box office and called the security manager, Tom Shepherd. As he expected and feared, there was no answer. The lure of this decisive game was too much for them all. To Marty Stang it made no difference who won or lost. He had only one concern and that was getting all that money into an armored car and on its way to the bank.

In exasperation he hung up the telephone. He thought of calling the scoreboard booth and asking them to page Shepherd but that would have made the security man angry, and probably embarrassed as well. He couldn't explain the feeling of presentiment that gripped him. He could almost physically feel danger closing in on him, danger he could neither anticipate nor delineate. For perhaps the fifth time he tried to telephone the Wells Fargo offices but even there could get no reply.

"The whole goddamn town has gone football crazy!" he growled in frustration.

Signals and one of his men waited until there were five minutes left in the first half. By now Brian Cotter had shocked Dallas by leading the Oilers to a seven-seven score over the vastly favored world championship Dallas Cowboys, who until now appeared almost a certainty for another Superbowl shot.

Signals stopped in the deserted hallway outside the stands and took the miniature transmitter from his breast pocket. "Stand by to cut all communications to the outside," he commanded.

Each one of his men reported back that they were ready to perform their long-planned functions in the overall Wildfire operation.

Out in the lower level stands Billy Weaver and his father were wildly cheering the feats of Brian Cotter and his Oilers. Billy's father had bet the entire fifty dollars on Houston with a seat neighbor, both of them having put up their money in cash and the Dallas bettor giving the Houstonite twelve points on Dallas. But now with Houston and Dallas, tied the Oilers not only looked as though they would not lose the game by more than twelve points but indeed win it. Bill Weaver was already planning what he'd do with his windfall fifty dollars. He could increase the liquor budget for the month by one bottle of bourbon and a case of beer. Also he could buy *Playboy* as well as *Penthouse* and maybe even *Genesis* too. And while he was at it he would buy *Forum*. Maybe if Mary would read some of that stuff she'd be as good in bed as she was in the kitchen, he thought. Then he turned his attention back to the field. Dallas had Houston down on their own twenty-five yard line and Roger Staubach was pressing the Houston defense.

"Defense! Defense! Defense!" the Houston fans implored.

J.J. Cookson was leaning forward, tensely watching the superb efforts of Dallas to score before the end of the first half. The skybox butler came up to him, asked him if he wanted another drink and J.J. nodded without taking his attention away from the Astro turf below.

"You can bring me one too," Cookie ordered. J.J. turned to his daughter. "Goddamn, you drink that bourbon and branch like a man. You never did that before Mike got back from Spic-land."

"Well, Mike will be out of the army tonight," Cookie replied airily. "We'll celebrate by drinking nothing but champagne. Would that make you happier?"

"I got to tell you, Mike's not getting out of the army tonight or tomorrow or next week."

"You know something, Dad," she said. "I'll bet you some money on that."

"How much do you want to bet?"

"Thirty thousand dollars," Cookie replied. J.J. Cookson wheeled away from the game and stared at her. "What did you say?"

"You heard me, thirty thousand dollars."

"We only bet with cash here," J.J. snapped back at her. "I wouldn't let you make a sucker bet like that anyway."

"I thought that was the story of your life, corralling

236

suckers, getting them to bet with you when you know you're going to win."

"Young lady, I'm gonna teach you a lesson. I'll bet you the thirty, if you've got the cash."

Cookie had been carrying a large leather handbag over her shoulder, a bag almost as big as a small suitcase. She took the bag off her shoulder, put it in her lap, opened it up and started pulling out thousand dollar bills. "Well Dad, I got twenty of it in cash right here. Where's yours?"

"You're not kidding, are you?" J.J. replied. "What makes you so sure?"

"Mike told me he'd be out, that's why I'm sure."

"Oh, so you're betting on what Mike's telling you. OK, I'll trust you for the other ten and bet thirty."

"Where's your cash, Daddy?" Cookie replied defiantly.

"I got most of my cash out on bets," J.J. replied ruefully.

"Well, if you can't put cash on the table, forget it," she challenged her father, eyes blazing.

"Jesus Christ, she's just like her old man!" Cookson laughed appreciatively. "Alright young lady, I'll put twenty with your twenty and you trust me for ten and I'll trust you for ten."

"You got you a bet, Daddy."

Cookson produced twenty one thousand dollar bills and shoved them into Cookie's pocketbook. Then as an afterthought he took the bag from her and held it in his own hand.

"You don't trust me, do you, Dad?"

"I trust you now. Sucker bet."

"Well, eight thousand dollars of that cash is Mike's.

237

He gave it to me to bet that he'd be out of the army by tomorrow."

Cookson looked at his daughter thoughtfully. "Well, I'll be go to hell. If he's out tomorrow he knows something that Vogel doesn't know."

"All I know is he told me that when the game was over, when the halftime show was over, we'd all know he was out of the army."

The skybox butler arrived with the drinks and handed one to Cookie and her father. Cookson took his with a grunt and gulped at it greedily. "Maybe I got mouse-trapped," he muttered and turned his attention back to the game.

The great Houston defense held and now at seven-seven with two minutes left in the half, Brian Cotter was sparking his Oilers toward another touchdown. There was no time to try a running game now. The Dallas defenders knew every play would be a pass. And each time Brian Cotter took the ball from center and faded back to throw, he hit a receiver. They were short passes. Rifled six and seven yard aerial gains. Then the long pass floated toward the Dallas goal line and Cotter's wide end scooped it up and was tripped on the eight yard line. With fifteen seconds on the scoreboard, Cotter himself dove the ball across the goal line in a quarterback sneak.

The thunderous shouts of joy from the stands threatened to rattle the thousands of square glass window panes out of the roof of the Astrodome.

The kick was good and Houston ran off the Astro turf at the end of the half, ahead fourteen to seven.

The kickoff after the touchdown was a mere formality. There was no way the Oilers were going to let Dallas run the ball back to score. A long kick was caught behind the goal line by the Dallas kick-receiving half-back who futilely rushed the ball forward and was brought down on the eleven yard line. The half ended there.

In Big John Dykes' box Larry reached over for Tom Dunning's attaché case and hefted it for a moment. "Just getting used to the feel of it, Tom," Larry gloated.

"The game isn't over yet," Dunning replied grimly. "I'll just hold onto that case until the last play of this football game." Dunning retrieved his attaché case.

As this exchange was taking place Signals gave his men the order. Within seconds all outside communication from the Astrodome, with the exception of the television broadcast was cut off.

In the box office a frenzied Marty Stang, at last putting a call through to the State Police to find out what had happened to the Wells Fargo armored truck, suddenly found himself holding a dead phone. No signal. "Oh Jesus Christ," he muttered aloud. "This is it. I just know it."

As Billy Weaver and his father were excitedly jumping up and down and J.J. Cookson's party left their seats to relax the west gate of the Astrodome swung open. In the scoreboard control room the announcer picked up the typewritten sheet prepared for him by Signals and prepared to read it over the public address system to the spectators.

Clearly any type of military demonstration was anticlimactic after the thrilling final seconds of the first half. The elated Houston fans and shocked Dallasites were standing, stretching, and many of them heading for a refreshment area. In the skybox circle all the affluent spectators were leaving their seats to discuss the first half of the game and enter into new betting combinations around the bars that were now receiving maximum attention.

CHAPTER THIRTY-ONE

"Ladies and gentlemen," the announcer's voice filled the Astrodome, "the Houston Astrodome now presents for your halftime entertainment a demonstration by a special unit of the United States Army which is stationed and is training near our city. The Wildfire unit will now give a demonstration of their training exercises for the special mission assigned them, the crucial seek and destroy operation, an option now available to the United States in case of a special international emergency. It has been perfected by the Wildfire team you will now see perform. Wildfire is under the command of Houston's own Major Mike Snyder and is part of the Sixth Division commanded by Major General Lloyd Vogel who is here with us today."

Up in the skybox Vogel turned from the bar, leaving his bourbon and water for the length of time it took him to walk to the door and receive the accolades from those nearby. J.J. Cookson was the first to pat him on the back and shake his hand.

Cookson and Vogel, and the others who weren't otherwise engaged in making bets or drinking, looked down at the Astro turf before them. Fifty men on foot double-timed into the Astrodome through the west gate taking their positions along one of the sidelines. The action caused little excitement among the spectators. Vogel turned and went back for his drink, followed by Cookson who was saying, "Hey Lloyd, my daughter seems pretty certain that Mike Snyder really will be out of the army tomorrow. How come she's so sure?"

Vogel shrugged. "I can't understand it, J.J. There's just no way, no way at all."

"Well, you'll both see soon enough," Cookie said positively. "I don't know what it is he has in mind but he sure was positive about it. It's the first time I ever saw Mike bet his own money on anything." Vogel gave her a patronizing smile but Cookson could not hide the worried look on his face. Something, something way beyond his control was happening, he sensed.

Marty Stang was not one to give up easily. He locked and double-locked the door to the box office and then walked up a ramp to the line of telephone pay stations. When he saw disgruntled fans banging at the phone boxes he was more convinced than ever that something was terribly wrong. He bolted back down the ramp and out into the parking lot beyond the Astrodome which was filled to the limit with automobiles. His worst fears were confirmed when he saw bearing down on the box office through a lane in the parked cars the awesome tank which clanked inexorably towards the lodging place of the day's receipts.

Marty crouched behind a car as he watched the tank

head toward his preserve and stop directly in front of this office. In a state of shock he watched the cannon depressed so that it was lined up directly on the box office. Then he turned and sprinted towards the outer edge of the parking lot looking for a phone booth that had not been disabled. He now realized that some strange force had cut off communications between the Astrodome and the outside world. The first inkling of the nature of the disaster at hand permeated his mind. They were going to rip off the Astrodome! But who were they? It didn't make any difference, really. He had to get to a phone and get help, a lot of help. His state of mind was further discombobulated when he heard the chuffing sound of helicopters and looked up to see two choppers, armed helicopters with men sighting along heavy machine guns from the open doors of the machines and realized that this was no ordinary hold-up. This was some kind of full scale military operation mounted by madmen.

"Oh Jesus Christ!" was all he could keep repeating aloud as he headed for the outer reaches of the parking lot and the street beyond.

Young Billy Weaver was one of the few spectators still staring at the Astro turf and the military demonstration. Although all about him he heard disparaging remarks about the military in general and why the hell should they be subjected to some army exercise which was taking time away from the scantily clad leggy Dallas Cowgirls halftime show.

The general apathy among this typical slice of American sports fans was reflected throughout the Astrodome. Shouts of "Who needs this? Bring on the Cowgirls!" could be heard throughout the stands. And nowhere was the disinterest reflected more conspicuously than in the ring of skyboxes overlooking the Astro turf. Even General Vogel was more interested in talking to J.J. Cookson and the VIPs he was entertaining in his skybox which included the Governor of the state than he was in watching the performance being staged by his men below. It was enough for him to know that his division was being recognized and that even if it was only for five minutes the President of the United States and for that matter the rest of the influential people of America, had become aware of his division and his name.

Vogel hoped Mike Synder would make the demonstration quick. They'd been allotted five minutes. He had cautioned Mike Snyder not to go beyond the five-minute time limit, since both the Dallas Cowgirls and the Houston girls who made up the cheering section of all the nearby colleges were waiting to strut out onto the field and be seen around the United States.

Cookson, on the telephone that connected the skyboxes to each other, was calling around trying to get more bets down on Houston. At this point he was asking for no point spread, just a straight bet. "You've got to bet on your own!" he announced jubilantly to his guests. "Can I get up ten thousand among all of us here to bet with Mark Phillips' box? He's got all that good Republic Bank money from Dallas down here in Box 18."

There was considerable excitement in Cookson's box and in moments J.J. had the ten thousand pledged. He turned back to the phone, "OK Mark, you got it—ten grand from Box 10 on Houston." There was a pause, then, "No, I told you. No point spread now. You got it?"

Cookson listened, grinned broadly and turned back

to his guests. "We got 'em!" He put an arm around his daughter. "Even Sally's got her money up for this one along with all of us," he said proudly. "Another drink, darling?"

"Sure, Daddy, why not. Then I want to go out and see what Mike's doing."

"He'd better not go over that five minutes," Cookson remarked. "One thing Dallas has got, they got those Cowgirls."

Hardly noticed by most of the occupants of the Astrodome was the main force of Wildfire which had been grouped just outside the west gate as it made its way into the Astrodome. First there were a half dozen armored personnel carriers followed by jeeps with machine guns mounted on them and then the new T-75 light tank. Standing in the turret of the tank, a grim smile on his face, was Wildfires's commander, Mike Snyder. The armor proceeded through the west gate and into the main part of the stadium. Even before it reached the west goal post, at a radioed command from Mike to his squad leaders, his one hundred repellers who had already secured their ropes to beams at the top of the Astrodome grandstands and fastened their harness clips to the ropes, their rifles now assembled, pitched off the top balcony of the Astrodome and slid down their ropes into the middle of the audience. Every section of the stands was suddenly converged upon by these spidermen slithering right into the middle of the spectators, most of whom were still unaware that a military exercise was in progress, so absorbed were they in the implications of the last Houston touchdown.

The first person to become aware of what was happening was not even in the Astrodome. The producer

245

of the network sportcast was watching the monitors on his television cameras and was horrified to see camera four focused on the armored personnel carriers and the tank. "My God, they're going to rip up the Astro turf!" he shouted.

Before his eyes the tank crunched onto the edge of the green artificial grass, tearing it up.

"Camera four, get a close up of that!" the producer ordered. As the cameraman zoomed in the extent of the damage being done to the turf, the possibility that it would be destroyed beyond repair in time for the second half horrified the producer into action. "Doesn't anybody in there see what's going on?" he screamed.

In the television control room Powell Purcell was giving a wrap-up of the first half to his millions of tele-viewers around the United States. "It has been, indeed, an amazing first half," he singsonged. "And when Brian Cotter went over for the second Houston touchdown of the first half, with only a few seconds left, he accomplished something of a miracle. We never thought Brian Cotter still had that left in him. Yes, he showed up great against Denver last week. But we never would have thought that Cotter, in his late thirties, still had that much steam left in him." Purcell paused, distracted by his director. The director was furiously motioning at the field below and behind Purcell, who was staring into the camera in the control booth. Purcell turned, looked down and saw what was happening. The armored personnel carriers and the tank were crossing the end zone line and heading right down the middle of the football field. "Something strange, something very wrong is happening here, ladies and gentlemen!" Purcell's voice rose to a pitch of excitement tinged with very real fear. It was a voice Purcell's fans had never heard from him before. "Some kind of an emergency is happening, ladies and gentlemen. I don't know what it is but we'll keep you informed."

In J.J. Cookson's skybox the phone rang furiously and Cookson pulled it off its hook. "Yeah, what is it?" he shouted. He listened a moment, his face taking on a stricken look. He hung up, rushed to the door and looked out at the scene below. He saw the tank and the armored personnel carriers entering through the west gate and crossing the Astro turf.

The Governor was beside him as they stared at the shocking scene below. As one, they turned to General Vogel just behind them. Pointing at the tanks and APCs they shouted, "Wildfire was not supposed to use vehicles. They'll rip up the turf! Get them off, Lloyd." The cigar, twitching in Vogel's mouth, dropped to the cement below them.

"Oh my God!" Vogel shouted. "What are they doing? What's that son-in-law of yours up to? Good God, don't you understand? The President is watching!"

"Do something! Stop them, General. Get them out of here!" the Governor yelled.

General Vogel clamped his gold encrusted bill cap onto his head. "Where's the public address system control room?" he shouted. "I'll order them out. Just get me to a microphone."

J.J. Cookson shook his head. "Now I know what Cookie was talking about." He turned to his daughter, "Did you know what he was going to do?" he cried.

"No, Daddy, of course I didn't. I didn't know he'd gone crazy! What are we going to do?"

"We've got to stop them!" the Governor answered and dashed back into the skybox, reaching for the phone. "I'm calling out the National Guard."

He pulled the phone from the hook and dialed zero for an outside line. He listened a few moments and then in a shocked tone called out, "Dead. The phone's dead. They've cut off all outside communication. What the hell are they up to?"

And suddenly a wave of awareness and apprehension swept through the sixty-seven thousand people in the Astrodome. One by one, then hundreds by hundreds they started noticing what was going on below. This was no ordinary military exercise designed for five minutes of recruiting propaganda. They watched in awe as the cannon in the turret of the tank now directly underneath the gold posts on the goal line raised slowly toward the top of the Astrodome.

Mike Snyder raised his right arm and the cannon emitted a loud explosion. All apathy was gone now. Every eye in the Astrodome followed the trajectory of the shell as it slammed into the gondola suspended from the ceiling of the Astrodome above the middle of the field. The large gondola, which provided the illumination for the middle of the field and could also be lowered as a platform for speakers, suddenly shattered. Pieces of it fell onto the field below. Simultaneously over the public address system and in lighted letters on the scoreboard came the shattering announcement. "This is a hold up! Everybody stay calm and there will be no casualties." The authoritative voice continued, "This is no war game. This is a military combat operation."

From outside the Astrodome the spectators suddenly heard another explosion that sounded like a bomb. Women screamed and men shouted at each other.

The tank that had trained its cannon on the box office had fired. Two men jumped out of the tank, rushed to the box office, entered through the destroyed wall, and quickly scooped up the entire receipts from the rush seat spectators who had waited so long to purchase for cash a ticket to the big game.

Within a minute of the time the cannon had been fired, over two hundred thousand dollars was gathered from the money boxes and carried back to the tank and thrown into the turret. The tank continued to squat malevolently in front of the main portal of the Astrodome, its cannon now covering on the entrance.

Spectators who had reached the portal and observed the cannon pointing at them turned and ran back inside the Astrodome.

In the Houston Oilers locker room, isolated from the confusion outside, Brian Cotter was talking to the coach and trainer who were slapping him on the back, congratulating him on his brilliant first two periods of the game.

In anticipation of what he knew he would be forced to do in the second half he complained, "I did something to my arm on that quarterback sneak. They hit me hard. But it was the right play."

"It certainly was the right play," the coach replied. Then worried, he asked, "What about the arm?"

"I don't know, it feels numb," Cotter replied. The coach turned to the trainer.

"See what you can do for his arm," the coach commanded. "We're gonna need that arm at its best."

"I'll give it everything in the cabinet," the trainer promised. Cotter was already pulling his jersey off over the shoulder guards and was giving over care of his bare arm to the trainer.

In his earphone Mike Snyder heard the call from

Signals. "We've taken over the scoreboard control room and we have two men behind the board to make sure only our signals get through. The team is taking over the television control room right now. Go ahead Mike, it's all your show. You are patched into the Astrodome public address system."

Mike Snyder took the microphone from its hook on the turret and pressed the hand switch.

"This is Major Mike Snyder talking, commander of Wildfire. If everybody cooperates this exercise should be over in an hour and nobody will be hurt. But we are not going to fail. And if success means we have to shoot to kill, we shall do so."

Out in the audience the spectators listened to the words coming over the public address system. Billy Weaver looked up at his father, frightened. "What's happening, Dad? Are they going to kill us?"

Bill Weaver surveyed the scene out on the vast disintegrating Astro turf. Then he turned and saw the trooper who had just descended from somewhere above into the group surrounding them, his carbine with a thirty round banana clip cradled in his arms.

"No, Billy, they're not going to kill us. But I'm sure as hell going to be out fifty bucks." He wrote off the little additional comforts he had already mentally acquired for the coming month. He'd have to pick between *Playboy* and *Penthouse*!

The voice of the Wildfire commander reverberated through the covered stadium. "Keep calm and nobody will be hurt. We are not terrorists making political demands and holding hostages until those demands are met. We are only soldiers that America wants to forget. So we're leaving. And we felt that the good, patriotic,

250

generous people of Houston and Dallas would not want
those of us who served their country well in the recent
war in Southeast Asia to leave the country financially
embarrassed. This exercise today is a simple matter of
acquiring money. We are sure that you fine people in
the Astrodome today wish only the best for me. However, to insure that our mission proceeds smoothly and
that no outside interference is offered by either the
state or the federal government, we have taken one
precaution."

With that, a flat bed military truck drove through
the west gate and into the middle of the field parking
on the fifty yard line. Secured to the flat bed of the
truck with metal brackets was a tall cigar shaped missile with four fins at its base.

"Ladies and gentlemen, you are looking at a tactical
nuclear artillery missile," Mike announced. The yield
of this particular nuclear warhead is approximately fifteen megatons. That is, should it explode it would deliver a force equal to the explosion of fifteen thousand
tons of TNT. This would be sufficient to destroy everything within a radius of approximately a quarter of a
mile from the point of detonation. In other words,
should this device be triggered, the Astrodome, the
amusement park, the motels, and all the automobiles
around us would be destroyed." An audible groan filled
the covered stadium. Mike held up his arms.

"There is no reason for this to happen. Let us all
pray that some irresponsible political idiot far enough
away from where we are gathered to insure his own
safety does not order military or police force to be used
against us here. Needless to say, the men of Wildfire
are anxious to complete their mission and get out of
here. Certainly we do not want to destroy ourselves

and you. I have in my possession a remote detonation device which will explode this missile at the touch of a button. This remote detonator will work at a distance of six hundred miles from Houston due to the relay system we have set up. So even after we leave the Astrodome we hope that we aren't pursued."

Mike reached down and held up the black box. "Before we allowed ourselves to be apprehended we would certainly detonate the device you now see on the fifty yard line."

From up in the ring of skyboxes, the richest, most influential, and powerful citizens of Houston and Dallas watched the proceedings with awe. The most stricken group of spectators in the entire Astrodome were those in and around J.J. Cookson's skybox.

"He's a psycho, a goddamn psycho. I knew it, I always knew it," J.J. Cookson shrilled.

"Do I win my bet, Daddy?" Cookie cried hysterically. With that she gulped the rest of her bourbon.

"Shut up, Sally," Cookson snapped. He turned to the Governor. "Any suggestions?"

"Do you think that's really a tactical nuke?" the Governor asked.

"I sure as hell don't want to find out," Cookson replied. At that moment armed troopers of the Wildfire team burst onto the Astro box circle. The boxholders reacted like woodchucks at the sight of a farmer with a shotgun. They ducked into their boxes, slamming and locking the doors behind them, in many cases not even waiting for all their guests to enjoy the apparent safety of the enclosures.

From his tank command post Mike Snyder looked directly up at the Astro box circle. "All you skybox people, there's no point in trying to lock yourselves in.

You might just as well stay outside, keep your seats, and watch this historic occasion. If we have to blow the doors off of skyboxes it only increases the possibility of injury to those inside." The men and women who were futilely pounding at the doors to the skyboxes to which they had been invited ceased their efforts at these words and turned to look down at the situation unfolding below.

"Now ladies and gentlemen," Mike Snyder continued, his voice cool, almost hypnotic in its calm appraisal of the situation, "to assist in the collection process, to help you make your contribution, which must be the sum total of all money and valuables you have with you, Wildfire has enlisted the aid of the Reverend Joshua Carey, the distinguished Evangelical minister of the gospel to lead us all in prayer and hymns as the men of the Wildfire team circulate through the stands collecting your offerings. And please, so that there are no injuries or more serious casualties, do not hold out on the Wildfire collectors. Any attempt to withhold money from them will be considered a hostile act."

In the television control room Signals and two of his most technically accomplished cohorts were directing the electronic coverage of the Wildfire operation. "I hope none of you will make us resort to violence," Signals said softly to the technicians and television executives standing about nonplussed. To Powell Purcell, Signals went on. "Now Powell, just figure you're covering a big news event, OK?"

Purcell looked at the menacing gunmen who had captured the booth. He nodded agreeably. "Anything you say."

"This is the only outside communication with the

rest of the world," Signals went on. "All phone lines have been disconnected. Just keep the coverage going as you would any other halftime show."

"Any other halftime show?" Purcell repeated incredulously.

To the director Signals went on, "You can now order your remote camera crew to go directly to the presidential suite which is about to become Major Snyder's command post for the remainder of this operation. I understand that the president of Network Sports is here today. Is he one of you in this booth?"

A network executive, who had been standing in the corner trying to be inconspicious, realized he was trapped. He came forward and faced Siganls. "What do you want?" he asked.

"We'll need your cooperation totally in the next hour," Signals replied. "Will you order your producer in the network sound truck below to set up a direct television feed between here and the White House?"

"What!" the executive almost shouted.

"You heard me. I should think you could do that in about three minutes at the most. We wouldn't want some rash general in the Pentagon to force us to detonate that device."

The network man looked out over the field at the nuclear warhead and nodded understandingly. "Oh, of course not. I'll take care of it." He turned to one of the technicians. "Give me your mike so that I can talk to Dan down in the truck."

In the scoreboard control room other members of the Wildfire team had taken charge. And suddenly echoing throughout the huge enclosed stadium the strains of the great Astrodome organ resounded. On the field a station wagon drove out onto the Astro turf and parked beside the tactical nuclear warhead. From the station wagon stepped the Reverend Joshua Carey. He walked around to the rear of the station wagon and ascended a small aluminum ladder which had been fastened to the rail on the roof of the vehicle.

Reaching the roof he accepted the microphone handed to him by another member of the team. The Reverend Carey began his evangelical exhortation.

"Ladies and gentlemen, brothers and sisters, if you are one with the Lord have no fear. For it is God's work that you see going on about you now. The experience you are sharing is that of the Lord working in mysterious ways, his wonders to perform. Yes, that's right. These men of Wildfire and their leader, Major Snyder, were motivated by the Lord to carry out His work today and in the years to come. This great nation of ours plagued by the bedevilled leaders who could not see the big world picture, who could not recognize Satan's threat to destroy our globe, these leaders who have no perception that the United States has indeed become Sodom and Gommorrah, these leaders of the United States who punish the men that fought for their country overseas, in Asia, for ten years, these leaders who have constantly demonstrated their contempt for such men as these of Wildfire who risked their lives many times and saw their friends killed, these men who are ignored and penalized by an unappreciative society today. The Rev. Joshua Carey paused, then, "It is their mission to make known to all of the world, not just the United States, that we must understand right from wrong. That we must understand that the godless Communist enemy is the devil's right hand. Yet those Americans who continue to fight this disciple of the devil are themselves the victims of persecution. Now, as they move among you, see them as they are, the personification of God's soldiers neglected by those for whom they fought.

"God asks for peace, not violence. Therefore do not challenge these men, and thus God, causing violence to happen. Do not challenge God's word, and remember it is far more blessed to give than it is to receive."

The Reverend Carey was well known to most of the patrons of the Astrodome. Therefore it was understandable that Cash and Carry's sentiment was greeted with a certain amount of skepticism. However, the awesome sight of the Bible-quoting, gospel-shouting evangelist standing in the very shadow of the nuclear warhead could not but exert compelling impact on the crowd in the Astrodome. The Reverend Carey turned slightly, looking at the tactical nuke taller than he was and felt all eyes in the Astrodome following his.

"Let us all pray that this dire device, the personification of the power God has put in the hands of man for self-destruction, let us pray that we never live to see it detonated. And while we pray, let us give, not merely generously but totally, everything we have, to further the work of the Lord being carried out here today and in the future."

Now the Reverend Carey turned from the nuclear warhead to the scoreboard above the west gate. "As you see in lights the figure fifteen million dollars represents the sum we will collect today to insure that these men of the Wildfire team are enabled to carry out their work. And that work is to fight the godless Communist oppressors all over the world from a new base of operations they are establishing. So I tell you, give everything that you have. If you brought money to this place for the purpose of betting it is no sacrifice for you to donate it to a higher purpose. It will go to further the Lord's will and not into the sinful practice of wagering money on sporting events. Now at the bottom of the scoreboard you see the figure two hundred and fifty thousand dollars. That represents what has been collected so far.

"Every few minutes the figure on the scoreboard will change and indicate how the Lord's collection is going. When you see that we have raised the figure of fifteen million dollars these soldiers of justice will leave the Astrodome and start on their crusade against godlessness and Communism. Do not allow time to run out. The crusade starts here. If it finishes here then that dreadful device of destruction will send us all prematurely to face God's judgment."

The Reverend Carey raised both arms. "Now as we give let us sing on this day of Thanksgiving, on this day that symbolizes the fall harvest, the harvest now being brought in as we stand here. 'Bringing in the Sheaves.' "

The great organ of the Astrodome, played by one of the Reverend Carey's trusted evangelists reverberated through the Astrodome as the spectators began to follow the words the Reverend Carey sang out through his microphone. "Bringing in the sheaves, Bringing in the sheaves, Bringing in the sheaves as the work of God we do."

CHAPTER THIRTY-TWO

In Big John Dykes' box located in the second most expensive section of the Astrodome, Tom Dunning surveyed the appalling situation around him. "How do we get out of this, John?" he asked plaintively. "We aren't giving them any of our cash." He turned to Larry. "You're so adept at threatening violence, let's see you do something."

"There must be at least two thousand people here today carrying handguns," Larry mused. "Maybe if there was some way we could get together we could take them."

"I don't have my piece on me," John Dykes replied. "But if I did I would know enough not to get into a fire fight with these machine-gun-carrying professionals. God help the first stupid son-of-a-bitch that pulls a hand gun on these guys."

"I can't let them take my money," Dunning's voice

was near to hysteria. "I'm getting out of here with my cash." He turned to Larry. "If you're afraid to use your gun, give it to me. I'm not going to let them take me. I'll be ruined forever. I've got to get a hundred and fifty thousand dollars into the bank first thing in the morning or I'm ruined. What am I going to tell them at home office if I'm caught embezzling all that money?"

"I don't know, Tom. What *are* you going to tell them?" John asked.

"I'm not going to tell them anything. I'm getting out of here with my money. All bets are off anyway, aren't they, John?"

John Dykes nodded. "I guess so. Judging by the condition of the Astro turf there's no way there's going to be a second half of this game played today."

"Do me a favor. Give me the other fifty grand so I can put it all back in the bank. Then I'll pay you next week everything I owe you. The whole fifty. But let me take it with me now. It will only be stolen from you by these hoods anyway."

John Dykes looked at Dunning thoughtfully a moment. "OK. I'll give you the other fifty now. But tell me something, Tom. What would you have done had you lost?"

"There was no way I was going to lose. You know that, John. For chrissake I talked to Brian Cotter just like Larry here told me. Matter of fact I was surprised you took that hundred thousand dollars of my action. You knew I got to Cotter."

"There's no such thing as a sure thing," John intoned. "That's the biggest sucker bet of them all. Maybe Cotter wouldn't have thrown it away."

"Look, John. He would have done it. Give me the

fifty grand and let me get out of here. I'll make him do it next week and you can clean up. He owes me a big one."

John Dykes reached into his inside pocket and pulled out a thick sheaf of thousand dollar bills. He counted fifty thousand dollars and handed it to the shaken and trembling insurance executive. Dunning took the money from John, snapped open his briefcase, put it in with the other hundred thousand, closed it up and then turned to Larry. "Give me your gun. I'll get out of here if I have to shoot my way out." Larry gave John Dykes a questioning look. Dykes nodded and Larry obligingly pulled a 38 magnum revolver from the shoulder holster under his left arm and handed it butt first to Dunning.

"Thanks, Larry," Dunning rasped. I appreciate this. And I'll give you the dope on the next game Cotter plays in."

As Tom Dunning started to leave the box he noticed the two Wildfire troopers in the box two down from them. They were not merely accepting the money and putting it into the huge knapsacks on their backs. They were at times brutally searching those they suspected of having concealed money from them. As he watched one man flatly refused to hand over his neat leather pouch which he carried with his left hand through the thong loop. They couldn't hear the words but the collector suddenly jammed the butt of his rifle into the stomach of the recalcitrant and gave him a knee to the chin as he collapsed forward and then took the leather pouch from the limp hand. Opening it the collector empted all the cash into his sack and threw the empty case down on the seat. Methodically, box by box, the Wildfire team was collecting every dollar in this undoubtedly the richest mother lode in the Astrodome aside from the skyboxes.

Major General Lloyd Vogel strode purposefully toward the scoreboard control room on the second level. Although he passed a number of the troops from Major Snyder's unit, none of them stopped him or questioned his progress. A sergeant, perhaps out of sheer years of reflex action actually saluted the general. Vogel started to return the salute and then cursed, "I'll see you in Leavenworth for life, if not in front of a firing squad, soldier," he shouted and kept going.

Arriving at the door to the control room he pulled it open, walked in and was shocked at the scene that greeted him. Three of Synder's men carrying automatic rifles stood inside the box and to Vogel's amazement he saw the man he'd known as Major Sorell in Vietnam. Sorell had been the chief signal corps officer in the division and had arranged all the clandestine communications between the search and destroy missions and Vogel's headquarters. After the Vietnam War Vogel was vaguely aware that Sorell had been RIF'd but thought very little about it.

"Sorell, what the hell are you doing here? Are you part of this treasonous operation?"

"Call it what you want, Vogel. Yes, I'm doing my old job. Commo. What brings you into the scorebox control room?"

"Give me that microphone. I'm stopping this thing right now."

"As soon as the Reverend Carey has finished his hymn I'll put you onto the public address system and you can talk directly to Snyder. But remember he can talk back to you also over the public address system.

262

Don't say anything you don't want answered," Signals cautioned.

"I don't know what the hell you're talking about, Sorell. Give me that mike."

As the Reverend Carey concluded the hymn Sorell handed the mike to Vogel who grabbed it from him and shouted into it. "Major Snyder, this is General Vogel. I'm issuing you a direct order. Stop this operation instantly and leave the Astrodome. You and all your men will consider yourself under arrest. I'm bringing in a full division to take you and all of your people to the stockade."

"The voice you just heard was that of Major General Lloyd Vogel," Mike Snyder announced. "If he should be stupid enough to try to bring in a division, which he can't do since there's no communications out of here except television, I would have to activate this." He raised the black instrument above his head.

"I don't think any of us, even General Vogel, wants to see it used. And as a matter of fact, General Vogel himself can take some of the responsibility for this action of ours today."

Vogel shouted imprecations into the microphone but they were not broadcast over the public address system. He looked balefully at Sorell. "Why aren't my orders going out?" he shouted.

"We can't dirty up the air, Vogel," Sorell replied. Impotently Vogel listened as Snyder was saying, "Remember the search and destroy missions you ordered in Vietnam, General? Remember Phui Ba or Tin Long to name a couple of operations for which you were decorated and nobody but Wildfire knew what happened. Either one of them would have made the My Lai massacre look like an accident at a church supper. We created an accurate body count of twenty thousand for you during the time you were commanding the division in Vietnam. You got your second star on the basis of that body count, didn't you? Anybody's body as long as it was Vietnamese, correct, General? Now let's get on with this operation so that we can all get out of here without my having to press the button on this little black box I'm holding."

The television control room was operating under the direction of two of Sorell's most accomplished communications experts. The director was calling to his cameramen to cover everything. One camera panned the audience, another played on Major Snyder in the turret of his tank, another swung around the field.

"Are you getting it all on video tape?" Sorell's deputy signal officer asked the director.

"Right." The director was absorbed in watching the five monitor screens in front of him. "By the way, they're going to wonder what's happening back at network. If you don't let us get through pretty soon they'll have a posse down here. You can bet on it."

"You'll be broadcasting to the whole United States pretty damn quick. Just take it easy until we're ready. Meantime look at what an exclusive you're getting."

"You got a point there," Powell Purcell agreed. "This is a big news story. And we got it exclusive. Maybe they'll shift me from sports to anchor man on network news after they hear me report this event," Purcell said to no one in particular.

"We're with you, Powell," one of the Wildfire guards said. "If you were giving the news I'd look at it. That dame you've got drives me bughouse."

"You're not the only one, trooper," Purcell agreed.

"OK, my creepy peepy remote man is ready in the presidential suite," the director announced.

"Mike, the new command post is set up. I'll meet you in the presidential suite," Signals called out over the Wildfire channel. Then turning to the director, "Just keep video taping it all. When the other networks put this on the news tonight they'll all be saying courtesy of ABC Sports."

"Yes, the voice of Powell Purcell will be heard on all three networks tonight delivering the Thanksgiving story of the century," the famous sports announcer chortled.

"Speaking of giving, how are we doing?" Signals asked.

A technician at the front of the booth looked out at the scoreboard. "You're up to half a million dollars," he reported.

"That gives us a long way to go," Signals replied grimly. "Of course we haven't hit the skyboxes yet."

Despite the threats, police and regular guards in the Astrodome tried to use their own radio channel to set up a rendezvous on the third level. Signals had intercepted their radio calls and directed a special squad to contain them there. It was just what Snyder hoped would happen. Get all the guards together in one place and neutralize them.

The Wildfire squad waited until the police had occupied the bar and then, machine guns at the ready, they sealed off both entrances. The police had taken their positions behind the bar and opened fire on the Wildfire. Immediately the special unit chopped away with their automatic rifles and machine guns.

It was like a scene from an Old West movie as the liquor bottles splintered and disgorged their contents on the police ducking behind the bar below the glass shelves of whiskey, gin, rum, brandy, and liqueurs. In moments the hundred foot mirror was shattered with bullet holes scattering shards onto the police and guards. One of the police officers shouted, "Cut it out. He's all yours. No more shooting!"

"The leader of the special guard squad yelled, "OK, cease fire. Hands up above the bar and come on around in front. We'll all just sit this out right here." Slowly the police complied. Several dozen pairs of hands appeared above the bar as the guards and police inched their way into full view of the Wildfire force. Reluctantly they emerged from behind the bar and lined up in front of it. The leader of the special unit assigned two men with automatic rifles to keep the police and guards neutralized and then the others went out to help in the collection.

Marty Stang had the right idea in getting away from the Astrodome just before it was captured. He dashed through the parking lot and ran along the highway trying to stop a car. The traffic whizzed by him, drivers looking at him as though he were a madman. When he finally came to a phone booth he found to his shock that he had neither a dime nor a quarter. Pulling a dollar bill out of his pocket he began waving at the sparse traffic on this holiday afternoon, trying to get someone to stop and give him a dime. For five minutes he waved his dollar bill desperately and finally managed to flag down a driver who had nothing better to do than see what this crazy man beside the road wanted.

"Trade you a dollar for a dime," Marty cried breathlessly. "I got to make a phone call."

"What happened?" the older man, bald, looked through gleaming steel spectacles at the crazed Marty.

"You wouldn't believe it. Just give me a dime please. Here's my dollar."

"Hell, friend, I'll give you a dime. But you don't have to give me no dollar." He fished in his pocket and came out with a dime and a nickel. "Here, take this."

Marty Stang thanked his benefactor, took the fifteen cents, ducked into the phone booth and immediately dialed the state police. The driver of the car, having already stopped, decided to stay on and see what happened. Curiously he observed Marty as he made his frantic phone call.

At the neat little frame house in Bellaire section of Houston, Mary Weaver had been watching the last moments of the first half. What an exciting game her boys were seeing, she thought. Despite her mother and father's complaints, it was worth holding Thanksgiving dinner so Bill and Billy could have this experience. She watched unemotionally as Cotter executed his quarterback sneak scoring for Houston and putting them ahead by one touchdown. She watched the kickoff and then the half ended.

An announcer began to wrap up the first half action when suddenly to her surprise and annoyance—she had been hoping that the television cameras would focus on the section where Bill and Billy were sitting—the screen went dead. For several moments she stared at the flickering pictureless screen and then came the words: STANDBY. NETWORK DIFFICULTY.

Mary Weaver dutifully stood by hoping soon to see the stands of the Astrodome. However it was almost a full minute before an announcer came on and reported that somehow they had lost contact with the Houston Astrodome but soon would restore communications. In the meantime the network was offering a sports round-up of all the other Thanksgiving Day games until the halftime at the Astrodome could be picked up.

In Washington, D.C. the President of the United States, also watching the game, was similarly frustrated when the screen went blank. He looked over at his national security advisor and asked what was wrong. The security advisor picked up his phone, made a direct call to the network in New York and learned that contact had been lost between the network feed and the Houston Astrodome.

"Has this ever happened before?" the security advisor asked.

"Not that I can remember," the executive on the other end admitted. "Certainly not from the Astrodome where we have the finest permanent set-up in the country."

The security advisor nodded, hung up, turned to the President and a group of his aides. "Like it said on the screen, network difficulty."

"Ah," the President's political advisor moaned, "I wanted to see all those Cowgirls."

"Well, you would have had to see some kind of an army demonstration first anyway," the security advisor said. "The way this volunteer army we've got is going, the recruiters need all the help they can get. We'll probably see most of the demonstration when they get the feed worked out. Some sort of a latter-day Green Beret unit doing its stuff."

The press secretary entered. With him was the President's new image advisor. "The TV crew is already for you to give your Thanksgiving Day message to the people, Mr. President. You'll go on right after the Dallas-Houston football game. We expect to have the biggest audience standing by in their homes to see you that we've yet reached."

Six minutes into the halftime, at which point the Dallas Cowgirls had prudently come to the conclusion that their antics would not be included in the proceedings Mike Snyder was seated in the presidential suite which had the most sweeping view of the Astrodome of any of the VIP areas. Signals had joined him, setting up his radio communications with the rest of the Wildfire team. Lieutenant Hackett reported he was standing just inside the entrance to the Astro box ring preparing to pluck the richest plum in the entire Astrodome.

At the two side lines of the football field two parachute canopies were open and stretched out. Into these two canopies the collectors periodically dumped their collected cash and then went back into the audience for more. Sporadic gunfire indicated the foolhardiness of some of the macho gun-toting Texans who felt it incumbent upon themselves to at least attempt to shoot it out with the Wildfire invaders.

So far the casualties had been light, Mike Synder was informed by his men. One policeman had been killed, a state trooper wounded in the shoot-out in the longest bar in the world. So far two Wildfire troopers had been wounded, one seriously, but both were under care of the Wildfire medic team.

Tom Dunning clutched his cash-filled attaché case watching the Wildfire collectors come closer to John's box.

"I wouldn't do anything foolish if I were you, Tom," John advised. "These people are not playing games, you know. They're desperate. For them it's life or death. And even after they get out of here they're going to have a difficult time getting out of the United States and to safety."

"They've got no more to lose than I do," Dunning replied grimly. "If I let them take this money I'm through at Mid-Texas. Not only that, they've got an open and shut case of embezzlement against me."

Dunning gave John Dykes a long searching look. "Did it ever occur to you how much damage gambling does to family life in America?"

John reflected on this homily a moment. "That's why I don't have a family life in the first place."

"Well, I'm getting out of here right now," Dunning declared.

"Good luck, Tom!" John Dykes watched Dunning leave the box and edge his way upward through the football fans actually climbing over the seats keeping his head down rather than walking up the aisles where he could easily be seen by the collectors. Some of the people in his path were helpful and made way for him. Others, resenting the fact that they had already given all their cash to a Wildfire collector were not prepared to see someone else getting away without paying up.

When Dunning had almost reached the top of the sixth level stands an irate Houston rooter who had just forked over almost a thousand dollars was obviously of the opinion that if he had been taken everybody else was going to be taken too.

"Where you going to, Mister?" the spectator shouted as Dunning stepped over the seat and pushed his way upwards through the crowd.

"What's the matter, don't you want to contribute to the good Lord's works?" another fleeced fan howled derisively. "All of us here shelled out. We put up our money to fight the godless Communists. What's wrong with you? You heard what the Reverend said. It's only money you were going to spend gambling."

"Yeah, why not let the good Lord win one?" another spectator shouted, letting out a long bitter laugh.

Dunning paid no attention to the cries, which were now taken up by all the stung spectators who didn't like the idea of anyone getting away with what they couldn't.

A Houston rooter who had selflessly, albeit under the barrel of a gun, given his all to the crusade shouted at one of the collectors and pointed to Dunning.

Alerted, the two Wildfire troopers, their automatic rifles in hand, gratefully thanked the spectators who had called their attention to this potential donor so reluctant to make his Thanksgiving contribution to the cause.

They watched Dunning move toward the last row of seats. As he emerged only a few yards from the portal into the outside edge of the Astrodome, they shouted at him to halt.

One shot was fired, missing him. The spectators screamed and ducked as low as they could in their seats.

Dunning made it to the outside gallery and ran towards the exit sign. Just as he threw the door to the stairwell open another shot rang out, chipping concrete away from the wall a few inches from his head. Whirling, Dunning drew the .38 magnum and started squeezing off shots as he backed into the stairwell. It was with some satisfaction that he saw one of the collectors go down, dropping his weapon and clutching his chest where the heavy, hollow-point bullet had caught him.

Dunning almost made it. Flipping his rifle to full automatic, the other Wildfire trooper, seeing his comrade was mortally wounded, pressed the trigger and a hail of bullets accompanied Tom Dunning into the stairwell which he had thought might lead him to safety. Or at least, he hoped, a place where he could hide until the raiders went away. But it was not to be. Slugs tore at him, whirling him around and ripping through his body. His last thought as he died was, if they got the money I'd be dead anyway.

CHAPTER THIRTY-THREE

Lieutenant Hackett and his handpicked group of men in Wildfire entered the Caribbean Room which was reserved for Dallas Cowboys' guests. Hack made his polite little speech.

"We'll take as little of your time as possible," he began. "I'm sure everybody here is aware of what's happening in the Astrodome at this moment. You can look down over the stadium and see how our Thanksgiving donations are coming in. We are now offering you the opportunity of making your Thanksgiving donation to our work."

"And what if we decide not to take advantage of this opportunity you so magnaminously extend us?" a suave white-haired ruddy-faced Texan asked.

"We feel sure you will give generously. In fact," Hack went on, "you, sir, will be the first. May I examine your wallet, please?"

"I suppose there's not much choice," the elderly man replied reaching into his inside jacket pocket pulling out a large wallet and handing it to Hack. He looked around the Caribbean Room at the armed members of the Wildfire team. Hack took the proffered wallet and extracted four one hundred dollar bills. Hack nodded to one of the two men he had brought into the Caribbean Room for this purpose. The collector walked over to the distinguished old gentleman. "Would you mind reaching in here and showing me what you have?" the Wildfire man requested politely patting the left pocket. The old gentleman reached into his kick and pulled out a thick roll of hundred dollar bills.

"That's more like it," Hack said, pleased. Next he turned to a lady. "Those are sure beautiful diamond clips you're wearing, Ma'am. They match your earrings perfectly."

"Oh no!" the lady cried, stricken. "These have been in my family forever," she protested.

The lady, realizing she had no choice took the diamonds from her ears and from her dress and handed them over. Then, briskly, she opened her pocketbook and took a card from it. "I would appreciate it if you would contact me here. I'll report this theft to my insurance company tomorrow."

Hack and his men collected over three hundred thousand dollars in jewelry and cash in the next ten minutes. Then, their loot in a canvas ruck-sack, they left. Hack bowed slightly and said, "At least you won't have to watch Dallas lose this game. I'm sure it will be postponed."

Hack glanced at his watch. It was now seven minutes and forty-five seconds after the first half ended. They were right on time for their entrance to the skybox semi-circle.

Two teams had been trained to divest the skybox patrons of their money and valuables. The other skybox team would start at exactly eight minutes into the halftime from the entrance opposite the one Hack walked through with his men. He was completely familiar with the skybox set-up having been to several football games in preparation for this moment.

As Hack entered the ring, the skyboxes to his left and the seats to his right, it was evident that these tough Houstonians were not easily going to give up all the cash they brought with them for the purpose of betting on the game. The first box was closed and there were no spectators in the seats directly below.

So, Hack surmised, everybody had crammed themselves inside the skybox and locked it after them.

Hack knocked on the door. He knew his voice could be heard inside. "It would be best if you would open the door. If you don't I have a detonating cap which I can tape against the lock and blow it off. It's up to you how we join up. Open the door!" After a few seconds he said, "All right. We'll just blow it open."

Almost instantly the door opened and the owner of the box confronted him. He stared at Hack a few moments, a puzzled frown on his face. "I know you. You've been up here before. I met you in J.J.'s box. What in the hell are you doing?"

"We are ripping off the Astrodome. What else can I tell you?" Hack's eyes narrowed. "We'll start with you, sir. May I have your wallet?"

The skybox owner obligingly pulled a wallet from his hip pocket and handed it to Hack. He took what money was in the wallet and handed it back to the owner. "Credit cards are no good to me. But neither does this rather paltry few hundred dollars add up the way it should." He nodded to his collector who stepped forward and frisked the owner. "Nothing more on him," the collector reported.

"We're not playing games here," Hack's voice cut through the general din that permeated the Astrodome. "You can make it easy or hard on yourself." He turned to his team. "OK, you know what to do." While one of the Wildfire troopers covered the dozen people cowering in the skybox, two others methodically searched the luxurious lounge. One collector pulled at the bathroom door only to hear a shrieking female protest. "The door comes off, Ma'am, right now. Either you open it or I'll pull it open."

"Now just a minute, my wife is in there," a man protested, hurrying up to the bathroom door.

"Well, you'd better get her out, sir. Because if you don't I will." The skybox guest looked at the Wildfire trooper, saw that he meant business and called through the bathroom door. "OK Emma, you'd better come out."

The door opened and a middle-aged woman looked around apprehensively as she sidled out of the toilet. The collector strode into the tiny comfort station and pulled the top off the water tank behind the toilet seat. Diamonds glittered under the water and around the flushing mechanism. He reached in, scooped up the jewelry and dropped it in one of the large patch pockets on his fatigues. The small medicine cabinet produced a diamond ring inside of a plastic bottle of pills. Moments later he emerged from the bathroom with at least twenty carats of diamonds. Meantime the other collector had searched the bar and other likely hiding places Hack had carefully catalogued during his previous inspections of the skyboxes.

"I wondered why you ladies seemed so bereft of fine jewelry," he remarked sardonically. The collectors were now frisking each man individually after examining their curiously thin wallets. All of them had tried to conceal their cash either hiding it where they could in the skybox or on their persons. It took one minute and forty-five seconds to remove twenty-five thousand dollars in cash plus far more than that in fine jewelry from the first box.

"We're right on schedule, men," Hack said in satisfaction as they knocked on the next door. "The plan is two minutes a box," Hack reminded his team.

Hack knocked again on the door of skybox two. "You can let us in or we'll blow the door open. Take your choice," he announced curtly.

He was beginning to feel anxiety at all possibilities that could occur to doom them and their project. The audacity of the outrageous bluff they were perpetrating with the tactical nuclear device down on the fifty yard line played on Hack's nerves. He knew he would be a little less polite with each succeeding box. Their chances of getting away with this were diminishing as time went on. So many things could happen. He was on the verge of actually blowing the door open with the detonating cap when somebody pulled it open and let Hack and his Wildfire team in.

"Well, I'll be go to hell. Son-of-a-bitch!" The President of the United States had never before been heard by his staff to utter profanity. "I don't believe it. This sort of thing happens in Latin America but it can't happen here!" The network feed had been recov-

ered from the Astrodome and the precision robbery
was now being broadcast throughout the United States.
"They can't get away with this! Goddamn it, I won't
allow it! This just can't happen in the United States."

Appalled, he continued to watch as the cameras
zoomed in on the Wildfire collectors throughout the
Astrodome. One camera was focused on the seventh
level skyboxes and the turmoil in the ring outside the
boxes as the wealthy citizens of Dallas and Houston
were either being ripped off, or were waiting to make
their forced contribution to Wildfire.

"*In flagrante delicto*," muttered the attorney general
who was watching the game with the President. "The
only other thing I've ever seen like this was the shooting of Oswald on television," he went on.

"Mr. President, they're ready in the television studio.
I think you should talk to this madman who's directing
the operation," the press secretary said.

"Don't call that a military operation," the President
growled. "It's an out-and-out terror act. And they try
to bluff us saying they've got a tactical nuclear weapon.
I'd know it if we were missing one, wouldn't I?" he
stared at his security advisor.

The security advisor twisted in his seat. "We didn't
mention it to you, sir, but a 15 metagon tactical nuclear device was stolen in Texas down along the Mexican border. It seemed like nothing more than a local
problem so we didn't bother you with it."

"You didn't bother me! A nuclear device is stolen
and you didn't bother me?"

"Well, basically it was an artillery piece and the Defense Department felt they could handle it without taking it up to your level."

The President hunched forward in his seat and

278

stared at the television set. Extracting every aspect of drama from the situation possible, one camera was now permanently fixed on the tactical nuclear weapon on the fifty yard line which was displayed in the upper left hand corner of the television picture.

"Goddamn it!" the President fumed. "The network's making a circus out of this."

"In all fairness, sir, I wouldn't say so," the press secretary offered hesitantly. "But they're certainly making the viewers aware of what a potentially explosive situation we're facing here."

"Tell me more about this nuke that was stolen!" the President commanded.

"It happened a little over two weeks ago," the security advisor reluctantly began. "A group of blacks took it. They were speaking some foreign language and the eyewitnesses felt that it was some African country, someplace like Uganda, that was taking it to use on hostile neighbors."

"The two security officers who were with the nuke when it was taken still haven't turned up," said the Chief of Staff who had just arrived. "We figured since it took both of them to set up and arm the weapon they were being detained for just that purpose."

"We have to assume that they've got the real thing out there then," the President replied. "Get me all the records on this Major Snyder. Let's try to see what kind of a madman we're dealing with."

The President glanced back at the screen. "So there they are in the Houston Astrodome, sixty-seven thousand people inside, God knows how many more within the lethal range of that weapon and a bunch of hoods are ripping the place off. What do we do?"

279

"Well, sir, I think you should negotiate with the man. The situation is that serious."

"Negotiate with a terrorist?"

"They don't consider themselves terrorists," the Security Advisor warned. "I think we should stay away from that word should you decide to go in to the television studio and confront them."

The President sighed deeply. "All right I'll go." He followed his press secretary out of the family quarters upstairs where they had been watching the broadcast and went down to the television room which had been set up next to the Oval Office.

In J.J. Cookson's box which he had not even bothered to close at this point, realizing the futility of attempting to keep the Wildfire team out, he and his frantic guests watched the television screen intently.

"The President is going to talk to him," Cookson exclaimed. He flashed another severe look at his daughter. "Are you sure you didn't know anything at all about this, Sally?"

"I swear, Dad, of course I knew nothing about it. You don't think I'd let him do something this insane if I knew in advance what he was thinking of, do you?"

"I hope not." Cookson turned from his daughter to the set. "How the hell does Mike think he's going to get away with this? He's a dead man. They'll shoot him down wherever he goes."

"So I win my bet, don't I!" Cookie exclaimed. "He'll be out of the army by tomorrow. Even if he's not shot. Don't you think?"

"Aw, shut up! The bets off anyway. This is no normal situation."

"You don't win bets on normal situations," Cookie argued.

Cookson turned on his daughter. "Jesus Christ Almighty. My own daughter! And, at a time like this, with an atom bomb out there that could blow us all up and probably will, she's thinking about collecting on a bet."

"Like father like son, or daughter in this case," some wag pronounced trying to bring a note of levity into the tense group. Cookson ignored the remark. And at that moment Hackett and his now experienced skybox heisters made their entrance. A number of prominent Houstonians had decided to take refuge in Cookson's box including the Governor. They reasoned that since the leader of this maverick military group was Cookson's son-in-law Mike would have decreed special attention, perhaps even immunity from theft for his father-in-laws' friends."

"Hack Hackett! What do you think you're doing?" Cookie shrieked. "You and Mike and the rest of you have gone mad. Crazy. Now I want you to stop this nonsense right away while there's still time. Daddy can get you all out of trouble. And the Governor here. But not unless you stop this right now."

"I can't make any guarantees, Miss Cookson," the Governor said sternly.

"Makes no difference either way, sir," Hackett replied.

One of the collectors pulled open the door of the toilet and began a minute search. The other collector inspected the usual possible hiding places and Hack addressed Cookson. "We might as well start with you, sir. Hand it all over."

"I'll do no such thing." He turned to the Governor. "He'll have to kill me before I allow myself to be made party to this terrorism."

"It's not terrorism. It's just collecting long overdue social welfare benefits," Hack shot back. "I'm sorry you're going to make it hard on us and yourself." He nodded to the specialist who had scooped a handful of jewelry out of the water tank.

"Everybody has the same idea," he remarked cheerfully. "Makes it easier than taking it off them." He dropped the results of his search into a pocket bulging with diamonds, then approached Cookson. "Sorry you make it necessary for me to use force, sir."

Cookson looked into the gleaming, fanatical eyes. He quickly changed his mind. Solemnly he reached into his inside pocket and pulled out the wallet. "Here. Just give me back my credit cards. Where you're going you won't need them."

"That's right sir." The collector opened the wallet and extracted a heavy sheaf of bills. He looked at them briefly. "Well, for the first time it looks as though someone's given me their whole bankroll." He shoved the money in his ruck-sack and handed the wallet back to Cookson. Then he took another step towards the irate oil man and began to frisk him. "Well, well, what d'ya know. He's got more." The collector started pulling folded wads of hundred and thousand dollar bills from Cookson's pockets.

"This must be the big winner today."

"Look in her pocketbook," Hack said pointing at Cookie.

"No, you don't get into my wallet," she cried. "Your boss is my husband."

"That's right, Cookie," Hack replied. "He's the one

who said to be sure to check out your pocketbook. He says there's six or seven thousand dollars of his money in there along with yours."

Before Cookie could reply the pocketbook was roughly snatched from her by the collector who opened it. He let out a shrill whistle. "For one young gal like this she sure carries a lot of the green." He stuffed Cookie's cash into his sack and turning the pocketbook upside down, spilling cosmetics and jewelry onto the floor. He knelt and picked up a diamond necklace, a diamond ring, and other valuables. Then he turned to the next occupant of the box, and held out his hand.

"Go ahead, Mr. Hodge," Hack said. "Give it to him. He'll only take it if you don't."

Henry Hodge laughed uproariously. "The only thing I've got is a checkbook. Old J.J. got all my cash when Brian Cotter scored that touchdown. Matter of fact he was just getting ready to start accepting checks from all of us who forked over our green."

Suddenly from the television screen an electrifying voice shot forth. "This is the President speaking. I am personally taking over negotiations with the—" obviously he started to use the word terrorists. But quickly he thought better of it.

The President paused, then went on. "I address myself to the paramilitary unit which is occupying the Houston Astrodome at this moment. The United States will not be coerced into condoning or in any way giving in to the sort of—" Again he all but used the word terrorist before sputtering out, "—the demands of those who would so flagrantly violate all laws, legal and moral, by which Americans live. But we do have a duty to those in the Astrodome, sixty-six thousand people I'm told, and their families. Therefore a resolution to this situation must be achieved right now. It is impossible for me to understand how you members of the United States Army unit occupying the Astrodome can rationalize what you're doing. Reading over the record of your leader, Major Mike Snyder, I find a military record impeccable in every respect. Yet it is this officer who has led this lawless attack on sixty-six thousand innocent people watching a Thanksgiving Day football game. Now, with no more comment I address myself to Major Snyder who is in the Astrodome at this moment directing his mission of plunder. What is it you want, Major Snyder?"

Hack nudged the collector whose attention had been diverted to the television set. "Get on with it. We haven't any time to waste. Snyder will do his job, we do ours. Forget the television."

The collectors went back to work trying to concentrate on finding every last hundred dollar bill in the box despite the distracting voice of their leader coming across from the television set.

"What we want, first and foremost, is to make America understand why we're doing what we're doing," Mike Snyder said in a clear, unwavering voice. "Sure, we want ten million dollars or whatever amount of money we can collect out of this operation. At the moment we have about two hundred men in the Astrodome and another fifty or so outside in tanks and armored personnel carriers sealing off the Astrodome from the outside until this mission has been completed and we get out of here. You ask us why? I'll tell you."

Mike looked down at the card in front of him on which he had scribbled a set of notes. Then he looked directly into the television camera.

CHAPTER THIRTY-FOUR

"Mr. President, think of this as a strike," Mike began. "A new kind of strike. We represent the forgotten and reviled soldiers who responded, whether or not we liked it, to our country's call. And now America doesn't give a damn about us. Those of us who went into universities after the war for higher education had to do so on our own. The GI Bill of Rights for the veterans of the Korean War and of course World War II do not apply to us. Those of us who need psychiatric care are denied it unless we are able to pay for it ourselves. And what makes things worse for us, Mr. President, is that the deserters and draft dodgers, those who refused to fight for their country are the heroes now while we hardly dare admit that we fought in America's most unpopular war if we want good jobs or a college education. And most of us who elected to stay in the military have been reduced in grade or rank. We are, even though still loyal American soldiers, looked upon with mistrust because of the fact that we fought the war America should not have started. But America did start it, Mr. President. And we did our duty.

"But it's more than the fact that today, the country we fought for repudiates us who fought and died in Vietnam. We have seen what happened to freedom in the Southeast Asian countries we fought to protect. But that's not why we are taking these drastic steps today. The country of which you are President, sir, seems to us to be doing everything in its power at your level to betray the values of those who fought and gave their lives beginning in 1775 so that there would be a United States of America.

"What we ask you, Mr. President, is, when will this country, and your administration in particular, stop treating what friends we still have in this world as enemies and giving our country away to the real enemies of America? America is destroying itself from within. Everywhere, we back down. In Africa we hand over strategic countries like Rhodesia who want to be our friends to local Communist dictators who revile us in the United Nations each time America is defeated in a vote. You, Mr. President, are leading us to another no-win war which will have to be fought someday because of the American giveaway that you are presiding over. Every man in the Houston Astrodome today collecting what we consider to be our rightful financial benefits so that we can go to another country—one you would give away to the Marxists—and fight the creeping anti-individual initiative of the Communists whose ultimate target is America. We are loyal Americans driven to extreme measures. We are convinced that we can help block the outside forces American policy is encouraging to undermine this nation. We hope that Americans who feel the way we do will want to join us. We will not be hard to find."

The President and his staff watched the screen incredulously as Mike Snyder articulated the rationale which was motivating Wildfire II to pursue its operation.

"The man is obviously insane!" the President declared.

"Perhaps, but we must deal with him," the security advisor replied. "His beliefs are not those of a narrow segment of our population. But I think we must reply to this maniac. Right now. And let him know he can't get away with it."

The President nodded and gestured towards the television camera pointed at him. "Put me on the air. Can this man, this Snyder, see me where he's sitting?"

"Yes, Mr. President. He has a monitor directly in front of him."

"Very well. Put me on." The President paused and then when he saw the red light on the camera he began his rebuttal.

"Major Snyder, this is your President. I will not waste time giving orders which I know will not be obeyed. There is only one thing I can say. You have no chance whatsoever of getting away with this madness. For the sake of your men who have been obviously misled by your misguided zeal I would ask you to release them from your orders and give up right now. There's no way you and your men will ever leave the United States alive. I can order out the Air Force, the Army, and the Marines if necessary, to say nothing of the National Guard. In minutes the Air Force can provide air cover to prevent you from moving beyond the area of the Houston Astrodome. So why don't you save your own lives and deliver the sixty-six thousand innocent football fans from terror by giving up."

Snyder, watching the President on the monitor in front of him, pointed to the director of the television coverage of the event indicating he wanted to reply. The red light came on and Snyder replied. "Mr. President, that's just what I wanted to talk to you about. As you can see, we have in the middle of the Astrodome a nuclear device capable of destroying everything within a quarter of a mile from where I now sit. If you are not aware of the fact that a 15 megaton yield nuclear warhead was taken from the Brownsville-McAllen security area, then your national security advisor has been grievously remiss in keeping you informed. I will ask the television crew to now give you a close-up of the device as I talk to you. I'm sure that your military advisors will recognize it as the missing nuclear missile which disappeared along with the two security officers escorting it just two and a half weeks ago. And I'm sure, Mr. President, if you will look at the instrument in front of me you, or at least your nuclear advisors, will recognize it as the remote detonating device to explode the warhead now sitting on the fifty yard line of this stadium."

Mike gestured to the camera to come in for a tight shot of the detonator in front of him. After a few moments of close-up on the detonator Mike turned to the director and asked him to send a tight shot of the nuclear warhead on the fifty yard line across the television cable to the White House.

In the White House the President and the rapidly burgeoning group of advisors arriving on the scene stared at the television set. "That's it, Mr. President. They do have the warhead taken on the 7th of November between Brownsville and McAllen."

"I thought you told me it appeared it was taken by some radical African group," the President said grimly.

"That's what we thought from the eyewitness accounts, Mr. President. It appears they used deception to make us think that Idi Amin or one of the many other unbalanced black despots in Africa had taken the device."

"Racist! I always said you were a racist!" the Ambassador to the United Nations shouted at the National Security advisor.

He turned to the President. "There is a clear indication of the racist nature of the man around you, Mr. President," the Ambassador shrieked. "The first thing he thought, the first conclusion to which he arrived was that it was blacks that took the device."

"Now calm down," the President said soothingly. "It was a fact that an all-black group actually took the device and the two officers in charge of it. Let's try to be rational about this problem."

Mike Snyder's commentary continued. "Since we acquired this nuclear device and the detonator we have set up a series of relay stations between Houston and our destination. Our escape route is covered every fifty miles by a relay system that can carry the signal, when I press the button on this box, to the warhead here in the Astrodome. It is our hope that you, Mr. President, will not, by calling in force of arms against us, cause this device to be detonated before everybody gets out of the Astrodome and far enough away so they will be safe.

"And even after the people have gotten out of the

Astrodome a nuclear explosion would cause widespread damage and loss of life. If this is what you want to be responsible for, then be my guest. Now, as I look out over the field I see by the scoreboard that we have collected a little over three million dollars. We still have a long way to go, Mr. President. So if you have any regard for the people here in the Astrodome and this great structure to say nothing of the families living within the lethal range of this device, you will order all American military units not only to stay sway from Houston but also not to pursue us. As you well know, when this detonating box is armed, as it now is, the destruction of it will automatically set off the warhead. Therefore it would be foolish of you to try and shoot down our escape plane. It is incumbent upon you, Mr. President, to aid us in every way in the completion of this mission and in leaving this country. Do you understand, sir?"

In the White House the President and his staff looked at each other. Nobody had a suggestion.

And in the skyboxes where the elite of the spectators in the Astrodome were monitoring the proceedings, taut attention was paid to the dialogue on their television screens between Washington and the Astrodome. Captain Hackett and his crew were within three skyboxes of meeting their counterparts who had started at the other end of the ring. All resistance, all the Texas macho impulse had now been quelled. What was important was for everybody to come out of this bizarre and perilous situation alive. Those with access to TV sets were privy to the conversations between the President and Mike Snyder and prayed that the President would expedite Wildfire's imminent departure from the scene with whatever loot they had.

290

Materialism had given away to pure survival. Throughout the Astrodome, spurred on by the Reverend Cash and Carry's evangelical exhortations, the football fans were eagerly giving every dollar they possessed to the Wildfire collectors in order to get the figure on the scoreboard high enough so that this desperate band of men would be satisfied and leave them to make their own retreat from the awful machine of destruction upon which all eyes were fixed.

The phone rang at the President's desk. He did not wait for anyone else to answer. He snatched it from its cradle. "Yes, this is the President."

"Mr. President, that is the warhead that was stolen. And as long as the two officers are missing we must assume that they have been forced to arm it."

The voice of the Secretary of Defense was unmistakable. And the intense alarm in his tone transmitted itself to the President's consciousness.

"Thank you." He hung up the phone.

"I think they're bluffing, Mr. President," said the Chief of Staff of the Army. "The procedural security we have developed would make it impossible for them to truly arm and detonate a nuclear device."

"Even if the two officers—whom nobody has seen or heard of since the day the device disappeared—even if those two men cooperated?" the President shot back.

"It's possible but the possibility is so remote that I would advise an immediate operation to interdict and capture those madmen!"

"And what if they were able to detonate it? Whose responsibility is it ultimately, yours or mine?"

The Chief of Staff shrugged and remained silent.

Perhaps never in his entire career had old 'Cash and Carry' put on a greater performance. The great organ continued to thunder out the stirring notes of that great Thanksgiving hymn *Bringing in the Sheaves*. And indeed the men of Wildfire continued to step down and deposit sheaves of bills into the open parachute canopies.

"I hope you enjoy that fifty dollars as much as I was going to," Bill Weaver ruefully said to the trooper who finally reached his row of seats.

"God bless you, sir," the trooper answered with a grin, himself overcome by the Reverend Carey's rhetoric. "Every penny of your fifty dollars will go towards establishing the new force to stop the godless Communists who would destroy America if given a chance."

"Amen, brother," Bill Weaver replied since he could think of no other retort. His only interest was getting himself and his son out of the Astrodome and home for Thanksgiving. If they got out of here alive, if they were eating that great bird he had purchased two days ago, he swore he would never again squander money on such items as *Playboy* and *Penthouse*. And instead of the weekly bottle of bourbon, he would put that money into a roast of beef for the family.

Joshua Carey was singing lustily over the public address system, "Bringing in the sheaves, bringing in the sheaves, giving to the boys who have given!"

By not the mood in the Astrodome had changed to one of virtual exaltation for the men of Wildfire. Each time the scoreboard racked up another hundred thousand dollars there were shouts of joy and applause throughout the stadium. Hack Hackett led his troop from the seventh level ring of skyboxes into the elevator which they had captured and down to the Astro turf level, then out onto the field to the open parachute canopies where Wildfire accountants, punching furiously at their Texas Instrument Company computers, were tallying up the score.

The cash alone collected in the skyboxes added seven hundred and fifty thousand dollars to the tally. When it was rung up and flashed on the scoreboard a mighty cheer, louder even than the accolades that poured out for Brian Cotter's touchdown, vibrated off the glass roof of the Dome and shimmered down among the spectators. Fear had given away to wild-eyed excitement. To the amazement of the collectors, fans from all over the Astrodome shouted to them and bade them approach to receive money they had missed the first time around.

When the jewelry from the skyboxes had been evaluated cursorily Hackett and the accountant agreed that it was worth a minimum of a million dollars when sold back to the insurance companies, and at least two million dollars if sold at even fence value. The million dollars was rung up on the scoreboard and again a mighty shout went up in the Astrodome. Even J.J. Cookson had been totally overwhelmed by the emotional hysteria of the situation. He pounded the bar and ordered another bourbon to celebrate.

Meanwhile in the presidential booth Snyder was continuing his dialogue with the White House. "Thank you, Mr. President. You have my wholehearted respect for making the decision you have made. I see from the scoreboard that we are now up to eight million dollars, still two million short. I guess we over-estimated the financial capacity of the yield here today. I can see we will not make fifteen million but we're certainly going to stay until we collect ten. By the way, I forgot to mention we also have a timing device built into the detonator. You know all about that. In one more hour the warhead will explode. That is, unless I order our nuclear expert to turn it off. And as you know, procedural security is such that only we who have set the timer can turn it off. So let's hope we collect the other two million forthwith."

A sudden chill gripped the occupants of the skyboxes who were watching the exchange on their television sets. The momentary exaltation turned to icy fear. "They've got to have missed a lot of money up here!" Cookson shouted. He turned to the Governor. "Help me. Let's get the rest and take it down to them. I've got another ten grand they didn't find." He went behind the bar and throwing a row of bottles to the floor he began twirling the combination on a small safe which Hack and his men had overlooked. Quickly he opened the small steel door and reached inside. Pulling out all the cash within he gripped it in his right hand and shoved his way out of the box and on into the next one. "Come on, get up the rest of it. No point in holding out now. Maybe I can talk to Snyder if I show some good faith money. Come on, come on!"

Sheepishly the occupants of the neighboring skybox went into hidden leather-covered pockets of their wallets and pulled back sections of the carpeting, retrieving cash hidden before the collection team had forced them to open up. The Governor followed J.J.'s example by canvassing the other boxes. The denizens of this, the richest circle of private viewing accommodations of any theatre or sports arena in the world, began helping to make the second collection a rich one.

Jewelry which even Captain Hackett had been too gentle to search for quickly appeared. Cookson rushed back to his own skybox, picked up the telephone which was operative on all calls within the Astrodome, and dialed the presidential suite. Hackett who had joined his commander in the command post picked up the phone. "Hackett here."

"This is Cookson, Hack. I heard what your man just said to the President. Tell him for chrissake to turn off that timer. I think we can come up with another half million in the next twenty minutes."

"Well, Mr. Cookson, that's a very fine and noble gesture on your part. We appreciate it. Just get in the elevator and bring it on down to that big white canopy you see. Major Snyder has decided, as you saw, to settle for a paltry ten mil. Bring it down. And let it be counted."

"I'm coming right down, Hack. Now be reasonable. Surely Mike doesn't want to blow up his wife. Maybe he hates everybody else in here but surely he loves Cookie."

"That's a moot point, sir. But bring it down." Hack turned to Snyder and held his thumb up. "Looks like your father-in-law suddenly got religion. I guess we underestimated the powers of the Reverend Carey."

"Well, Mr. President," Snyder exclaimed happily. "We are getting much closer to our quota all of a sudden than I had expected. Now sir, I hope you're doing your part and keeping any military or police operations from interfering with this mission."

"We will not interfere with you, Major Snyder!" Beads of sweat clearly showed on the television set as the President continued his negotiations. "Just get your money, de-activate the timer, and get the hell out."

"Precisely our sentiments, sir." Mike gave the director a sign and on the screen an extreme close-up of the nuclear warhead ominously filled the tube. "At the ten million mark we will de-activate the timer, sir. But don't forget, I can still detonate that device remotely from as far away as a thousand miles. As I mentioned, there is a relay device every fifty miles from here to our destination. And as your chief nuke kook can tell you, even the slightest tampering with that weapon before disarm time, set for six hours after we leave, will detonate it."

In the Oval Office the President looked over at the White House chief scientist who had just arrived. Dourly the scientist nodded his head in assent.

The President glared at his television director and made a gesture to cut off transmission. Then he turned to the assembled experts and political advisors. "What the hell kind of nuclear devices have we created that this could happen?"

"Snyder must have a very experienced nuclear weapons expert on his team," the Chief of Staff remarked.

"Oh my God! What has the world come to, what have we come to when we make such a thing possible as we're witnessing." The President turned to the television director. "Put us back on the air." When the red light blinked out of the front of the camera the President somberly stared into the lens. "All right, Snyder, we will not interfere. Haven't you taken enough loot already?"

Mike Snyder smiled into the camera and said to his director, "Put a shot of the scoreboard into the other corner of the picture."

Instantly in the upper half of the screen next to the cylindrical obelisk which was the nuclear device was displayed the scoreboard which indicated that nine million dollars had now been collected from all quarters of the Astrodome. Mike Snyder continued to address the President, "Even the management of the Astrodome was able to discover funds in the safe which they have contributed. It is gratifying that everybody here is anxious that we attain our goal."

In the barn containing the actual nuclear device a hundred and fifty miles southwest of Houston Captain Savage and Major Huntley struggled with the bonds holding them motionless as they watched the television set which their Wildfire captors had obligingly left on for them. "My God!" Huntley exclaimed. "Can't they realize it's a bluff? Surely the President, surely his advisors, can tell that's just a mock-up like the ones they made at Ft. Sill."

"It's a goddamned good fake, Major," Captain Savage snapped. "Looking at it on television it would fool me."

"We've got to get out of here, we've got to get to a phone. We can't let them get away with this."

"I'm open to suggestions, Major," Savage replied. "I'm making a little progress with the ropes around my ankles. If you could push your way over here maybe you could help me."

Major Huntley, digging his heels into the dirt floor of the barn, pushed himself as close to Captain Savage as he could. With their hands in cuffs behind their backs it was difficult, but together they worked at the hastily tied knots holding the Captain's ankles together.

All during the game the two officers had struggled to free Captain Savage's ankles. Their Wildfire captors had deliberately not tied them too tightly so that they would be able to escape from the barn in a reasonable length of time. Savage and Huntley had developed a workable rapport with the black troops who had captured and guarded them for the three week period between the theft of the nuclear device and the football game.

Finally just before the end of the first half the ropes around Savage's ankles had been loosened enough by the furious efforts of the two officers so that he could struggle to his feet and painfully hobble towards the door of the barn. First he had tried jumping, a sort of rabbit-hop gait, but he kept falling to the ground and having to struggle to his feet again. Savage discovered that he could shuffle one foot an inch in front of the other and then bring the other foot up to it. Moving thus he finally reached the door and threw himself against it. His Wildfire captors had not even locked the door and it creaked open enough to let the officer out. In dismay he realized how isolated the barn was in this desolate part of the south Texas desert country. Nevertheless, inch by inch he struggled towards the road which ran by the field in the middle of which stood the barn.

Hopping, falling on his face, struggling once again to his feet, shuffling and again hopping he fought his way to the road. One car went by without seeing him struggling across the rutted field. Falling and rising, Savage continued. And the more he struggled the looser the ropes around his ankles became. It took him half an hour to work his way to the side of the road and then, confronted with the heavy wire fence around the property, he was unable to go further. He pressed his face to the fence looking down the road for any sign of a vehicle coming by. It was not long before a decrepit pick-up truck bounced along the dusty road toward him. As it approached he banged himself against the fence, jumping and shouting at the top of his lungs.

As the pick-up truck passed directly by him he let out the loudest bellow of which he was capable, jumped up and then fell back on his head once again. Rolling over so that he could look out on the road he was elated to see that the pick-up truck had stopped and backed towards him.

A grey-bearded old man opened the door and leisurely strolled out of the car and towards the fence.

"What's the trouble, friend?" the old man called out, pushing his wide-brimmed hat onto the back of his head.

"Help me, help! This is a national emergency!"

"Did you escape from the county jail?"

"No! I'm a United States Army officer. I was kidnapped by subversive enemies of America. I've got to get on the phone to Washington right now."

"Well, I can tell you, friend, we're a long way from a phone. But I'll see what I can do to help you." The old man with surprising agility climbed over the fence, pulled a knife out of his pocket and cut the ropes from Captain Savage's ankles. "Can't help you with them cuffs but I'll take you down to the next police station we come to," the pick-up driver offered.

"Hurry! Help me get over this fence." With his legs free now and with the old man's help Captain Savage struggled over the top of the wire fence, fell to the other side with a groan, got to his feet, and shuffled to the car door. The old man opened it for him, helped him inside, then went around to the driver's seat and started to drive away. "I think there's a sheriff up in the next town. Maybe we can find him. I guess you're not escaping from a prison farm or you wouldn't want to go to the sheriff's office, right?"

"Just get me to the nearest phone." The tone of authority registered on the pick-up driver.

CHAPTER THIRTY-FIVE

A mighty roar burst from the lungs of sixty-six thousand football fans imprisoned in the Astrodome as the scoreboard announced the figure nine million seven hundred and fifty thousand dollars. Then under it in lights, "Thank you, we'll take it and go." In the presidential suite Mike Snyder looked from the scoreboard back to the television camera. "And every man, woman and child in the Astrodome will thank you, Mr. President, if you order all military and police units in the United States to stand down for the next four hours. Remember, sir, that even though we will de-activate the timing device we can still detonate this weapon from wherever we are. Also remember, for five hours it will detonate if tampered with."

On the field, with the precision of the trained military unit it was, the Wildfire troopers gathered up the great parachute canopies full of cash and jewelry and double-timed with them to the armored personnel carriers parked on the west goal line ready to take them out through the west gate and into the next and final phase of this operation. The escape from the United States to their destination!

From all over the Astrodome the Wildfire team streamed from the stands onto the field. Mike turned to the television director. "Okay, there's nothing more for me to say. You might as well concentrate on our exit. We appreciate your help." He turned to Powell Purcell who had, perhaps for the first time in his entire career, sat speechless watching the proceedings. "Powell, get back into the television booth and give a little narration of what you see as we finish this operation. Always the trickiest thing in Vietnam, after a search and destroy mission is to get out whole. It's easy to get in and find your target and destroy it. But getting out, there's where the discipline comes in. If nothing else I think we've repaid your efforts on our behalf by giving you perhaps the greatest exclusive news break any network ever had. Agree?"

Purcell nodded silently. He gave Major Snyder a feeble wave of the hand and then left the presidential suite heading as fast as he could for the television control room. On the field the Wildfire team had assembled in precision formation on the half-destroyed Astro tuff. At a command from Captain Hackett they all raised their right arms in a gladiator's salute to the Astrodome audience and then turned towards the west gate.

In orderly fashion, as the men on the forty yard line leveled their weapons, the men on the fifty yard line dashed through their cover and assembled downfield, pointing their weapons toward the opposite end of the field. The men who had just given them cover raced through their own covering teammates until they had reached the twenty yard line.

At the same time the Reverend Carey sang out through the microphone he was holding, "God bless you all. The Lord's work has been done. And now we leave you to contemplate what you have seen today. As I said at the beginning of this service, the Lord works in mysterious ways his wonders to perform!" With that the Reverend Carey jumped from the platform to the Astro turf and nimbly ran towards the goal line to the cheers and applause of the Astrodome crowd. From his seat below the skybox J.J. Cookson, holding field glasses to his eyes, watched this spectacular retreat. And then, to his surprise, he saw a civilian emerge from the stands and walk across the Astrodome to join the departing Wildfire troopers.

"Well goddamn! Son-of-a-bitch if it isn't big John Dykes! He's going with them! Now what the hell do you make of that?"

Cookie, standing next to him, said, "I won my bet, Daddy."

"The hell you say, daughter!"

Mike Snyder appeared on the Astro turf and to the cheers of the spectators double-timed to his armored personnel carrier parked underneath the goal posts at the west end of the field. John Dykes reached the armored personnel carrier at the same time. Mike gave him a hand up into the front seat, jumped in beside him and the vehicle started out the open west gate. At this point the entire company of raiders double-timed out the west gate after the armored personnel carriers and in the open air boarded the two-and-a-half-ton trucks and personnel carriers waiting for them.

Just before Mike's vehicle left the Astrodome he turned and held up the black box for all to see.

"Get a tight shot on the box," Powell Purcell barked. As the Wildfire team left the Astrodome, Purcell began to describe the scene. "Ladies and gentlemen, never in my career, never in all the time I've been covering sports events have I seen anything like this. And I'm sure you never will again either. I'll now try to recap everything that's happened in the last hour and a half and I have just learned that we will have a complete special broadcast tonight at eight o'clock showing you exactly what happened here at the Astrodome on this Thanksgiving Day."

On the highway outside of the Astrodome the Texas Highway Patrol was converging. No orders had been received by them to allow this arrogant gang of criminals to escape from Texas. As they were approaching, four great army engineer bulldozers were moving monolithically down the divider of the two lane highway. Each time they came to a light stanchion they drove through it, snapping the steel columns off and plowing them directly ahead into the divider. For a mile every obstacle that rose more than three feet above the ground was knocked down.

The Texas Highway Patrol cars, eight in number, speeding up from the downtown area of Houston formed a blockade of the highway.

Leaping from their cars, taking cover behind them, they leveled high-powered rifles and submachine guns at the oncoming bulldozers. It was a foolish move on the part of the police. Even as they began firing the armored tractors moved towards them and, undaunted at the fire pouring out from behind the police cars, they crunched into the vehicles, the great blades pushing them off the road. The police dispersed in all directions as with great metalic screeches their cars were crushed and moved out of the way. At the other end of the highway from this abortive blockade came the sirens of ambulances.

From out of the sky a giant Hercules jet transport came heaving over the Astrodome and squatted down on the highway in a perfect landing, all obstacles having been cleared before it. The ramp dropped from the back to the Hercules and the Wildfire vehicles careened up to it. The Wildfire team carrying their silk canopies bulging with stacks of currency, and jewelry ran up the ramp and into the belly of the mammoth troop transport plane. The ambulances passed through the Wildfire road block of tanks and armored personnel carriers and stopped at the ramp. Men in wheelchairs from the Veterans Hospital were wheeled up the ramp and inside the Hercules.

The remainder of the Wildfire team ran from their vehicles, blocking the highway, and climbed up into the transport behind the crippled veterans who had chosen to join them on their odyssey.

Last to board the plane was Mike Snyder himself. Having counted all of his men including John Dykes and the Reverend Carey, and still clutching the black box, Snyder ran up the ramp which was pulled-to behind him. Inside the overloaded transport he pushed through to the pilot's compartment and sat down in the engineer's seat behind Captain Murray. "OK, take off!"

The Hercules spun around on the highway and like a mechanized giant goose, all engines blasting at full power, the transport came roaring down the freeway and pulled off just before reaching the collection of tanks and armored personnel carriers and trucks blocking the freeway from any traffic. The Hercules struggled for altitude and roared over the Astrodome leaving the sight of one of history's most memorable heists behind as it pulled up into the air over Houston in the afternoon sun.

"Now for the hairy part," Mike said to Captain Murray as he pulled the transport up toward the stratosphere. "Let's just hope our bluff holds out."

The co-pilot handed Mike a portable television set and he stared at the picture being telecast from the Astrodome. The spectators were fleeing out all the portals but one camera continued to stay focused on the nuclear warhead. Nobody went near it. Screwing and earplug into his ear he listened to the narration delivered in sonorous tones by the famous sports announcer.

"The orders are that nobody goes on the field," Purcell told his audience. "Orders, I might add, which are unnecessary. Nobody wants to touch that thing out there. Major Snyder and his men are in the air now heading for where we know not. But we do know that Major Snyder has with him the black box which could detonate this device if he is pursued and feels endangered. The President has promised that no interference will be offered the daring men who just ripped off this famous sports arena, perhaps the most famous in the country, certainly it is now, for almost ten million dollars.

Well, fans, we are leaving too. We wouldn't like to be here if somethings happens to make Major Snyder nervous. We will leave all the cameras focused on the field and the scoreboard so you can see for yourself what's happening. Meantime, goodbye from the Astrodome for the time being. We will talk to you tonight at eight o'clock when all of the fabulous footage will be shown to you complete with stop action segments of some of the spectacular situations which we saw played out before us today. "Adios!"

Mike Snyder laughed. The Hercules turned off its course and headed out over the Gulf of Mexico. There were no fighter planes to be seen in any direction. Obviously they were being tracked by radar, Snyder knew, but as he looked at the television set on his lap, the spectral nuclear warhead in the upper left quarter of the picture always on the tube no matter what other scenes were being show, Mike knew they were safe.

The pick-up truck containing Captain Savage came to a gasping halt in front of the sheriff's office of the little town of Las Nogales. The old driver opened the door for the officer who jumped out, keeping his balance precariously with his arms still handcuffed behind his back. He rushed into the sheriff's office and found the sheriff and his deputy both staring open-mouthed at their television set.

"I've got to get a line through to the White House right now," the Captain shouted.

The sheriff and his deputy gazed dumbly at this handcuffed apparition. Finally the sheriff asked, "What do you have to talk to the White House about? Did you just escape from the county jail?"

"No, I just escaped from the people that are doing that," he inclined his head towards the television set.

"Sheriff, he just told me a story like you wouldn't believe," the driver drawled. "You better put him on the phone. He's got some important information. Something the President will want to know right away."

"I think you're both crazy. Lock them up, Jeddy," he said to his deputy.

"Don't be crazy, Sheriff. I've get to let the President know that that thing you're looking at on your television set is a fake. It's no nuclear weapon. The real one that was stolen is back ten miles down the road in a barn. I've got to let the President know so he can release the Air Force to go after them."

"Is that a fact?" the Sheriff drawled. "Well Mister, you'd better tell me a little more about this. And how did you get handcuffed behind your back that way?" He walked over to Savage, turned him around brusquely and examined the handcuffs. "Them bracelets are official police equipment. I think we better lock you up until we find out who's looking for you."

"Goddamn it, Sheriff, you will never have another job in law enforcement if you don't let me get through on the phone right now while there's still time to stop them. The Air Force could shoot them down right away."

"And have them press the little button?" the Sheriff challenged.

"I told you, that bomb is a fake. I've got to get through to the White House." He breathed deeply in frustration. "Don't you see the uniform I'm wearing? I'm Captain Don Savage, United States Army, nuclear control unit. Now get the White House on the phone and hold it for me so I can talk. Have you got a key so you can unlock these things that are holding my hands behind me?"

"And if I get the White House what's going to happen?" the sheriff asked.

"The Air Force will shoot them out of the sky wherever they are!" Savage shouted.

"Oh they will, will they?"

"Every second counts. Can't you realize it, Sheriff?"

"Lock this escaped jailbird up, Jeddy!" the Sheriff ordered.

"You'll regret this, Sheriff!" Savage shouted.

The sheriff's deputy took Captain Savage by the shoulder and propelled him into the back of the building towards the cells. He opened one barred door, pushed Captain Savage in, and clanged it shut after him. Then he walked back to join the sheriff and watch the unfolding drama on television.

"You know, Jeddy," the sheriff drawled. "That there individual just maybe might be telling the truth. Sure would be a shame for those fellas to get caught after all that, wouldn't it?"

"Yeah, I guess it would. Never saw a robbery like that one before."

"Yeah, I guess they deserve to get away with it. Now you take my boy, Bill. He was in Vietnam, two years. Can't get himself a job anywhere now. Everything those fellas said my boy Bill says. What'da you think Bill would think of me if I was the cause of that Major Snyder getting shot down by the United States Air Force?"

"I guess he'd never talk to you again, Sheriff."

"That's about right, Jed. Now get on the phone and call around and find out if anybody's escaped from the county farm or any of the jails. We sure got to have it on the record that we tried our damnedest to find out where this handcuffed fella escaped from."

The President and his advisors still stared impotently

at the television screen before them. "Well they're two hours out now," the Chief of Staff of the Army commented. "Everybody's left the Astrodome. Shall we send the Air Force after them, Mr. President?"

"He said he could detonate that bomb for four hours," the President replied. "We'll get him eventually but let's not take a chance on having the Astrodome and everything around it nuked."

"Yes, sir."

"Any idea where they might be going?" the President asked.

The Chief of Staff was looking through Major Michael Snyder's records.

"No sir, unless—"

"Unless what?" the National Security advisor asked.

"I see he was stationed in Costa Vacca right up until the time we cut off aid to them and threatened sanctions against them because of their violation of human rights. That Miguel Alamen, the president, thought a lot of Major Snyder. Just maybe—"

"You think they're heading for Costa Vacca? the President asked.

"Could be, sir. That Miguel Alamen is just crazy enough to go for something like this. He could use three hundred men like those."

"If he goes there we'll have him extradited immediately," the National Security advisor declared.

"We don't have diplomatic relations any more with Costa Vacca," the Chief of Staff reminded him.

"We may have to establish relations with Costa Vacca someday," said the CIA Chief who had responded to the emergency call from the White House. "Our information is that they are about to start lifting the highest oil production in this hemisphere."

"Anything would be better than having to deal with Nigeria," the National Security advisor commented.

"Racist!" screamed the Ambassador to the United Nations who had just arrived. "You have always been in favor of status quo in South Africa and Rhodesia and against our dealings with Nigeria," he shrieked.

"The problem at hand," the President cut in, "is that device we're all looking at on the screen. I suggest we send somebody out to have a look at it."

"If it's the nuke that was hijacked and they knew how to set the timer, then it will go off if it's tampered with," the nuclear scientist counseled. "And if they were able to hijack the nuke in the first place the chances are their knowledge of procedure is such that they can do anything the device was designed to do."

At the sheriff's office at Los Nogales the imprecations of the man who had been brought in handcuffed resounded from the cell at the rear. "The President will personally prosecute you!"

The sheriff looked at his deputy sadly. "No escaped prisoners in this part of Texas?"

The deputy shook his head.

"Well, let's see now," the Sheriff yawned, stretched and consulted his wristwatch. "It's been about two or three hours since they left the Astrodome. Reckon they ought to be wherever it is they're going by now. Get that man that calls himself Captain Savage out of the cell and let him make his phone call."

The deputy nodded and pulling the keys from his pocket walked to the back of the sheriff's office and unlocked the cell. He led the prisoner back into the sheriff's presence.

"We checked every jail and county farm and nobody

reports an escaped prisoner. Jed, see if you can find a key or a pick that you can use to get those cuffs off this man's wrists."

"While he's doing that, sir, please get the White House on the phone," the officer pleaded. "It still may not be too late. Once they get where they're going there'll be no way of getting them back, I know that from what the men that were guarding me said."

The sheriff picked up his phone and dialed zero finally getting an operator. "I want to make a collect call to the President of the United States," the sheriff announced.

"For chrissake, sheriff, don't bother with that. He'll pay you back a hundredfold."

"All right then, operator, make it a person-to-person call to the President of the United States." He turned to Savage. "If this is a big hoax and it sure looks like one, this office ain't getting stuck with a call to Washington, D.C., I can tell you that."

Hopelessly, in frustration Captain Savage stared at the ceiling a moment. "Can't you just get the White House on the line and let me talk to whoever answers?" Savage begged.

Up in the Hercules winging its way southward to Costa Vacca, Major Snyder left the cockpit and walked back among the Wildfire men cheering, recapitulating their experience with each other, and helping themselves to the liquor supply Major Snyder had thoughtfully removed from J.J. Cookson's vast store of potables on the compound.

Big John Dyke and Reverend Carey were earnestly comparing notes and discussing how they would apply their respective trades in Costa Vacca. "Well, Reverend, perhaps you could help me at the casino. I'm sure we could use a chapel adjacent to the premises."

"As long as I get them first," Cash and Carry agreed jovially.

Major Snyder refused the offer of a drink but encouraged his troops to help themselves. "We're not out of it yet, men," he cautioned. "But you've done your job, now it's up to me to finish mine and get us safely to Costa Vacca."

A cheer went up as the men lifted plastic cups to their leader. Mike Snyder went over to the crippled veterans in wheelchairs and also had a short conversation with three of the bewildered psychological cases. Then he made his way forward to the cockpit of the Hercules and once again took the television set on his knee. He glanced at his watch.

"In fifteen minutes our little message will come up on the scoreboard and the nation will see what we really did," Snyder chuckled. The co-pilot turned in his seat. "Sir, we've just made radio contact with Costa Vacca. Apparently the old man himself is leading a flight of fighter planes to escort us back to the base."

Snyder laughed, some of the strain now gone from his tone. "That's Miguel Alamen. As dictator's go, the best and most benevolent in the world. He only tortures Communists. And then only a little bit, just enough to loosen their tongues."

He looked down at the television set which had been turned to the nearest television broadcasting station in Mexico. The same picture was being carried from the Astrodome. Excited stacatto Spanish was being mouthed by the announcer. "I can't hear what they're saying but at least we can see the scoreboard and the device and the view of the Astrodome. I guess we've made worldwide news when even Mexican television is carrying it. I was afraid we'd be operating in the blind at this point." He glanced down at his watch. "Well, five minutes from now the world will know that the United States has been had."

Desperately Captain Savage, now in touch with the White House, having persuaded the sheriff to let him talk to whoever answered, was stating his case. The White House operators, used to every crank call in the spectrum of zaniness finally were convinced that this call should be put through at least to the National Security Advisor who was with the President at the moment. In the President's office the phone rang and a secretary picked it up. She listened, then nodded to the Security Advisor. "For you, sir."

The Security Advisor virtually snatched the instrument from her hand and placed it to his ear. "Go ahead," he commanded tersely. As he listened to the voice on the other end identifying itself and then articulating the procedural codes which would identify him over the phone as a nuclear strategist, the security advisor stiffened and listened intently. "Go on! Go on, Savage! You're absolutely certain? The President has made up his mind we will take no chances. You're certain!" He turned to the President and shouted into the phone, "Hold on!"

"What's up?" the President asked.

"I've got one of the two officers who was with the nuclear device when it was stolen, Mr. President. He just escaped. He says that what we're looking at on the screen is a mock-up and that the original nuclear device never left its case. In fact it is in a barn in Texas now. In other words, sir, they bluffed us."

"That was always a possibility," the President replied calmly. "But only a possibility. Any man fanatical enough to pull a Jesse James on the Houston Astrodome is crazy enough to have a real nuke in the middle of the field if he had access to it."

"Look at the screen, Mr. President," an aide shouted. "Something's happening on the scoreboard."

The President and his advisors looked at the screen. There the lights were spelling out something. And then they read the message from Major Snyder and the Wildfire team.

"Bang! Bang! You're dead!"

For some moments the assemblage in the President's Oval Office stared at the television set. Finally, in hollow tones, the President pronounced, "Well, the crisis is over. So they had us. But there were no injuries or destruction attributable to decisions made by us. I am satisfied we handled this matter properly and in the tradition of presidential judicial decision-making."

"Yes, Mr. President," came the chorus of accord. The President nodded in satisfaction. "We will determine how to deal with Major Snyder and his men in due course." He turned to his press secretary. "Call the networks and get a half hour delay on my Thanksgiving address to the nation. I want to rewrite it."

Five hours after their departure from the highway beside the Houston Astrodome, the Wildfire team landed at the Costa Vacca International Airport. The jet fighters which had escorted the Hercules the last half hour of the trip circled overhead as the giant transport touched down. El Presidente Miguel Alamen and his entire cabinet were on hand to greet the men of Wildfire. Standing beside El Presidente was his daugh-

315

ter, Miguelina. The men of Wildfire disembarked and followed uniformed guides past the welcoming committee of officials and the flower of Costa Vacca's maidenhood who waved and called to the men promising them a *fiesta magnifico* that night.

Mike went directly to Miguelina. The crowd was forgotten as Miguelina threw herself into Mike's arms.

"Thank God you are here, *mi amore*," Miguelina whispered huskily into his ear.

"After I pay my respects to your father we will have our own *fiesta magnifico*, my darling!" Mike kissed her again, reluctantly released her from his arms, and turned to El Presidente snapping a smart salute.

"General Mike Snyder reporting for duty, sir!"